ITCH

The Art of Possibility

Harper St. Clair

Blue Heron Book Works, LLC

Allentown, Pennsylvania

Cover design: Angie Zumbrano
Blue Heron Book Works, LLC
www.blueheronbookworks.com

For my mother, Theresa,

for teaching me to trust

in the magic of next

FOREVERMORE

For my husband, Scott, for

sharing the entrusted magic

EVERYWHEN

Table of Contents

ACKNOWLEDGMENTS

Various researched references were utilized throughout the novel, including tidbits from the likes of sources, people and places like Merriam Webster, OED, Jung, Yeats, Rumi, Proust, T.S. Eliot, William James, Wikipedia, Google and library archives, museums, art galleries, travel sites, auction houses and international designer portfolios. I consulted hundreds of random sources for historical content from books, magazines, articles, quotes, media, interviews and web sites while envisioning the story's design.

My goal was to pose random facts and fictional tidbits to align the narrative with historical realities to expose both the trusted and supposed reality. Since accomplishment never happens alone, the novel was written with the assistance of many generous inspirational sources. I'm grateful for the contribution each has provided on the way to publishing. You all know who you are and how much you mean to me.

Deepest appreciation to my husband and the steady company of my faithful dog, who sat with me as I wrote. And to my 3Ms, and certain family members (living and dead) who have accompanied me along this windswept journey of magical discovery.

Part I

When you change the way you look at things,
the things you look at change.

Albert Einstein

1 Knitch

New York

It's tough to square but growth requires pain, which is woven into the fabric of our humanness. If you can't swallow that, you'd best find the exit ramp to that bustling village called delusion where you can mingle with others who live safe lives of insignificance.

And so as it was, I chose the journey of painful growth. Though the pain that called me forward wasn't the physical kind, it didn't hurt any less. My pain was a much subtler concoction, one shot angst, one shot agita and two shots compulsion for unquenchable success—and a hearty splash of ego just to top it all off. This neurotic cocktail was so cleverly mixed however, I thought it worthy of my undying commitment, though the price required nothing short of selling my soul.

The customized composite was uniquely equipped to cast its spell on me for decades. But of course, it too cradled a fated hamartia— the fatal flaw which is the exact cause of a soul's undoing. Like a tracking cookie that grooved with my yearnings, I played along for as long as I could until in classic anagnorisis, I was forced to face my resident monster. And once you meet this storied creature face to face, there's no going back.

And so, this is my story about how a portentous blend of cosmic forces, one fine day, came a knocking on my chamber door. And how by way of many a strange convergence, I embarked on the only journey worth taking; one which was nothing short of the literal search for my life.

Though curiosity may be the typical way by which most journeys begin, how I got to where I am today is another thing entirely. You see, my journey began with an itch! An eccentric energy of underground forces mixed with cosmic hints, stacked like tiny twigs banded together in a trusty knitch to ultimately create a fire that burned inside me.

It was as if the universe was providing me with a tiny key to a panorama of possibilities, ones I never would have suspected were feasible. Notoriously though, this itch came to me just as Kierkegaard attested, *"A possibility is a hint from God. One must follow it."*

2 Mitch

New York

My baptized name is *Michello Marco Bonaventura,* but everyone outside my family in Italy calls me Mitch.

At 42, I'm a reluctantly single resident of Soho, an outlier gem in the urban sprawl known as Manhattan. Professionally, I'm an artifacts dealer, that is, an old-world cognoscenti, a bona fide virtuoso of art and antique treasures.

Since the age of seven I've been wired to live for the *tesori nascoti,* as we Italians say, or life's hidden treasures. The potent combination of spiritual enrichment and visual enchantment is my real jam. Naysayers may refer to my dealer trade as the underbelly of the art world, but they have no understanding of what it entails, especially amid the fast paced, cutthroat, greedy groove of high dollar trading. The hunt for treasure is surely a most compulsive business. Anyone who pretends otherwise is a liar and there are plenty of dissimulators in my trade; the liars being dealers who can't admit that it's not the high-minded quest for beauty alone that drives them.

Trust that the level of artifact I deal in has long tentacles like octopi, with heirs and disgruntled governments constantly stalking the unmet potential.

Appearing to democratize the partaking in further drama; you'll find Dorothy's ruby slippers sold for over a million, but the buyer still can't find Oz. But these types never wander into the darkest catacombs, nor do they veer into the lesser known underworld where true treasures tend to burrow. And it's true you must be somewhat of a loner to jive with this inimitable schtick of mine. As a hunter, a seeker, an excavator and aficionado, there's sundry ways in which the treasured unveiling can occur. But in the throes of steady practice, the pace of pressing design project deadlines on top of balancing one's incessant curiosity and the daily grind knows just how and where to rub you raw.

Though we Italians like to say, *tutte le strade portano a Roma,* no matter where you think you're headed, in my twisted world, all roads lead to a roundabout of possibility, where the opportunity for amplified creation circulates like fresh air.

Despite—or because of—its potential for danger, I'm well aware that the treasure hunt makes my blood race. But I wouldn't put myself in this kind of danger for just anything.

Though my surname, Bonaventura, conjures good luck and makes me sound much more personable than I am, I must clarify my truth: I like people, but I love, rare and beautiful things. Mix the cocktail, danger in the service of beauty, and I'm all in.

I first caught the bug as a young schoolboy. Early on, I could be found traipsing through trinkets and treasures with my Italian father who was an artist, loved antique books and made a living running two legendary shops in Genoa. My spirited mother hails from Biella in Piemonte where she studied fashion merchandising and taught me how to appreciate a worthy textile, not just with my hands or my eyes, but with my soul. She believes it's this artistic passementerie that makes the soul sing; hence also her passionate regard for my father. Her family has worked at *Vitale Barberis Canonico* for generations. They speak of wool as if they were poets touching divine threads. This is probably when I first became aware that if certain wools were an evolutionary miracle as she claimed, then perhaps everything around us must also be much more than it seems.

My mother saw everything through the lens of fabric and bemoaned that humans didn't wear as well as fine cashmere, that is, never to wrinkle, naturally opening ourselves to tentering, while remaining strong and durable, woven of threads that last the test of time; and not least, retaining all our memory. In later years and in lonelier moments, I could see how my mother's pronouncements have shaped my bachelorhood because one must also contend with that pesky problem of mortal wrinkling.

My only other female role models were an astute covey of European nuns who ran my prep school, Academia di S. Maria Assunta. They had a knack for divining not just the Almighty, but that elusive handsome chap, human potential. The sisters infused learning with story lines, which captured something in me and what they referred to as holy imagination, which provided the foundation of my fondness for the art of discovery and a deep love of the unexpected.

The Sisters of the Assumption (an ironically apropos moniker for the Order since they were cheerleaders for the grand assumption of possibility) had uncharted rooms of stuff dispersed throughout unnamed buildings on the waterfront campus. This un-inventoried surplus was never locked away; rather it was accidentally billeted into tangential offshoots of dormitories and main thoroughfares. For me, just like the forgotten film footage that doesn't make its way into the final cut, these dark rooms materially cradled a store of sacred potential.

These unattended storerooms in alcoves contained antiques, desks, exotic doors, statues, lamps, smelly hard cover books, frames, and storybook chairs, like the one Goldilocks might sink in to, eating a bowl of porridge of just the right temperature. There were also darker corners hiding a cadre of mysterious things like locked metal boxes, tarnished coins, spool of threads, typewriters, gilded chests and bookshelves half-hidden in inches of caked dust. I remember wondering if all this dust was the same stuff they used to put on our foreheads on Ash Wednesday. Some afternoons, I'd spend hours searching for photos in library books, hoping to identify something, anything resembling what I'd uncovered.

The Sisters were easy to converse with, and I could have asked any one of them for the history of this trove, but I thought it best not to divulge my secret pastime. Speaking aloud might diminish its creative force in my still adolescently assembling head. Italians regard the *l'arte di arrangiarsi* as the talent for making something out of nothing opportunistically. A source of national pride it speaks to the art of possibility, the art of arranging yourself and the art in figuring it out yourself. It may take a while to get the hang of it, but once you experience it, you too will be infatuated by the pursuit forevermore.

Rest assured, there's a big difference between junk and the common finds that might be called junk by untrained eyes. What Jean-Louis Remilleux said is true, *"Antiques are not dead things, they have a lot to teach us about how we lived and thought."* What the nuns lodged wasn't cruft. Most of it was usable stuff of some value. And their stash was of a far different constitution than the likes of what's kept mindlessly in American storage units; like the ones they spend $7 billion a year renting; to hold mostly worthless things; things they can't cull in order to afford real space in their lives. Though the propensity to tolerate endless clutter may seem innocuous, as a designer, I've seen it do some serious damage.

And then came the day when I found my life's calling. Potting around, I spotted an old frame with an oil painting inside it, turned to the wall shoved behind some dressers. It was an abstract landscape with a particularly generous use of blues and greens, but I had no idea what it was or who painted it. It wasn't signed so I went to the library and looked through picture books to see anything that resembled it. I spotted a plat du jour; one in the style of an underappreciated fellow named Vincent. The rendition was comprised of thick globs of distinctive paint.

I proceeded to check out a book about his art and eventually took my underground mystery to my father. When I described the painting, he came to school to see it for himself. Then, he immediately made an appointment with the Reverend Mother and brought my Uncle Gio along. I sat silently with them, as my uncle explained to Reverend Mother what it could be. Her eyes popped out of her head as if she'd seen a ghost, or more appropriately in her case, a Holy Spirit. My uncle, who was an esteemed architect with famous artist friends had them render a qualified opinion.

My father praised me for being an artistic sleuth and said though I wasn't a painter, I had a good eye. He said that while he could create a body of work with his paints, I didn't have to paint in order to utilize my talent. With a good eye, I could see the beauty in all things, in a never-ending way, without the burden of physical inventory. That same night, he gifted me with a first edition volume of Edgar Allen Poe and in thick black ink on the opening page, he quoted Poe: *"The pleasure which is at once the most pure, the most elevating and the most intense, is derived from the contemplation of the beautiful."*

In a family of artists, an approbation in the realm of beauty was intoxicating and I accepted his pronouncement of my being an appreciator of beauty as foreordained destiny. Initially they thought the painting could be a hearty fake. By the time I'd heard it wasn't, I was already halfway through the next grade in school. And ever since that day when it was authenticated, I was hooked.

Most kids up to bat wait for such a storied pitch. They secretly anticipate getting that itch or the calling that's distinctly meant for some mightier swinging to show. This kind of itch, unlike most things in this topsy-turvy world, doesn't run the risk of being outgrown. As it turned out, the painting was a lost canvas from Theo Van Gogh's personal collection and determined to be by none other than the post-Impressionist anomaly, his brother, Vincent. It was titled "Sunset at Montmajour" and the indelible impression it made on my mind's eye will stay with me till I cease to breathe, spurring me on to chivy the recesses for a lost ideal, the promise of finding treasure.

When the nuns found out what the painting was worth, they funded the future of their order, granted me a scholarship, and invited me to the otherwise all-adult unveiling party. I was introduced as the finder of the work of art, and everyone clapped, a little surprised that I was just a scrawny kid. Though my mother always had a gleam in her eye whenever I was in view, on this day I think she wore borrowed wings from on high.

How could I know that I, like a fine swath of cashmere, was being lovingly tentered? And this is exactly how talent works. Your particular gifts grab you even when you don't know they're yours yet. They may sneak up on you but usually they're not too far off from where you're centered most days.

From here on, my artistic education became a family priority. Not only was I personally motivated but now my father and his fraternal entourage would schedule monthly expeditions to historic churches, castles and museums. It was a lot of fun to see so many beautiful things and to hang out with my crazy uncles who were funny, smart, old-world fellows. Somewhere in between the array of artistic assimilation, I made room for this future self where the spectral spirit of connoisseurship invited me in by name. As a result, I saw firsthand how designed spaces could be created to transport guests to fantastical worlds; and that by passing through them, their spirits could be altered forever, enabling hearts to make room to possibly pursue an enriched and aesthetically fulfilling life.

As if this wasn't enough boyhood stimulation, this fraternity also had a notorious fondness for gourmet food en route. My father would routinely inspect the veal and mozzarella for freshness while interrogating the chef on gastronomic procedures, agreeing to sit across from the stove—the uncles watching with eagle eyes as the chef prepared our meal. The fraternity talked of complementary flavors as painters talk of colors, impressing me with the idea that any skill raised to a high-level of aesthetics was worthy of the gods.

My father was compelled to instruct me about the art on the walls, while my Uncle Gio was intent on instructing me on what he called the bones of a space. I learned how light and shadow work together to fill cavernous spaces. Though I listened intently to their ideas, I was always intrigued by the furnishings and how individual pieces each had their role in addressing the inner lives of empty rooms.

Uncle Gio, my sage Italian godfather, saw the itch coming for me early on. To commemorate my high school graduation, he gifted me with a portmanteau, a plush, chocolate brown, leather travel bag. The designer let the craftsmanship of the timeless piece do the talking; the Cucinelli is a beautiful creation. More so, this poetic gift foretold my future. And it continues to reveal its light to me through the years. I would travel the world in pursuit of beauty. The gift was, of course, accompanied by a precious and prophetic letter.

"To my Godson and Trusted Famulus:

Now that you are entering the larger world, you must become adept at utilizing both the art and the luxury of the portmanteau. The bag has two compartments for a reason. It tells that nothing out there (which you will experience) will ever be of only one thing. Rather, everything is comprised of a glorious gallimaufry; facets of tiny, glimmering wisps, rolled, stuffed and folded into a unison of telltale revelation. Though all things awaiting you are comprised of such multiples, among various parts and pieces, the real magic only happens when they come together. Though you may not understand them all fully yet, rest assured, you'll have to carry them all with you until you do."

The second part of his sentiment was characteristically just as moving.

"The more good things you can carry with you, though they may seem like disparate bits and pieces at first, the more they will eventually come together in order that you can create something beautiful with them; something which you cannot imagine may be possible now—something which will become art for your soul in all your days to come.

May this lush, little bag be a companion to you for all of your life, as you come and go, both here and there. May it always provide a secure space all your own, for packing all that you will need as you travel into your bright future, blending this and that into your unique creation of a life well-loved."

Everywhen,
Uncle Gio

3 Kitsch

Italy

Today, I'm off to my annual pilgrimage to Salone del Mobile in Milan, known as the tentpole of Milan Design Week. The Salone draws thousands of exhibitors from all over the world. It's heaven for design devotees who, like me, adore credible collectors showcasing the budding trends their creations are forecasting. A gold mine, where sensory overload's a given, I never miss it because despite the work it requires to take it all in, it gives back tenfold in inspiration.

Interestingly, the psychology of design and the analysis of acquisition bump right up against other weighty mathematical areas like the geometry of desire and the calculus of accumulation. If this were a movie, you'd hear "My Favorite Things" as musical background. First, however, you must analyze why you classify certain things as 'favorites'. If you step through it, you'll be amazed. No matter how well you know yourself, some reasons will surprise you.

The matter of why we like what we like is fascinating. Most people are uncomfortable confronting their tastes because it exposes too many illogical vulnerabilities. This tiny transport into and out of our deepest secret likes and longings is what maps the routes by which we emotionally navigate our lives. I know first-hand that only love and one's collections are as purely personal as it gets, no matter who you are or how much you're worth. Stuff is a vital part of our human make-up. We all have a soft spot where we're compelled to indulge, but it doesn't mean we can logically explain or account for it. The oddest realization is that we come into this world with nothing and yet we spend our lives behaving as if we can take our accumulations with us when we leave this world. Despite impractical indicators, in that fleeting moment suspended in egomaniacal acquisition, no one knows for sure if it means anything or whether we just think it does.

And you might consider this when it comes to acquisition. It's comprised of a chaos of sorts; a bubbling broth of conscious and subconscious urges. They flavor each other until you can't taste them individually anymore. Still, it serves as a tiny port of departure outside the restless eye of your always less than perfect storm. And when it's said and done, we must face that the real point of every journey is all about the deep-seated desire entrenched in us to fall in love.

Ephemera stands for things that were expected to be relevant or in demand only for a short time, but nowadays all bets are off about projecting longevity. Ergo, this 1960s renaissance at the Salone. Eras become enchanted in cycles. Older designers had already written the 60s off as kitsch. In the design spin, we say kitsch is the junk you can sell for a profit because it may have associative value to a few.

But the textbook definition of kitsch is a thing (to borrow the Yiddish term, a *tchotchke*) that appeals to popular or lowbrow tastes. Nowadays, in the global world of commerce, junk is still junk but kitsch isn't junk at all. Rather it's something with an appeal beyond its objective worth; a token of temporary relevance beyond what it is, something of value that isn't valuable. Whatever that means.

As a dealer it makes perfect sense, but to put it bluntly, I don't deal in kitsch. I've learned to 'ditch the kitsch' even when it can seem temporarily compelling. My clients are hobnobbing moguls who relish the stability of things with tangible value; as in things that hold their worth on the world market, in much the same way an Hermes Birkin bag continues to appreciate in a diva's closet.

But listen, there's really no accounting for taste. Take for example, a client of mine who incessantly buys porcelain figurines from Spain, often travelling to the village where they're made which is not far from where she hails in Valencia. She relives her past through her proximity to their creation. An enormous estate piece that was commissioned just for her is the largest and most expensive Lladro ever made in the history of the brand. It's not something that would appeal to most, although there is poetry in it: the porcelain which begins as mineral rich mud, experiences a magical transformation by crafting. But that's not its value to this particular collector. This piece is a passionate memento of her time with her deceased billionaire husband and their storybook life together. Its scale is as grand as their courtship, forever a symbol of the experience she lived when he was alive.

Just as her collection represents her days as a young girl, this piece speaks also to the aspirational quality of collecting memories, a time when she coveted unobtainable treasure and promised herself that one day she would own such beautiful art.

To this day, her home is filled with these mementos and the grand centerpiece graces the stately foyer of her Texas mansion. There's no amount of money in the world that would allow her to love any piece more than this one, even though its value, outside of her own heart, abides in its size and historical uniqueness.

I can understand the sanctity of the longing, but my personal inclination happens to be as far from this position as I can get. I keep a large Buddha in my bed chamber to remind myself what a sticky fellow Attachment is. And while it's neither tasteful nor prudent for me to be this frank with most clients, the art of unbridled attachment doesn't speak to anything artful at all. It's more about a sentimental connection that enables one to crawl into an emotionally locked space filled with objects that enable their owner to pine, identify and sometimes obsess on some phantom ideal.

Most clients do a decent job of managing their wants, while others operate like addicts, preoccupied with filling an emotional need by way of material things. Getting enough is impossible because there's nothing in this physical world to remotely reach the depths of that spiritual void. Ironically, it only leads to more obsession and isolation. As you see in my field, I must pay serious attention to both psychological and aesthetic matters, putting them in a context of behavioral economics, to better address the marketable opportunity with a client. Much of what happens when purchasing the artifacts I sell is akin to a subconscious tug of war in the head of the buyer. And the struggle between the emotional and the rational mind will never end in a tie.

Research shows that the *precuneus* is the precise section of the brain where all autobiographical memory resides. It emotionally colors its own data constantly, so much so that on a factual basis it can't objectively be trusted; except for the simple fact that it's all any of us have to rely on.

Truth is, what we ultimately hold in our hands is the result of a balancing act that's neither random nor rational. Though unabashed clarity isn't a welcome sentiment in the world of high dollar demand; my job is to demonstrate how selectivity creates beauty beyond what was believed possible. Your job is to learn to appreciate the white space.

4 Rich

India

Though it appears that I wander the world haphazardly, being called here and there on whims of the rich and famous, chasing intuitive leads for treasured finds; nothing could be further from the truth. Rather, I've a roadmap in my head at all times and the path is one of strategy, not happenstance. I couldn't cover enough ground if it were otherwise. So today, to juxtapose the order of Milan, I'm focused on taking in the creative chaos that is India. But whenever in doubt about one's direction, I've come to trust that most of us are perpetually headed in the direction of some sort of marketplace. And I too am about to venture in.

The energy inside this market hive is dense, almost stifling. It wrestles with itself, holding the atoms of sleepy hollow, beehive, raging river, Sufi den, ancient temple, classical theatre, royal palace, whore's quarter, political enclave, destitute slum, broken piggy bank. As everything in India, all the juxtapositions create a new stew.

This leg of the trip is about a sourcing strategy I've developed to snag some specific finds for a picky client, a famous American icon who insists on furnishing her fourth home, on a septentrional strip of California coast, with only the most exotic art and treasure intended to create a colorful but spiritual space; one conducive to relaxing, but in a chic and provocatively sensual style. But she does give me free rein. So much so that from Rome to Rajasthan, I've been treasure hunting with the creative license only known to those who happen to be travelling without keepers.

I appreciate her faith in my vision. Though the best work is derived from collaboration, the more leeway I have, the likelier it is that magic will happen. Although my clients realize this, it usually doesn't stop their interference. But here's the thing: something extraordinary can only emerge from an uncontrolled process as it often reveals something grander than what they intended. It's precisely at this creative crossroad where a project can expand beyond the confines of the client's original vision, morphing into something greater than mere accomplishment.

My medium is the objects that I introduce onto the live setting; the objets d'art that transcend the confines of a space. This connection is the real source of all magic. It is the spark of soul that we long for; one that speaks of the art of possibility.

Besides my own projects, I do this for a few of the top names in the design business who refuse to schlep through endless markets, auctions, and thoroughfares to deal with cunning, belligerent merchants which I find part of the adventure.

There's also a thrill in knowing people who you, dear reader, only know through tabloids. For example, the woman I'm shopping for? The one who gave me carte blanche to buy what I wanted? She goes only by a first name and is revered as one of the world's biggest pop stars. And one of the most difficult to deal with as she eventually articulates her vision after I've been creating it for months without her input. You would know who I'm talking about immediately if I gave you the first initial of her name, which I won't.

India reminds me that the brighter the light, the darker the shadow. And shadow all too easily masks underlying beauty. One reason I'm so drawn to its contrasted showcasing is its drama of vibrancy and filth; the coexistence of sandwiched forces, butt-up against each other like lost siblings just reunited, yet not. They sit side-by-side in this dysfunctional mosaic of quotidian life, conjuring magic out of a befuddling and flawed coexistence. My father likes to say that Saint Bonaventure said that shadows are the literal footprints of God and that we should not be so ready to forego probing them more intently. But this same disparity resides inside every tiny transaction, no matter how infinitesimal the coined exchange. Embracing today's energy, I'm compelled to bargain down to nearly nothing for a certain something, fully aware that my cosmopolitan client will never be concerned whether I saved fifty thousand US dollars or five; the savings buried regardless in my mark-up for the transaction.

In the heat of this lambent Indian morning, I'm devoted to probing the recessed doorways that evaporate as soon as they appear. From the start you must acknowledge that every way out may also be a way in. This is the only way in which real treasures are found. Therefore, like a kite catching the lift of a steady breeze, staying present and open to the possibility in the now is key to catching the winds that await. Every impression triggers an association: Eerie sounds with no physical origin, the pending negotiations, this shopkeeper's bad breath, the dynamic of our pantomime exchange, the waft of curry, the inside feel of his tussled shop where I might stumble upon something extraordinary by fated accident.

Indeed, I come upon a hand-carved, hand-painted set of ancient wooden temple doors; capable of creating a gateway to an artistic assembly brought to life for a project that sits poised above the Pacific's blue cradle. I firmly believe that artifacts have their own spirits and that their magic arrives for us always at street level, in some pedestrian marketplace where the magic of inanimate creation is relegated.

Moving through the maze, I dart alongside aromatic and displaced scents among random fixtures, taking in the waves of spice, tinged body odors, and the fragrance of flowers surrounded by junked options. I see collectibles that might be fun as fillers, like barbotine plates in a French country kitchen; or old Guerlain flacons from the 1800s to inspire a bored little shelf in a surly client's guest bath; or an intricately opulent thick blue vessel of glass-blown composition with just enough grace to enliven the lonely recess of a grooved, antique ebony credenza, a possible solution for a stark wall in a client's Tuscan estate.

But rooting out the artful from the marginalia is essential. So is being open, perhaps enough to welcome an unexpected bit of potential that might alight my path on this ordinary Tuesday morning. Though I've no idea where I am, or exactly what I'm seeing, I'm consumed with finding my way inside the belly of this funky medina. Feigning an insider's familiarity, I proceed.

Among labyrinthine successions, I hear a haunting but recognizable muse mumbling from somewhere inside the assorted collections. The invisible spirit stays close by, keeping perfect pace with my steps as she follows. Present in the best possible way, it's as if she's guiding me through a secret door and I've suddenly become part of an obscure but metaphysical unearthing. Though the entity is unknown, I feel almost a part of releasing some 'thing' trapped too long in a masked existence, begging to come to light or to be celebrated through the simple act of physical discovery.

The steadily abiding nuance and the satisfaction I have from taking it in, continues like a shadow following my every move; until a randomly abiding Hindu god, cast of stone, points me to exactly where it is I need to be.

I trust that all things have their distinct energies. And when working amongst them as regularly as I do, I'm attuned to the contagious ripples they stir. Despite barriers of language or issues of private access, this is how I roll.

And then there's this little nuance. Just as easily as any one of us can be categorized by passers-by on any street, the well-tuned merchant is innately aware of the precise moment when an interested atom from inside a passing stranger will show itself. Mind you, this happens long before any tangible transaction germinates; well before the buyer officially acknowledges any interest and way before eyes meet to reveal a subconsciously gestured clue.

The market dance of the reveal finds its form, ever so slightly conveying one's buying sophistication or lack thereof. It earmarks your essence, revealing your unspoken intent, foretelling how much you want something, even how much you have to spend. The seasoned merchant is like a blood hound, smelling when you're in range of an object of desire, and assessing if you're an able, rich amateur or a superficial browser, and most importantly, what your real business with the merchandise is. It's not much different than when you're in a busy metro; how it is that your dress—your coat or shoes or hair style—tell more about you to the casual observer than you intended to share.

The unspoken intention of a buyer is worn upon their sleeve, and I'm painfully aware of exactly how it is I choose to wear mine. For me, appearing unfocused is a coy line of defense. I visibly flirt with things I do not want, a healthy dose of detachment being essential to a successful encounter. Each attuned merchant I pass has trash and treasure amply mixed, a time-honored ritual of unbridled, democratized participation.

There really is some 'thing' for everyone; though this isn't as important as realizing price will be the key factor in determining and sustaining interest. Regardless of the outcome, the unfolding hope of interest hovers like smoke in a poorly ventilated room above the buyer's currency and the seller's reach.

In India, one's wealth might be the equivalent of a week's wage, so foreign travelers can be presumed wealthy by local standards, and yet the wealthy here may not be considered so by Western standards. Whether buyer or seller, we all don many hats. In the marketplace, I'm the buyer, but later with my client, I'm the seller; the histrionic roles cycling back and forth until no one is purely one thing. So, long live the marketplace, a place where you can never really know what will find you. And what role you may be destined to play.

But on the last day of my meandering, it's difficult to keep existential weariness at bay. As I stumble into an indoor-outdoor configuration, longer than it is wide, two vociferous brothers greet me, incanting gibberish to everyone in earshot. I try to ignore them to make my way past the narrow rows of their shop where I might be harder to track, secretly hoping to claim my thoughts again. But the incessant haggling continues, and the brothers show no sign of abstaining from their accented repartee.

I stumble upon a small henge of stone statues that pique my interest. I think these figures might show well in an estate garden or peristyle. There's a half dozen of the alluring figures, all in the vicinity of about five feet tall. Out of the blue, without knowing why, I instinctively go in to strike a deal with the shortest of the brothers. I'm ready to take four of the six at a shamefully low price, given their age, size and condition. I'll pass on the two taller ones to afford me more placement flexibility. I act disinterested in everything else once I've secured a firm price for the steal. In a *wabi-sabi* way where a perfectly imperfect order is trusted, the same brother, who I now know to be named Shams, portentously reveals an unexpected nuance, in his heavily accented broken English.

"Ah, you, you know, they no can be separated or no sell."

This caveat is a most unusual one coming from a merchant in any land. Plus, these stone icons seemed to be randomly placed and weren't presented inside his shop as an honored grouping.

"I don't understand," I respond.

The elder brother, Pradeep, jumps into the discussion more animated than Shams and speaking much better English. Grimacing with every muscle in his lower jaw to make his point more visibly apparent, I realize his misplaced anger isn't coming from a place of rage but rather from his intent to make his point understood.

"Are you stupid, or no?" he asks abruptly, his lack of tact taking me by surprise.

I retort inoffensively, "What if I am?"

There is an abrupt silence that lasts a little too long, as if he believed that I could be.

"Why don't you tell me why they cannot be separated, since I only want four, not six, and that already separates them, no?"

Adding bold gestures to his repertoire, Pradeep insists I am not to take his warning lightly. "I tell you. But I will only sell in pairs. Two yes, but not one. Got it. Not three, but four is good. Know if you take – you are to keep together. If you understand, good. Done."

"I see there are three sets of two, yes? Or, three pairs? Two are paired, for example, like male and female, a couple, a set, or matched pair?"

"Yes, maybe, why?"

"Pradeep, tell me, are they perhaps gods, or lovers, or ancient royal dancers? Which ones go together best in twos? "

He looked at me blankly.

"I tell you, only in pair. Only in two. This important. Who they are not much matter. Two yes. But no to one or three. You good now, yes?"

"Or what?" I spout. "Pradeep, I'm asking you to tell me what it means if I separate them."

"No good. No pull apart. I know it. They be not happy, and they make big unhappiness yours. If you do one, they make you not happy. Okay? That is all."

It seemed obvious to me that this was a ploy to make me take all of them. "So, you want me to take all six, right?"

"I no trick you. No. Why I want do that? You already buy enough. No trick."

If Pradeep was trying to make me uneasy leaving two of the statues behind, it was working. I felt the unfamiliar grip of superstition. "You admit that this pairing sounds a little crazy for stone statues? Please, tell me, where you heard this story?"

"No story. Real. I learn hard way after I buy."

One thing that all dealers, me included, have is the honed instinct of a poker player. We can read who is holding a winning hand, who is bluffing. Pradeep wasn't bluffing. "Tell me more of what you know," I pleaded.

"Ah, you see, I buy six. I put, one here, see, this one there. I make room. I move one, put there, yes? No, no, not good. Things go down, bad things, no good." Pradeep pointed to his heart. "I say what I know. I put in two, there, and poof, all good. Crazy no more, no joke, boom, it stop. I try more later, because I no belief. I test what man say; keep them in two. I tell you. I test. I put in one and one; not two. Ask Shams, he know. My shop burn in fire. I lose all money. Baby get sick. I put back here, see two by two and boom, sales good. I keep six by two. Why chance? All good; happy, no problem. Best."

"Okay," I conceded. "But why would you hide them back here and not keep all six of them all together up in front?"

"Aye, see all in here, there, mister, to make room, no easy. You say, oh, go, make room; here best. Not so easy, you know? Do is hard."

His brother cautioned deliberately in better English, "These be heavy things, like life. See. All so many people here, there, all people no doing. See, beggars there, nothing? This is life, mister. You get? I ask, what so special? Nothing. You see? Only life here, no more."

Acknowledging his deeper point, I ask the more expressive sibling. "Tell me more of what you know about the statues? If I buy them, I must know what you know."

"I know, what I say. All by two, or no go. Period. Or, you get pain."

"No more to know," said Shams chiming back in. "Keep in two, all good. You know why? Know. You see? One is looker with eyes to see, and other, you know, do like Bollywood, actor, dancer, I think. They work in two or no good."

"So, I must think of them as sets? Heads/tails, night/day, dark/light, male/female?"

"Good/evil," said Shams.

Pradeep fumbled for words, "All is creation. Everything. Poof." He gestured in the air while making the sound with a deliberately percussive P. "One see. Clap hands, good. Or what? Nothing. You see? You, me, all see in two or not real. No do alone. We know, God want two."

"Tell me why you say that one is the actor?"

"One makes show, do, clap, laugh, cry. By two, we make art. Art good."

I finally understood. "I will keep them in twos and honor your wishes; one as Watcher and one as Actor."

"No, no, no." Shams blurted emotionally, "No good. No say one out loud. End or you get pain, my friend.

"Why pain?"

"Because you hear me say two, out loud. I tell you. You know. Pain. Period."

"This thing, ask why I not want more big price. I need you go and take away. Big worry if I keeping. See, all good stone, maybe 1000 years old. No more for me to keep. They be like women. Trouble, here, trouble there, Ooof. You no believe me?"

"No, no I do. You are telling me that these statues are magical, yes?"

"Oh, I no say magic. No thank you." He pointed his index finger in my face, moving it down to my shirt with a poke. "No, I no say magic to you. What is magic? I tell only what I know."

"I stay by six statues long time. You want? Good. Take. Lucky you. – You good price. All yours. Your statues."

"I assure you Pradeep, I won't separate them, and I will take all six from you. Okay?" I put up six fingers to be clear.

"Good," said Shams.

"Yes. Thank you," Pradeep added.

I was beginning to feel I'd entered an altered reality. I wasn't sure if I was really buying into their crazy tale or not. I was reminded of an advertising truth: facts tell, but stories sell. "I want to be sure with you that not all six must stay together, right? Only twos is good?"

"Yes, two, two, two, all good."

"Tell me," I said, "how long have you had them?"

"Not year. No sell. Customers only want one or three. You pick good number, so I make deal. I no want on my heart, no more, you see?"

"Are they likenesses of gods?"

Shams laughed. "Oh, Hindu gods, who knows. Too big to count. Confusing. Hindu gods all change this, change that, all time. Too big to know. Gods all good – yes, but you know, gods want things."

"Gods all want more, more all time. God is merchant. No, nothing free."

"I know gods be women." Pradeep spit on the ground to make his point. "You laugh? But I know true."

"Why?" I asked.

"Too hard to make happy."

As our fandango concluded, I made arrangements to ship all six figures back to the States, and since our spiritual incompatibility couldn't aid me in accomplishing any more today, I'd come to the marked point when it was time to hightail it out of wherever the hell I was. But in India, unlike in America, you don't have a social equivalent for letting someone politely know when you're ready to leave.

I'm so reliant on not having to say anything directly when in the Western process of preparing to leave. It's a little detail that reminds you where you aren't. And being so culturally Italian, our trusted adage, "*La gentilessa apre tutte le porte,*" also doesn't hold water in this novel marketplace where kindness is not a door opener or a door closer.

The art of the ditch. Like when it's last call at a bar, or Cinderella is watching the clock turn 12, or a salesman cuts you short because he's got a more promising buyer waiting. If you're older than sixteen and on a date, you too know the drill. When it's time, it's time. If your first inclination is to preemptively cut and run before the curtain drops, this is an acceptable choice, possibly for reasons you may never fully articulate.

Life is strange, but in the marketplace the potential for oddities seems to double. As the brothers weaved a tale, whether fact or fiction, it did compel me to take all six. I hoped to have better luck deciphering the encounter later, perhaps under a full moon, accompanied by my Manhattan poison of choice.

Don't get me wrong. All days should be this charming. I got what I came for, and then some. Though I've done my pedestrian penance, I hope I didn't miss something essential and that I ditched out on today's deals at the right time, on my own terms, and possibly also unscathed. That is, unscathed from those invisible, oblivious, unnamed things that lurk where buyers buy and sellers sell, and in that mystical somewhere, the limbo in between the worlds. It's always the case as Plato warned: "*Everything that deceives must be said to enchant.*"

5 Niche

California

In the design world, there's one thing that's understood by all who partake. A design has either got soul or it doesn't. Boom. End of story. As you approach the project finish line, if you've applied your talent truthfully in service of an inspired objective, a soulful essence makes itself known. Art is created when simple space becomes a vessel for holding the will of imagination and vision of the creator for the joy of its inhabitants. We can only wish that our lives will work in the same way, eventually disclosing a positive reveal.

Wanting to fill every niche of our lives with our idea of art is in our bones but having a sense for the art of proper placement is something that either comes naturally or not. Teaching the eye is not possible. There really is a place for everything, and everyone can, and does, partake in this labor. But only a talent like I possess can make this art.

Which is why, when I presented M with the Middle Eastern vision I had for the many niches in her Malibu retreat and she screamed, "I said Turkish! This is Mediterranean, you imbecile!" I knew that not only was I dealing with someone with absolutely no sense of historical design, but also someone with no sense of the art of the niche. Incensed, I pulled the handkerchief from my jacket as gentlemanly distraction, camouflaging my outrage, but only for now.

Her assistant, Candy, who moments before had insisted on plunking the sugar cubes into my tea herself, rolled up the design prints and handed them back to me without bothering to put them in their sleeves.

"Come back when she's in a better mood," Candy whispered as

she showed me the door. "She just got panned in *Rolling Stone*. They called her a…" she leaned in closer, "a washed-up diva M! She's an artist. They can't treat her like that."

I nodded as if I agreed with Candy's assessment. But I did not. Did Candy not know that I, too, am an artist and can't be dismissed like that.

My usual method of—mentally adding surcharges to the hefty retainer—didn't stop the bleeding this time. It hit me hard that though most of my clients think I might design for God, there are a few annoying narcissists who think of me as hired help. I thank God for the crashing waves, so Candy couldn't hear me curse the aged icon in four languages.

After the M encounter, I rang up Jonathan, an established California Coast designer and long-time friend who's kind enough to acknowledge that someday he hopes to be me. Little does he know yet today that I wish I could be him. His huge gift is being hard of hearing, so he never has to listen to what his clients say they want. His profound realization, to his great success, is that he discovered that at a certain income level, all California homes look the same; so he just replicates the indistinguishable style in each abode. His only point of departure is rotating the art with up-and-coming artists, which thrills the artists and makes his clients feel that they're in on some soon-to-be holy secret.

Being hard of hearing also makes Jonathan the perfect luncheon companion when I need to vent. Jonathan, the native Californian, ordered a filet and a glass of Opus One. I went with the Power Paleo and most appropriately, post M, a power shot of Lagavulin 25 to quench my outrage.

"It's always the damn niche that causes the unforeseen trouble, isn't it, Mitch?" offered Jonathon in associative support.

"I know. The focus on the finite space pushes some over the edge. Why, the larger the space the more they can pontificate endlessly about their vision."

"And by the time we get to all of it, they've forgotten where we started anyway."

"Jonathon, truly I should have been a psychologist."

"No, you're too busy being a naughty patient."

"Mitch, you know of that Swedish design concept: *lagom* that neatly conveys what's required for the proper utilization of the niche? The 'not too little, not too much' idea that aims for just the right balance between things to create a composite of both order and grace. I'm consoled knowing that every culture has its own take on the imperative of ordering."

"Yea, my very good Muslim friend informed me that a wall niche is a regular feature in most mosques. It's called a *mihrab* and the niche is a dedicated space that serves to pinpoint the direction of Mecca or *Qibla*."

Jonathan nodded occasionally, though you could never be sure about what he heard or disregarded. When he pushed the check towards me, he let it rip. "Cut the crap, Mitch. M isn't your problem; she's her problem and you know it. Let me give you some real practical advice, pal. You need to see Athena." He politely shoved at something that looked like a bean—his hearing aid—in his right ear.

"Athena who?"

"There's a long wait list, but I can get you in."

"Why would I want to get in?"

"Trust me, you need to see her. You're letting the hoi polloi define you."

"Did she define you?"

He laughed. "Of course! She helped me find my proverbial niche. She got me to see something I wouldn't have paid mind otherwise."

"Pray tell, Jon, what was that?"

"It's complicated but just look at my before and after, and I think you get the point. Look at how my work no longer consumes me and how balanced I am now."

"You mean how balanced you appear to be now, don't you?"

"Whatever, balance is good anyway you can get it." I studied Jonathon's expression, and he was dead serious with an air of gratefulness when mentioning this Athena. I wondered what he had in mind. You see, I'm also painfully aware of something known as the *dark niche.* I have one. Everyone has one. For some, it's an infinitesimal space. For others, it's a regularly frequented over-sized chamber having enough square footage to harbor some resident evil: a black hole in one's heart or soul lacuna, an emptiness demanding to be filled that the wisest among us know is part of the human condition, whose siren call is denied at one's peril."

"Yea Mitch, the wise ones work to vigilantly tame its tug and learn over time, with practice, the dark niche will diminish in size and become less and less habitable."

"But back to the not-so dark niche, Jon. I know you agree that minimizing any part of the whole is a flawed design practice."

"Yes, every bit of our space and who we are needs its due. But some clients like M won't pay you or it homage. Addressing the niche is an instrumental part of our business both artistically and monetarily. After all, many a priceless piece sits graciously in a once forgotten space, exposing the beauty of the newly observed space."

"And you know I needed to converse with you today just to wet my whistle again with a sane comrade. Without getting too esoteric Jon, I still believe to my core that we are divinely entrusted to illuminate the power of beauty and ordering human spaces."

"And that my friend, is why I want to be you in my next life. But in this one, you work way too hard and way too much. You know better than to trust all your clients with the truth. Some of them only want you to control the delusion. It's your job to let them or to just walk away. Like most of your conundrums Mitch, you just don't want to admit what you already know you know."

6 Witch

Greece

The word witch could nowadays be considered a retronym, because old definitions about what it meant don't hold up. Take, for example, the Salem, Massachusetts Witch Trials in 1692. These witches, or women with deviant intuitive inclinations, were burned at the stake because they were a threat to the brittle norms that were upheld by the Puritan pilgrims of the time.

I can't help but noodle the irony that today about 1.5 million witches live in the U.S., a pantheistic anachronism sprouting exponentially from our current cultural miasma. Comparatively, there are only 1.4 million Presbyterians in the U.S., so it seems the tables have turned by volume in favor of the ranks of witches and their broomsticks.

The behavior of burning witches at the stake was fueled by the social premise that the avidly conservative Puritan way of life was to be unquestioned and that any deviation from its norms was to be interpreted as condoning permissive behavior punishable by death. Keeping 'the order of things' was the priority of communal rule. The chaos this caused among the communal ranks, however small, was a powerful source of disruption to the whole. Capital punishment cannot expunge what a deviant is secretly thinking.

Creative expression as we know it today wasn't allowed to show itself until almost a century later, though glints of what was to come were abundantly apparent through tiny keyholes; and oddly it's the glimpse through the keyhole that's the precursor of what's coming.

We modernists are spoiled because creative thinking, artistic expression, and intuitive heresy are praised and encouraged by the elite.

The tattoo craze, graffiti, rap music, multi-genderism all spin in greased grooves that back in the Puritan's day would have caused a scourge of flaming flesh.

Today, it's openly admitted by its enlarged definition that there are witches of every stripe among us. Whether it's a person who openly practices Wicca or is engaged in some form of occult practice, or a dabbler in the tarot, astrology, fortune telling, alchemy, or a student of the mixed philosophic and religious bouillabaisse among classical disciplines—Beware the witch!

There are white magic witches and black magic witches. There are psychics, shamans, soothsayers, healers, and mystics among us who do not claim to be witches at all, though there's a blurred line in terms of how the many practices intersect.

From tiny African villages in Uganda to Hopi reservations in Arizona, to Cairo, Israel (the land of Kabballah), Buenos Aires, Los Angeles, New York, Miami, Istanbul, Zurich, Mexico City and Montego Bay—occult practices and rituals abound, both in and out of the public view.

A mystical thread is well woven into our human heritage; a deep-seated desire to engage in meditative and esoteric behavior that ties us, if not to each other, to something beyond the here and now. Whether we're trying to contact dead ancestors through Hindu Pitritarpana or seeking answers through the Catholic Pope or Buddhist Dali Lama, or consulting ministers, rabbis, mullahs, mental health gurus, or our horoscopes, every human life inherently makes peace with aspects of the mysterious. No matter what we think we know or how smart we are, the biggest part of all our lives remains a vast and untidy mystery.

All of which was on my mind on a temperate azure day in a tiny town by the sea in southern Greece, where for all I knew an ancient god or two might still be in residence. I was here on the advice and advance booking of my friend Jonathan, searching for the abode of a renowned tasseographer, someone who was beyond famous with a jet-set clientele, and I was late for the appointment. I wondered if that would affect any prophecies or interpretations of my affliction.

The study of tea leaves or coffee grounds has a long broad history, but the practice is especially grounded in the country the ancient gods called home. Like all mysterious practices, the draw is that we can possibly learn more from the guide than we know by ourselves, and that there's an undiscovered potential that we can access via the guide. In order to better interpret the events in our lives that appear happenstance, the guide can disclose how they actually may be rooted in a master plan. And I, grounded in the yes or no finalities of my trade, and a bit surprised at myself, am not immune.

As I checked the street numbers along the way, I knew I was near. At the end of a turnabout stood a tiny, bright white house with the numbers 22 (two two, a good omen) barely visible on the wall just behind a tall blue pot of Golden Esperanza in breeze-blown full bloom.

A laughable aside on my desire to meet her was that I usually take my tea in bags rather than loose, and though I like the aroma, I never drink coffee. I flew up eight steps to a shiny bright red door where I was greeted by an attractive older woman with a full head of smooth white hair. Her luminescent face was tanned, and she had the most astute eyes I'd seen in quite some time. Petite and unassumingly fit, she was elegantly postured like a dancer and seemed to be someone who knew important secrets but would never tell. Her pelagic eyes held my attention with a gaze of someone half her age. They danced with the rhythm of her voice, like an obliging partner. But it was the melodic charm of her soft accent that warmed my heart most, and her impressive command of English was unexpected accompaniment.

"Hello Mitch. I've been expecting you. Tell me what brings you to my door?"

On any given day, no one loves a veiled greeting as much as me; but this one resonated differently, giving me an inkling that something else was awaiting.

"So nice to meet you. I've anxiously awaited our meeting, though admittedly with some trepidation. Tell me, how long have you been reading leaves?" I asked, trying to atone for my tardiness with small talk.

"I see that you like to answer questions with questions." For a minute there was silence. It was the silence when two discerning souls meet for the first time and are making space to let the other in. Like soft vapor, it lingered between us, just above where we stood.

"No worries today, Mitch. I think we are going to get along just fine. I've been reading leaves for as long as you have likely been alive. I am Athena, but I prefer that you not say my name aloud unless necessary."

"And why is that?"

She lightly laughed, "It's not for any occult reason, if that's what you're wondering. It's more practical. I get distracted personally when I hear my name. I try to keep the reading apart from me so I can channel the information I receive on your behalf without static or interruption. You see, these kinds of connections are very fragile things, like silken threads."

"So, string theory is real?" I cajoled.

"Exactly." She laughed, seeing I could flow with her mystical sentiment.

"Your English is so unexpectedly good," I said.

"Yes, my father was American and my mother, Greek. Knowing both languages helps me figure out more than I can handle most days," she said as she walked me through a breezeway into a garden that opened to a surprising view of the azure sea below. The expanse was far more from what it appeared to be from the street.

"Your home is lovely, and the view is so surprising."

"Yes, I like it when things are more than they seem and not the other way around."

"Me too."

"I think it's why you made an appointment to see me. No? You must also be one who is open to the unexpected."

Her candor caught me off guard. "I surely hope I am. At least I'd like to think I'm open to the unexpected, but of course I'm also not as brave as I seem."

She smiled.

"If you want the cosmic truth, you don't seem brave at all to me.

What I'm telling you isn't judgment; just my sharing with you what I actually see. Is that good with you?"

"That's why I'm here. Your honesty is most welcome, but I still hope that I am somewhat brave." Her pronouncement left me feeling unusually insecure.

Kindly she offered, "Yes, and there's nothing wrong with your thinking that unless you're trying to get to the truth. Bravery isn't your gift. You're quite the calculated personality, well-rounded, nicely balanced for a man your age. Your soul is older than you credit it to be. You have been born many times."

"I'm no stranger to earth then?" I asked.

"I said you have had many lifetimes. I never said they were all here." She let that sink in. "You study and organize everything in your mind well before you attempt it; so you see, bravery doesn't have much to do with your personal energy. But let's say that bravery isn't something you should concern yourself with. Or better, it is not something you should use your energy working on."

"Oh," I said, at a loss for retort.

"You know there is only so much time and energy we have in this life? It is best not to waste your energy on things or people, where there's no authentic or special calling, or itch, or karmic need. Not when it can be better spent elsewhere."

Athena smiled. "To know thyself is never an underrated advisement. To accomplish it, one needs to be either a demi-god or a purveyor of magic. For a mortal, I think you are doing just fine."

As Athena invited me to be seated at a weathered, round teak table, she began arranging the table top with a gentle back and forth motion which consisted of her moving things about in a mesmerizing way: an off-centered candle upon a hand-woven artisan cloth burned intently with gold and silver talismans sprinkled about it; tiny shells were spread nearer to her side of the table than mine; ornate flowing scarves, one blue, one green, in umbra shades, were loosely draped on the backs of our chairs. Wistfully, they were caught in a balmy breeze, like expansive wings reverently attending our seated selves.

The garden was well-tended with flowers, rosemary, mint, basil, lemongrass and a neat patch of some mystery herb I didn't recognize. Contentedly growing nearby in rows of symmetrically placed pots were plentiful pink, purple, and blue flowers that made the sequestered space feel alive and magical.

I pointed at a foot-high plant with yellow flowers I didn't recognize. "What's this one?"

"That is henbane, a somewhat weedy annual."

"I love how you've created such an inspiring garden. I have profound appreciation for the study of space and artful placement." I felt a pang, not owning up to the profound insecurity that drove me here. "I love what you've made possible."

"Thank you. I can already tell you are an artist, by both your hands and your eyes. Do you find when it comes to designing spaces, it is about just listening to them? They tell you what they need to be, like ingenuous little children, if only you will listen."

"Your point of view reminds me of my godfather."

"I can't take all the credit. The faeries are also very fine communicators and far more willful than one would believe. They especially love the amaranth. You know, it's the plant of immortality from the Garden of Eden, so it makes sense to me."

As she laughed aloud, I pondered if perhaps she was serious about her garden helpers.

"Before we begin, I should let you know about the henbane shrub you asked about."

"Yes."

"The ancient Greeks say it is a key ingredient in witch's flying potions. Of course, there's a supportable medicinal reason for that. It's a relative to belladonna. Anyway, I only mention it to you to illustrate something about these readings. You see, just like herbs, well, let's just say, these readings have a life of their own. I cannot tell you how long or how short the reading will be or exactly what we will accomplish. Some of it may come now and some of it may choose to follow you after you leave. You see, it depends on the energy we both bring and what it is that

I can see, what I can find and then also, just you, and how open you are to the spiritual energies. It's important you are comfortable with this. If you have doubts, it can interfere with what it is I receive."

"I understand. Don't you think this is exactly how it is in life? You know, that it is very much a continually fluid process?"

"Yes and no. Both answers are true. It all depends on what, who, and also when."

"I think I understand, but regardless, I'm ready for come what may. Please do your thing and know that I'll be open to whatever you find."

"It is only because the time is right that we are here and together now. Because we are both fully present, we can make something happen." Athena cupped a small handful of aromatic herbs into her small hands and rubbed them in her palms, mashing them together three times, and then she set about sprinkling them about the table. I could smell the pungent rosemary as she began, "First, one question: Is there anything that you would not want to know?"

"I'm open to you sharing whatever you see. I would actually prefer to know, if that's what you mean.

"I only ask you this because we cannot un-know anything once we know it."

"I assure you, I'm fine with knowing."

"That makes it better. By now, you can probably see how it is likely that you might interpret your reply back to me as a further indication of that bravery ideal of yours—because you honestly do want to know. But, you probably can also see my earlier point. You are an intellectual, a thinker, a planner. This speaks well of your academic mind, but I assure you, your wanting to know is not about bravery at all."

"Your particular gifts are much more a matter of artistic assembly—rather than one or two great gifts, actually yours are based on the gift of congregation. The gift is comprised of many qualities, but as a matter of degree and not from one tangible force, say like bravery is. Your gifts are a blend of energies that collectively comprise a curious whole; a unique concoction but not exactly, all together, easily identifiable as anything in particular, or for that matter, well understood. Your true energy is mostly about divine curiosity. It's what moves you and what has gotten you where you are today. You have a burning desire to create, to discover, and to explore; in short, you do want to know. I think curiosity may be at the center of it all. It is what drives you, deep in your soul. I see it is what enables all your other gifts to come to light." She moved the herbs around. "Know that it is best not to interrupt me once I begin your reading, unless of course I ask you something. Otherwise, you should wait until the end before asking me questions. For this reason, I tape the reading for you, as sometimes it comes fast, and it may be difficult to recall, and I really want you to remember."

Listening to Athena so intently, I no longer felt myself anchored in my chair. Clearly, I was in the presence of a powerful personage, a virtuoso who was wise and respectful of both her gifts and mine. With a mix of excitement and trepidation I focused with all of me as Athena began our mystical exchange.

"Actually, you happen to be akin to sea glass. I don't think you know this."

"I'm familiar with sea glass. Washed in the ocean as salt and tide erode its surface, they become opaque, their sharp edges rounded. I collected colorful pieces as a child with my grandmother. Why?"

"I say this because though your edges are smooth, you are a less transparent character. You are open to taking 'in' from all around you. You must try to settle closer to the sea, compared to the big city where you reside. I see you are deeply involved in the arts. This is good for you and your constitution. It is as it should be, but you are not only creative. You have a good deal of practicality mixed in. You're successful whenever you allow your gifts to guide you."

"Business is good, but lately it is more a means to an end. You are essentially creative, but simultaneously internally analytic. Still, you are personally underleveraged, and this is despite all that you have achieved. Unfortunately, other than in your work, you don't spread yourself out much. This is sad for those who will miss out on your company, and vice versa. You have more to give than you actually do.

This can be an issue. You are always busy and I mean, all the time. I see the practical need for temperance. You are misunderstood because though you appear extroverted, at heart, you are more introverted than you admit. You may not have realized this until very recently. Though when a child, you were rather quiet and somewhat of a loner, yes?"

"Well, I was an only child, but I never felt alone."

"This is because you are followed by several dedicated guides. That and there is always a lot rumbling up there in that head of yours. I mean this literally. It is not a particularly restful place up there during the day, plus you have company too," she said as if she had known me for years. "It's a nice place - up there, if you don't mind busy. I do not think you know what procrastination is or what it is made of."

Then, suddenly, without warning, on the inserted count of three, she abruptly ceased her train of thought and adopted a somber tone, as if a heavy curtain fell before us, between acts.

"We begin now with a cleansing prayer."

I thought we had already begun.

"Mother of God," I exclaimed silently to myself, petitioning with the traditional Catholic exclamation for divine help for tightening my seatbelt. The roller coaster car was about to leave the station.

Athena firmly closed her eyes and gracefully began moving her hands over the tabletop in horizontal circular sways. The scent of vanilla, lavender and mint were aromatically wafting as she spoke; now speaking only in Greek, delivering a melodious sing-song chant that rolled off her tongue in easy recitation. Her Greek blessing contained the snapping of fingers in between the longer series of words. She closed with a single quiet coming together of her hands without the sound of an actual clap. She opened her eyes but after this point, she no longer made eye contact with me. Instead, she looked down or across the table or intermittently closed her eyes, as she continued in full flow. I marveled that she began without cups, tea leaves or coffee grounds, as I assumed would be the traditional norm.

"You are comfortable in what you do. You make easy decisions for most things. I see you drift among historical pieces and luxurious artifacts. I see you not in museums, but rather curiously in exotic places, in palaces and large estates all over the world, as well as in antique-like surroundings, in caverns with valuable treasures, ornate furnishings and old books. Your education and your work are tied together. They are all of one piece, like cloth with no seam. This keeps your true self grounded because there is no radical impasse between them; but this can be somewhat tricky. You are not destructive, and you are not in any physical danger. But you live too little outside of your head. Do not get me wrong; the weather is good in there, but it doesn't have enough comfortable chairs for the good company you still will need in your life. I am not recommending quantity over quality; you of all people, need quality. I appreciate your selectiveness, but while it seems harmless, it is also deceptive; because you are not aware of how much this is a larger truth for you - or what the ultimate consequences will be."

I felt a sudden quiver of intuition in a way I hadn't experienced in years.

"You mostly live in the worlds of others, somehow, but not as much as you should in your own. Your own world is smaller but more precious. You must learn to make space there, inside this particular place in your life of which I speak. You are the only one who can choose to make this possible for yourself. This sacred space is calling for you but you have yet to heed its prompting. It has been calling you for some time, though you continue to ignore it. Know that it will not wait forever. I think you may be an Aquarian, the water bearer, maybe February?"

"Yes," I said, "Actually, late January."

"I see your personal planets now and what occupies your orbit, Mercury, Venus, Uranus and Jupiter. This is why you appear paradoxical, though despite it, you happen to not lack for popularity. You are surrounded by distinctly forceful energies from the motions of the angelic universe. They are around you, in a constant circle. They mesmerize you some, but occupy most of your time, though you use them mostly to sort through work ideas in this alternately temporary and practical realm."

"These actions in which you engage; they are set in motion more so by many 'others' who are outsiders no doubt but respect you and your product. You must learn something critical. Life is not a business, nor was it ever meant to be. It is important to manage life but make no mistake, it is not the real work of why any of us are here. In fact, Mitch, you need to work on doing less and being more. Making a living and making a life are two very different things. The latter is far harder but could appeal to the artist in you, if you will let it. Focus on this idea, almost like a meditation. Creating a beautiful life could be your greatest work yet."

The muse continued without pause. "You delude yourself thinking you have your life under control; yet there are boxes inside you that you store but are afraid to open. You prefer not to think about what is inside these boxes, even though I know you know the boxes are there and none are empty. You would rather do your usual business instead, but deep down, you know these boxes deserve your attention. You must make the space to contemplate what it is that you inadvertently avoid. Among all the fine treasures I see around you, the most valuable thing you will ever own is your own intuition."

She continued, barely taking any breath between the words that poured out, like water tipped too intensely from a pitcher. Her messages fell upon me, flooding my mind. I became full past my brim, as the liquid drenched my psyche.

"You work with rare things. Perhaps you are wealthy because of the goods I see surrounding you? These things are only common among royals. But curiously, I am not sure much of it actually belongs to you. Enthralled with the study of ancients, these things, they comfort you emotionally, much more than you attest. They are like substitute companions. But you are missing – a certain something you are yet to find. This is not love exactly, though it will lead you perhaps to real love, if you choose to be open to it."

"You aspire to be spiritual, but you are afraid of all you bring to that table. You like being free, but you are deeper than you appear, though not yet ready to embrace this hidden side of yourself. You keep it at bay, except intellectually, where you access it as an inner source of accomplishment. It is as if God also resides only for you in artful places. You hide keenly behind your charm and likability. However, you cannot hold your awareness back much longer; for soon you will see that it will draw you out. Only you can say yes or no to the call."

"This unknown entity, this circling dervish mystery – the testament yet to come, the one to still be revealed, it will show itself to you – but you must be ready to accept it. If you do not meet it boldly, when it first knocks upon your door, just like an itch that is there and suddenly gone – it will not return to you. I mean, ever again. You could lose this rarest strand, a starter thread that you ideally would know to follow."

"This thread of which I speak, it is illusive and different but very real. It is the start of creating a new life for yourself. It will require risk, but it will be good. You know, this is always the nature of all of the really great gifts."

"You must remember that each life has one central crossroad; a critical point where the journeyman must risk going either left or right. Little forks are usual, but the big fork only comes once. Trust that other forks are small by comparison to the big one. The crux comes fast and without warning, and whatever you do next, just after receiving it, is what determines all the rest of it for you. We all have this marked spot of demarcation, but it happens at different times for each of us, according to our path. You, Mitch, almost now directly upon it. If you choose not to pay attention when it calls you, there will be, of course, other opportunities, but lesser ones which are not as fruitful. If you miss it, down deep, you will know inside what you have missed. This very turn could make you physically ill right after, or worse case, years later, or you could die unnecessarily as a result of it before your time. If you accept its invitation however, you will venture further and wider, past your current understanding of how far is far, and how wide is wide. You will live to the end of your eighty-ninth year; forging a way of unexpected joys from the mythical and benevolent Jupiterian sources that faithfully abide with your Jupiter placement; I think perhaps, in Pisces."

We sat together in a strangely quiet limbo now as I realized I was barely breathing.

"Wherever it is you live today, it will become but a port of call. I see you are up in the clouds, but you must soon be seaside. I see a woman with you near the ocean. Her name begins with the letter C. You do not have children of your own, but your life is rich.

"You clearly have a deeply woven celestial bond with your mother and your father; perhaps because you are an only child. There is cooperative work they will assist you in doing here even after they are gone. They were promised to you, beyond the bounds of here and now, and will continue to be with you, often in your dreams, even after they have passed. Your father passes first and then your mother, but years later. You will spend time where they live, and there is great joy there still to come."

"You have a dependable energy at your core. Your early goals were grossly simplified given your aptitude; maybe for you to better fit in, or to be understood or to be at home in your smaller world of that time. Today, you choose a larger world and aim to claim it for your own. But somehow, it is still very much the world of others. It is a royal world; not really yours except by association. This connection or actually also, ironically, this non-connection, it consumes you. It must not be confused with your making your own life. I cannot stress this enough, or you will come to know as an old man what it is to regret."

"Your work is challenging but it doesn't scare you. In fact, you are well suited for the part you play, still, you must know, you are only the actor in that play. Eventually, you must come off stage and live the other side of the curtain. You must find that certain other – the very one who sees you for you and watches for what you can become. This essential connection is for true fulfillment. Beyond the relationship you have with yourself, this watcher is critical to you and to your awaited potential. You are gifted, but you will never find the great treasure solo."

A sun shower had started suddenly from a bank of clouds that had stopped above our heads. As the last tiny drops of rain fell onto the table, I knew down deep what she was seeing was true. I must prepare to follow a life to the unknown great treasure, no matter whenever it calls for me. While caught in my own antics, the steady grind, the successful entrapments, the habits, I've absolutely no idea how to navigate the treacherous path of creating my own future.

But the relentless Athena did not cease. "Oh, you like the game, the competition of your work but you have no idea what you are really dealing with yet. There is another game that you are unknowingly part of that rules your work world, far beyond your spiritual understanding. There are things with real powers that you will come to know, beyond the goods that may be prized. This other side, it is not about success or earnings. Many will miss the very point that you will come to see. You soon will have to face it, whether you want to know it or not."

I wanted to stop her now to process her relay in more detail, but I knew I must hang on to her words as best I could.

"With this awareness, you must make personal decisions, ones you never thought would be yours to make. Some will shake you at your core. Though you prefer to stay at arm's length, these decisions will come at you with your name clearly upon them. They will be directed only to you for the required action. They will be big to you but will make no sense to anyone else. Whatever you do, do not abstain from facing what is presented to you, no matter how bizarre it may seem. And know from the start that you will be in over your head, more quickly than you believe."

"You will feel alone but you won't be. You are not alone in any way but only spiritually. In fact, you are followed by guides who have you in their line of sight. Among them is one Sacred Guardian. Be ever so thankful for this great gift which you have earned from a past lifetime. Ready yourself, for the piece of a great mystery coming your way. It's been tracking you to some extent for a while now. It is not clear to me what it is. It is complicated to know. It is not stalking you but rather, will call you out, because of what you do, what you already know and where you must go. When it appears, a not so gentle wind will blow inside your skull, filling every miniscule, mystical crevice between your bones; hinting something not yet acknowledged that you instinctively know about this life. Some of this is not pleasant to be entrusted with, but it is part of your lesson."

"Your journey takes you all around the world. No one that you thought you could count on will be there for you, that is, not in the way you think they can be. Though possibly the one whose name begins with C will eventually be, if you decide to let her in. She may be Sagittarian, if that helps you find her. Anyway, she is of December energy."

Athena was speaking so quickly now I could hardly make out all her words.

"Once you face the darkness—if you accept it—then everything you need to know will follow. You do not need bravery to succeed, only focus, intuition and tenacity. Oh yes, and the ability to ask yourself while upon the path, *what is true,* but only what is most true for you. You must trust only your own vision."

As I heard her words coming forth in sound, I sat mesmerized by what was happening at this tiny table by the sea in this lovely garden with this magically deep Greek stranger. I wondered how much of it was coming from me and how much was coming from her, and what exactly was making itself known somewhere in the place between us, in a requiem of trance-like, operatic, spiritual disclosure.

I saw the glimmer of delicate rain shower remnants, half-droplets clinging to the surrounding foliage and the dainty pastel flower petals. Athena's cryptic revelations about the Actor and the Watcher that I'd encountered in India took my inner sense of balance away. In a bout of emotional vertigo, I struggled to stay focused and upright in my chair. I felt that I was back to being six years old, when I was once stupefied by a magician. Only a few feet away from me, he was engaged in contrived legerdemain, while I remained ignorant of the concealed possibilities.

Simultaneously exasperated and energized, I knew that a pure magic dwelled in this place and that there was a reason why I was right here, right now, with Athena, who was revealing the opportunity that was almost before me, in such a way that I too saw its significance. However surreal, I knew this was all real because unlike a dream, it was palpable and my understanding of it came steadily in waves, not in encoded whispers. It demanded I pay attention in order to remember all of it, not in parts and pieces but rather as a whole experience.

I knew in this moment that the essence of life itself is meant to be just like that of pure magic. I felt the raw power of its evolving promise inside me, in a way I never had before.

Something was literally opened-up inside me, for the first time. I wanted to speak of it aloud, but I couldn't find the means. Instead, I sat numb, unable to disturb the flow of this magical thing I was somehow swept up in. But I also realized with trepidation that this psychic Greek sage wasn't done with me yet. I second guessed myself, wondering if I had made a mistake earlier by telling her so surely that I wanted to know everything. In this moment I realized the witch was right. I wasn't nearly as brave as I once thought I was.

Athena forged forward. She directed the message across the gap between us, and I saw it rise up in to the air, into the blue sky above our heads. As I saw the Aegean in the distance, I knew the ocean heard her words and it was holding a piece of my aspiring truth within its lunar tide.

Then, suddenly just like the Venus rising from the mind of Botticelli's canvas, Athena rose like a weightless muse and ceremonially began to pour tea from the antique pot on the side table just behind us.

In a low voice she explained, "This is a white peony tea. I prefer to look into the symbolic associations to find your true unfolding. I intuit which type of tealeaf to use, but only after I meet you in person. I promise you, this one is all yours."

The cup and saucer were delicately hand-painted with pastel pink flowers and wisps of soft green and gold, like faerie kisses on white porcelain. She didn't speak but motioned for me to drink, or at least I got the message to do so. As I raised the cup to my lips, I closed my eyes, relieved it wasn't hot which was good, because my heart was beating in anticipation of what was still before me, which was also begging to be swallowed. What was to come, I did not know, but my interest was so deeply piqued that I felt at one point, if I couldn't take it; in that moment, I might fly away on a wind that would surely catch me mid-air. As I took the last sip of warm liquid, I passed the ground-strewn cup to her, and she began.

First, she spun the cup three times and asked me to take the cup, turn it over and quickly right it. Peering inside, she gazed without hesitating as if the cup had turned into a large storybook and she tumbled inside, headfirst, into the thick of it, only to reveal some remarkable half-hidden truth.

She stared at the leaves. Athena carefully named specific letters aloud. "I see these individual letters in your tea leaves. It will be up to you to determine what they mean." She pronounced each letter slowly, one by one: M.A.N.I.T.C.H.

I had no idea what they meant or what they referred to or what I was to make of knowing them. These would be letters I would have to add to my lengthy list of mysteries to decipher later.

"I see you walking through a market, more slowly than you normally would. Pay the time of day no mind. Let yourself wander into alcoves, intuitively without agenda. Do not drive yourself through collections at the Gemini-like pace that you often exhibit which can make you appear superhuman with a list in hand. Instead, here you must stroll like a novice, not with the baggage of your artistic expertise. Try to flow in and out, weaving about and through, letting certain coteries speak to you. Wait until you hear your name. You will pass behind a certain blue door to see. By passing through, you may find the treasure of your life, but it is not about money or worth. It is through this entry that your future will officially begin to become known to you."

Athena abruptly ended our session. She lifted her head and looked me squarely in the eye. "And so be it. It is." She rubbed her hands together, palm to palm, gesturing that we were done.

"That's all of it." she smiled, "I would ask if you have questions of me, but it is of no use. The open window has already closed." She laughed. "I cannot answer them anyway. What I told you is all I know about it. Hopefully, it will make some sense to you."

"Well, yes, wow, certainly, I hope so." I said, taking in a hugely deep breath in the hope of re-setting myself back into the here and now. "Thank you so much. I mean for everything. I'm in shock, actually. I've never been privy to this kind of mystical mastery. How is it that you can know these things? I'm dumbstruck, realizing what I must learn about my own life."

"And may we never lose this quality that stirs us from within." she teased. "You know, I only tell what I see before me. It falls into me and then out of me, as it comes into view. It is like photographs in an album, until it is done. It goes away as suddenly as it comes, and then, it ends. Now, it is all yours to process for yourself. Actually, your part is the hard part."

"Mitch, life is a carousel. It goes round and you need to move about it freely while not getting off the platform. Some horses are better than others, for you that is, so find your best ride. It is still all about the ups and downs. The carousel keeps turning and we do not get off until we die. But, you, you my friend, are due for a real change of horse. Is this helpful?"

"Beyond my comprehension at present."

"Trust that it can only make real sense to you. But it does mimic how life works. You know how it has you completely in its throes and then when it's done with you, goodbye, and suddenly your run of show is over, and it's the big farewell. This is how all of the big things work. Just like hurricanes. Entrances and exits must never be minimized."

"Or, for that matter, in my case, anything in between."

Amused, she assured, "I have the comfort of knowing some of life's secrets. Unfortunately, everyone wants to know the secrets, but actually, few will ever mind them. I know for sure more than half of life involves accepting things on terms that are not yours. However, if we can surrender to this and stop trying to take control, we can have a pretty good run."

Stuck in my own tracks, I questioned, without trying to sound as if I was begging, "So you really can't answer questions about anything you said?"

"No, I really cannot. I'm sorry but the gift didn't come with that kind of ribbon on the box. It is only exactly what it gave you directly, no less, no more. But hopefully, as you ponder it, your awaited question will be answered – by none other than by you, because you see, the actual asking is the key; that is, ultimately, asking yourself something you are not asking of yourself already. My clients tell me, without these readings, those important questions would likely never come up, let alone be confronted. Rest assured that many commit to the asking part but very, very few commit to the knowing part."

"Yes, I see how that would be the case. I admit, this wasn't on my radar, but it is now. If it was remotely on my radar, say maybe subconsciously, I hadn't realized how significant it is."

"Oh, but it was on your radar the whole time. You just did not know it."

"Or in my case, it's more like I didn't want to admit that I knew."

Athena smiled back sincerely, "We all have the answers we need; we just need help facing how to go about confronting them. Keep in mind that everything I can see has to be coming, somehow from you and your radar. It is all you. Every single part of it is you. That is the magic and the miracle of it. The subconscious is where we secretly are all waiting to be found."

Athena handed me a tiny pouch. "What is it?" I asked.

"It's called Meadowsweet. It will make you a fragrant herbal tea that you're likely to be glad you have later tonight. It will help you settle and dull the sting of realization some."

As she led me back through the hobbit-like garden to her front door, I said her name for the first time. "Athena, your name is certainly appropriate. Like the goddess of wisdom, you are one enlightened lady."

"We all have the names we need in this life and the experiences we need to grow for they find us, just as the names do. A name is not anything to be diminished. We have that tendency as human beings, you know, to miss the miraculous for the mundane. You know, Mitch, most mysteries aren't mysteries at all; they are just things we can't accept yet."

She pressed, as if needing to impart something essential for me to understand, "Unearthing what is buried is always a worthy pursuit. You must not dismiss what you do. Your work may be the metaphor you need. It is all right before us, as I see it. If we follow our personal clues, a commitment to live vibrantly will emerge. You know, the uncovering is both a restoration and a discovery of one's authentic power."

As she handed me the cassette of my reading, we hugged and I left her sanctuary, a disoriented, befuddled, but somehow relieved man.

Half behind the parting door, Athena warned, "Don't forget, Mitch, like sea glass, you are where you need to be, but you must prepare for what the sea has in store."

7 Twitch

Greece

In the aftermath of my otherworldly reading with Athena, my head felt literally shrunken. I was spinning too fast to wind myself back to wherever it was I was meant to be. Plus, I also felt a slight constriction in my chest. She'd obviously hit a nerve for me to have such a marked physical reaction.

Missing the comfort of my previous nest of certainties, hell bent and accompanied by my trusty portmanteau, I hurriedly checked in to my hotel with the intention of sinking my weary bones into a plush pillow of solitary refuge. A massage seemed most prescriptive since Athena's reading was still in the process of settling into my muscle tissue in untold ways. It was my only hope of releasing the tension that docked itself into the harbor of my right shoulder.

Since departing down those eight fateful steps from the witch goddess's house, an uncanny grip had hold of me. A persistent twitch that wouldn't let up. It made regular rounds from my head to the base of my neck and back again, in a karmic figure eight. I'm hoping it's only one of those twitches that comes from the weariness of carrying too much baggage, both the metaphysical and the physical kind. But ironically, my gut also tells me I'm twitching from some secret inner delight from the unsettling data I received, a portmanteau with its two packed compartments chock full of possibilities.

The distinct pronouncement of my lack of bravery tingled like a pernicious itch. In emotional terms, this assessment translated into unease that it won't be long until I'm officially in over my head. I recognized that I was working myself into a fit of hysteria, the kind I'd always observed in others with distain.

"Hello Mr. Bonaventura, welcome to the Grand Resort Lagonissi. It's a pleasure to have you with us again. We have your preferred room," said the dark-haired Grecian beauty at the lavish reception desk. In my abnormally aroused state, her pulchritude created a momentary priapic distraction which she acknowledged with a smile as she continued bent forward over the computer screen.

"Thank you and please be sure to place a do not disturb sign like a marquis over my entire stay. Oh, and I'll also be needing a cassette recorder, delivered to my room, as soon as possible, please."

"Yes of course, but let me verify first that we do have you here for two nights?" She peered into the computer portal. "If you don't mind my asking, sir, what do you do?"

"Well, I guess you could say I think about where things go all day."

"Are you a philosophy professor or a psychologist?" she asked.

"Only peripherally. Rather, I think about invaluable objects all day, like a designer and collector. I find them and hunt them down. Some would call me a Revealer.

"Sounds both exhilarating and exhausting." She finished up on the computer."

" It is," I confirmed. "Things have a way of sucking the life out of you."

"Like people?"

"More so."

"Oh dear. More than people?"

"Oddly but often, yes."

"Thank you, sir. I appreciate the insight. Oh and of course, the antique recorder you requested will be brought to your room within the hour. Have a restorative stay."

Recognizing her Millenial dig as a signal of what I was already feeling in my physical body as the effects of simple aging, I entered the chambered nautilus of my alcoved room. Folding the panoramic balcony doors to open wide, I marveled at the scintillating view.

There's something magical about being perfectly perched, just high-up enough to see through the catbird's eye, but basal enough to spot the full panorama in human context. I tell myself that this is how I precisely want to operate when on the low ground as well; high enough mentally to be above the clutter and misery, but low enough to be in mortal proximity of the goings-on.

The sea breeze calms me as I take in adjacent aromas from the shade-loving foxgloves and ivies gracing the terrace walls, grounding my vista in the Platonic ideal of essential Grecian beauty. Plato understood the importance of aesthetics in a well-lived life. It's the same kind of appreciation of beauty that Keats prized via that Grecian urn. One's soul's semiotic bark, the compelling reason the gods chose this place and why they decided to make it home.

As for Athena's assertion that courage wasn't my specialty, I trust that given my many shortcomings I can hope to let this one skate by. Since I've so many to choose from, why would I settle for focusing on only one? But what's most annoying is I've always been a fan of the classical Greek definition of character. The Greek code stresses honor and courage as flagship. Though all the ancient ideals are worthwhile, the Greeks chose these two as the essentials a man needs to carve out a decent life from the chaos that makes its way in. Ah well, Athena assured me that gifts are the clothing of one's character, which in my case, she said, wasn't courage but rather, was divine curiosity. I could only hope that honor was still intact.

But what in God's name do those letters, M,A,N,I,T,C,H mean? I was sure I was about to find out. But despite the Apollonian beauty all around me, I spent my night gazing at the dark sea, intermittently replaying Athena's recorded words; dabbling with a divine room service meal, except for a disappointing Greek salad. The namesake salad is nothing like the ones in New York delis. So how is it that the Greekiest Greeks no longer own their signature creation? Yet, another great wonder of the beguiling isle of Manhattan that bustles with creative impersonators of their ancestral lands. But then, is it not the very nature of creativity to have no bounds and to remain a fickle companion? Right when you think the creativity goddess is all yours, she exercises her inclination to be reborn on some distant shore.

Random ruminations aside, though I miss the appurtenant vibe of the Big Apple when I'm away, I won't indulge myself further about the stupid salad tonight. There's not room enough inside my uncourageous mortal veins for accommodating one scintilla more of anything. Besides, early tomorrow, I'll be visiting two highly praised procurators for clandestine showings. Later, I'll be off to auction for three highly desirable pieces, including a Roman bronze balsamarium, with a hunting scene in the round, hailing from the second century, that I've been eying for more than a New York minute. A beautiful object that will make a client's lonely niche come to life, in a stairwell of a Brooklyn Heights brownstone.

Tonight's the first time I can recall when something personal has taken disruptive precedence over my broader focus. I'm quicksand stuck in a state of panic juggling another design project, a Parisian penthouse, simultaneously. Needless to say, I must purposely honor every last painstakingly picayune detail in order to meet the desired oeuvre for both. Ultimately the goal isn't an easy task; just conjuring an organically inspired mindset, to call forth a celestial order with a dash of unbridled imagination.

The toughest part of the entire design process is that it all momentarily becomes tentative. I've had projects come and go in two days, but with others I've been stuck in mud for months. One consoling thing I know is that the better you get at something, the subtler the things are that make you good. The art of everything resides most in the subtleties. Whether it's a subtlety of physics and the disconnect between relativity and quantum, or the subtlety of perspectives of law in the Supreme Court, or what makes Levine the grand maestro of symphonic splendor, though seemingly there should certainly be others. The minute details of excellence elude all rhetoric. No matter what the language, outlier mastery is just like magic, it defies logical explanation.

If you hear something called an effortless work, it's a ruse. Real work is never effortless, and as anyone in fashion, physics, or design can tell you, the more effortless the work appears, the more work it required. If it's not truly a calling, no one of sound mind would want to do what it demands or requires with any regularity. However, if it's a calling, then one can't actually stop oneself from pursuing it endlessly until you're finally either feeble or insane.

All chatter aside, in my mind I'm flashbacking in real time, contemplating those two damn Indian brothers and their forewarning about the six stone figures that continues to haunt me. It's compounded further because of Athena's reference to the two respective co-dependents, Actor and Watcher. Like player and audience, subject and voyeur, alpha and omega, victim and abuser, dark and light, or the Ouroborus, the snake eating its own tail, it's all too apt to be accidental. One thing of which I'm certain: I don't plan on separating them outside the space of compatible coupledom. Let no man interfere with such a fragile thing as the holy order of two.

Consumed with my involuntary twitching, I wonder if Picasso had it nailed. "Art is the lie that enables us to realize the truth." Torn on the point due to my father's cherished influence, I'd prefer to favor Goethe on the matter, although my lower self better aligns with Picasso's existential stance more than the good poet's wisdom.

"It is not given to us to grasp the truth, which is identical with the divine, directly. We perceive it only in reflection, in example and symbol, in singular and related appearances. It meets us as a kind of life which is incomprehensible to us, and yet we cannot free ourselves from the desire to comprehend it."

It finally dawned on me to learn more about that little henbane shrub in Athena's garden, wondering if it had anything to do with my twitch. Turns out the wicked little plant has a life all its own. Witches favor it for their flying potions because when taken in a non-lethal dose, it makes one feel dizzy, intoxicated and mimics the feel of flying. I found nothing mentioned about twitching, but it sounds familial and feels close enough.

Luckily, I remember the Meadowsweet tea and pour myself a cup. An herbal precursor to aspirin, I welcome the infusion as Athena advised. Though nothing sinister happened at my reading, apparently she knew the simple burden of facing hidden truths is jarring to more than one's mind.

8 Pitch

Greece

Throwing the right pitch in just the right way to the specific batter calls for nothing less than string theory or particle physics or quantum gravity.

Athena threw me a curve ball, and I must admit that it, as well as my recent fast ball from M left me discombobulated. I felt like I had to recalibrate everything based on what I already knew. So, back to the carousel.

In my gig's circle of influence, whether I'm buying or selling, things change hands quickly, and often millions are at stake with every move. Whether I'm designing peripherally or centered on the mound, smack dab in the thick of a big negotiation, throwing the right pitch with adept strategy to whomever is at bat is essential to the outcome. My arm's got to be warmed up, ready to perform at a moment's notice. It's forever the outlier masters, who have the power to shape the game.

I can't help but toy with the metaphor even when I'm not taking in a Yankees game. I'm a rabid Yankee fan and believe that once a pitcher - whether of design ideas, or monetary deals; or a stitch-seamed round object hurled across a 17 inch square home plate, one is always wired thusly. My trade, like baseball, is all about the universal way of utilizing specific techniques designed to accomplish certain things that have stood the test.

Though it's the pitcher who first determines what comes next— what pitch will subdue what batter—the best batter will have studied the pitcher he's facing – his tempo, his tendencies, his endurance in late innings, what pitch he's likely to pitch when he's two strikes ahead. A deal you're ahead in can collapse with a single pitch, and boom, out of the park.

Just like in baseball, every pitcher is judged by his fastball, and every batter on what he can hit, meaning his conviction that what he's selling is irrefutably worth what he's asking. But the advantage is still the pitcher's. What Ted Williams said still holds: hitting a fastball is the hardest single thing to do in sport.

Baseball is a fascination of mine. It's rise-to-fulfill-the-moment heroics. It's science. Scientifically, it should be impossible to hit such hurling heat. Consider that today's best fastball pitchers throw at a high speed of 105 mph. Unlike in other sports where records are regularly broken, the physical dynamics of throwing the fastball tap out at the physical ceiling of 105 mph; the arm ligaments and tendons can't take much more.

On the flip side, the batter has 200 milliseconds to decide whether to hit a ball coming in at 100 mph. He has 50 milliseconds for his eye and brain to register the pitch and only 150 milliseconds to swing the bat. Hitting a fastball at 105 mph should be humanly impossible, but if both pitcher and batter are simultaneously in what sport science defines as a zone, possibilities all their own present themselves.

Thankfully, not every buyer requires a fastball; a change-up may suffice; a pitch that looks like a fastball when in fact it's about 20 mph slower; literally, a ball coming in slower but with the illusion of speed. It can throw a tired seller off his game. What baffles most is that no matter what you throw, the ball doesn't care. Pitches that worked yesterday can have a terrible tomorrow. And majorly, it's also all about whereabouts. The place colors things in strange ways so that things wield a mysterious hold on other things. Ask any Yankee about how the home play advantage factors in. Geography matters even when you don't think it's a determining factor. At the end of the day, all mark-ups are local. For me, buying in the States, is almost always going to go down one way, always a curveball. In Europe, it appears to be upfront, like either a high or low fastball, but rarely with any middle ground. In Asia, the rules you think you know don't apply. In Greece, it's all of the above and then some. In Istanbul, the art of the deal keeps an invisible vigil half the time so you're never sure what happened until it's done.

To paraphrase Athena, it's my ballgame to win or lose, so own the mound without sweating the outcome. But my knowing the right pitch to throw isn't always enough against a gifted batter. I've got to have tricks up my sleeve. The best one happens to be the toughest to do and at just the right time, which calls for advertising what the pitch is. Why? Because it's so damn good that batters still can't get a piece of it. They call this particular spin-sorcery perversion the ghost pitch, and emphatically it knows just how to haunt.

Generally, there are two types of spin: transverse spin, which is sensitive to Magnus Effect and makes breaking balls curve and fastballs rise. And gyroscopic spin or bullet spin, which is what makes footballs fly in a spiral. The latter isn't affected by Magnus Force. In the marketplace, just like with those best on the mound, the transverse spin is key, but what's paramount comes down to deception. Hence the magic of the ghost in this realm. Now you see it, now you don't. Though I marginally regret having to resort to hide-and-seek to beguile an honest seller, if you're in my game, you play to win or get a nine to five.

Regarding the gifted batter perspective, it's an art to be able to wait for the fat pitch. You have to have the confidence to wait, but you also need to have the brains to recognize it when it's there and the sheer guts to go for it.

Such is the conundrum of each of our games. For those of us who have to bat for our gains (that is, not those just born on third, thinking they hit a triple), every day calls for applying ourselves with outlier creativity.

Today, the game has officially begun, as I'm about to enter the auction house to plan my line-up. As I scan the crowd, I see that because there's a host of good auctions in the area, many rival buyers are there.

Specifically, I'm here to acquire an exquisite Etruscan bronze group of Hermes and Penelopeia from the fourth century that will perfectly complement an insatiable New York client's collection. Next up, a Greek pottery pyxis, with the bust of Nike gracing its lid, making this third century rendition of divine power a fortuitous find, and a sixteenth century Rococo bookcase, both with the same client in mind.

Though I only came to this auction to purvey the three pieces for my New York project, in my business, just as it is in life, you often don't end up with what you came for, so I unexpectedly also set out to secure a Roman mosaic glass patella cup with a millefiore decoration from the first century, the very earmark of when we began counting our human years anew. Finding a home for it is a gimme.

My motto, besides only buy what speaks to me and absolutely nothing else, is keep my personal impulses at bay. But today, to adduce what I mentioned earlier—that what you buy is often somehow lurking in your subconscious—today I intend to make an impromptu purchase for myself.

It has something to do with the juxtaposition of two ancient pieces, poised together. It's as if I recognize them from another life. I want them both and for no logical reason. A charming antique oak and pine French cupboard, perfect for storing champagne, even though it was originally created as a silk weaver's worktable. It holds an old world elan that speaks of something spiritually misplaced, probably within me. And an adjacently set Roman iridescent green glass lacrimarium from the third century. When it came up to bid, I heard it literally call to me aloud, and not once, but twice.

Keep in mind, this is a new twist for me and possibly a tell of Athena's foreshadowing that I'm evolving beyond my awareness. I mean, I love horses, but I don't want to own one. Eventually, it's a fine line though for all of us, isn't it? My line has suddenly without my permission become a little finer. But as is the usual means for me, I'll table this for tackling later.

But these particular finds speak of something else; as if I was abruptly consumed by the need to act at precisely the exact point where awareness intrudes against a distinctly different adjacent force; you know what I'm saying. Yes, right there, at that magical point where the force of both energies creates a collision which creates a whole new dimension. Each piece mirrored some hidden secret about the other; something which could only be seen or realized by way of their adjacent contrast.

I know too well that God or the Universal Divine, whatever name you give the Ineffable, speaks to us through the nature of things and through the sheer subtleness of juxtaposition—to ourselves, to each other, to the world around us, and also to the power that we attribute to the Master Designer of the Great Beyond. Understanding how nature allows them to coexist holds a fertile lesson. Physicists like Hawking tell us that atoms never work alone because creation requires collision. And so does creativity. The intersection of ideas, the chemistry of opposites, and the inherent juxtaposition of energies, are the very ways by which all human glory is manifested.

Though I happen to have the perfect place in mind to nestle the blue-green glass treasure—in an open niche, along an elongated wall—I believe it was my recalling Athena's sea glass analogy that compelled me to buy it.

But as I bid, it's clear that something else is at work here, independent of my covetous response. Perhaps I'm engaging in a subconscious attempt to create a symbolic still life of my new awareness. By enacting the act of ownership for myself this time, I'm securing Athena's words to me, further binding my way into the miracle of recognizing new visual anchors that might remind me of what it is I heard here in Greece and what it is that I must remember, and at all costs and forever. I know surely now that absolutely nothing in this life is ever, ever random. And though this auction was lucky for me—the bidding rivals arriving too late and the best buys, my buys were already seized for a cosmic pittance. But I also realize that on another day, a batter I cannot strike out also awaits his turn. Lest we may too easily forget that both the pitching and the batting are good.

9 Bitch

Turkey

On my way home from Greece, I take an impromptu detour to Istanbul to explore an old haunt that's proven to be both provocative and lucrative; but then the nature of lucrative is always provocative.

Greece influences visitors to passionately want to hunt things. It's only natural for its ancient elixir to seep into mortal pores as we yearn to take some of the classic cradle home. I'm excited to search for the next dredged find, and I can't help wondering when that blue door will show itself. I tell myself I'm ready for the yet-to-come, but truth is, I've absolutely no idea about my capacity. All I can do today is to breathe and stay open, acknowledging that there's not much in my control.

On my way into Istanbul via my proven samsara routes, those demanding twins, Chaos and Turbulence accompany me. And there's good reason. The city on Bosporus Strait named Istanbul was once known as Constantinople, back when it became the capital of the Byzantine Empire. Before that, it was called Byzantium and its history is nothing if not exotic; filled with mystics, wars, secrecy, and infighting. Over time, the name Byzantium became synonymous with anything characteristic of the empire, from its architecture to its intrigue.

En route into the figurative swarm that is Byzantium, I also happen to be engaged in the recovery of the traveler's trifecta: a mishandled ticket, a botched seat assignment, and a seatmate of robust girth who's left me pinned in and also happened to innocently spill hot coffee on my lap; which happened to be cradling a beloved out of print book, by Goethe, no less. The antique book is one my father gifted to me on my 25th birthday. I snatched my precious book, splayed on the aircraft floor, hoping to wipe it clean. But when I placed it back on to my lap, it had remarkably opened itself to a resonant page. Through the Faustian coffee stain, the German poet's lines eerily signaled like a bellwether.

The ancients never really stop talking to us one way or another, it's us who try to stop listening. There's nothing like a well-timed reminder when one's en route that *"what's done is yet to come."* Although I may have circumvented a Faustian bargain or two on my way; some days you just can't be sure of exactly what's coming for you, or better yet, what you might have fallen blindly into.

And once in the air, Goethe's Faustian lesson illuminated itself to my road-worn soul like footlights along a stage.

Through many a long day you'll be taught
   That what you once did without thinking
     As easy as if it were eating or drinking
       Must be done in order: one! two! three!

But truly, this thought factory of ours
   Is like some weaver's masterpiece:
     One treadle stirs a thousand threads
       Ties a thousand knots…

The philosopher steps in
   And proves to you it had to be so;
     The first was so, the second was
       And therefore the third and fourth were so.

If the first and second hadn't
   The third and fourth would never have existed.
     And this is praised by every scholar
       But never a one becomes a weaver.

Encheiresis naturae, chemists call it
   And fool themselves and never know it.

Part II

Everything you want is out there waiting for you to ask.

Everything you want also wants you.

But you have to take action to get it.

Jules Renard

10 Whip Stich

Turkey

If we're successful, a good design awakens something desired yet unrecognized by the space's inhabitants. When we're moved and comforted by a space, it awakens something deeper in us; we can feel immersed or thrown in to the possibility of increased self-awareness or better yet, a spiritualized kind of realized experience.[i]

In design theory, *Heidegger* first started with the idea of *dasein,* his term for the concept of "being in the world." Likewise, *Norberg-Shulz* expanded the dynamic and calls it "thrown-ness." I love the term because it describes how human experiences come at us. We don't see them coming, we don't plot them to happen, but they come at us, and we're literally thrown right in to them. While it's true that what you're looking for is looking for you, what's looking for you can only find you on certain days. Though you can't know when it's about to happen, it tends to meet you just as you're open to receiving it.

The operational mandate requires an openness to receive, or as Gio would likely say in kabbalistic jabberwocky, you must only be present to let it in. Perhaps this is how I've come to love the art of design so much and how it is that I've taken my godfather's architectural lessons and applied them diligently to my work. Applying them to my personal life of course is another matter but admittedly, I'm just another work in progress, riding that carousel to find my best horse.

Gio would say that everything involves some philosophy in its belly. Like architecture, design theory has profound underpinnings of

69

philosophy and psychology; much the same way that art and literature are central to understanding artifact. Of one thing I'm sure. Everything has its story, and every story is itching to be told.

And so this free-form day continues to unfold by my being 'thrown in' literally into a hot kettle overflowing with that cloudy stimuli of my own potential. With an obtuse promise of some illustrious possibility, like spotting a random thread to pull out for myself, I await the arrival of a prized weaver.

Most difficult for me is to be at ease with Athena's prophecy of the tsunami awaiting me on the other side of that blue door. I try to reassure myself I'm ready for it, but I've no idea what to expect, which according to Athena is the deliciously scary essence of being alive.

I just read the quote of the day on my iPhone from the Greek philosopher Heraclitus of Ephesus, the one who exhorted that fire is the fundamental principle of the universe. *"No man ever steps in the same river twice, for it's not the same river and it's not the same man."* I wholeheartedly can relate.

Abuzz in the 'thrown-ness' of the Buyuk Carsi, Istanbul's Grand Bazaar, I realize I'm just one more vulnerable schmuck among its half-million annual visitors who can't help catching the local fever and getting swept up. The GB, being smack dab at the nexus of the ancient trade route between the old East and West, is the oldest and largest covered bazaar in the world, having come into its own in 1455 after the Ottoman conquest of Constantinople. Spanning sixty streets and over three thousand shops, it lays east and west between the mosques of Beyazit and Nurosmaniye.

I've got random things to hunt for today but no absolutes, minus one personal exception: my compulsion for hand-made cowboy boots is front and center. Athena would be pleased that I'm attempting to further make room for the personal. Besides the old-world cobblers in Le Marche, there's no more inspiring spot to snag artfully paired leathers than on the streets of Cukurcuma. When I approach the familiar place, the smell of the glue will lure me in. If only life were so forthright in telling us exactly where it is we're meant to go.

Eyeing the vast seabed of Turkish carpets, perhaps I'll find a solution for a stateside project that's torturing me. You see, a carpet is the foundation for a space, an essential basis for whatever is to be put upon it. Like an underlying principle, it functions to hold or anchor whatever is yet to come. Since I don't have time to take the hop to Hereke, I'll have to stay attuned to what's here before me.

This day reminds me of the whip stitch, typically used to sew two disparate pieces of fabric together. If both pieces are lined-up, then the stitch can loop around the edge of the material. It's fully the case today that I should mind all my edges.

As I move away from the pedestrian groove of the bazaar, the ancient art of carpet wrangling itches for my attention. Funny thing, but carpets don't make for easy company. When eyeing them in lots they emit a distinct energy, dictating more than you realize until you're standing on them. And carpet wrangling's a tough sport, demanding a lot of hot tea plus the Olympic stamina of a professional wrestler or a jacked psychopath. Buying a carpet here is especially grueling because like a high school prom, the pain and suffering involved in making a deal can last too long with no easy way to gracefully exit the dance floor with everything you came in with intact. Plainly, this is no place for textile virgins.

To break the spell the carpets were weaving, I decide to meet a perspicacious old friend at Hagia Sofia; hoping to dabble in the inside scoop for what artifacts may be floating about a la Subterranean. Civilized cultures demand sharing libations before sharing professional intelligence, so we find a one-table café where we have tea of course, accompanied by *lokum*, the illustrious Turkish Delight which lives up to its reputation as a small piece of heaven, a comfort to the tired throat.

After cleansing our emotional palettes and catching up on local gossip, he informs me that tonight there's an invitation only auction featuring seven pieces never before alluded to on the open market. Tonight's showing is a rarity and I appreciate the referral. I might get lucky but if it's not in the stars, I'll trot back with a trace of remorse to my favorite Istanbul nest, the Four Seasons at the Bosporus. Even a bad day that ends up there knows how to turn itself around.

I leave him and continue my meandering through alleyways. I spot a metal Anatole France plaque on the entry wall of a shop containing a referential ditty: *"Wandering re-establishes the original harmony which once existed between man and the universe."* So it is that the very act of searching randomly is therapeutic, but when embraced in an exotic locale its value exponentially doubles. I buy the plaque and plan to hang it on the wall opposite my bathroom's mirrored sink. Another attempt at personalizing my life with more profundities. Funny how we surround ourselves with profundities to perform our toilette, as if their worn wisdom shores us up better than a close shave.

Personally, wandering feels particularly pleasurable, my body in tune with my spirit, reminding me how everything in the world is ruled by invisible forces. Most days we're so preoccupied with our relationship to the visible, we can't stop long enough to ponder that it's precisely the invisible that calls to us. Being an esurient buyer, I happen to know it's true because sometimes you're just meant to own something. I'm sure you know this feeling too. Although you've got to be prepared for the flip side, when the art of letting go is essential to accepting a harder truth, like the price; but if everything falls into your lap easier than it should, it's a sign. Well beyond your own effort, if you can stay out of its way, this is when you might experience the incoming ownership of some timeless and magical things.

Later this evening, I hope to secure a work called "The Nejad," a bluish canvas of abstract composition by the Istanbul artist, *Nejad Melih Devrim* that's likely to command a $700K entry. My securing it would complete a design composition for a discerning client who's given me the green light to go to $800K if need be.

With the bazaar closing at four, I mosey in and out of cramped corridors, dipping in among merchant hives, hoping to save some gas in my personal tank before hitting the auction tonight as finale.

My mind races to keep pace with my footsteps, until out of the corner of my eye, something arrests me—a hint of a protruding carpet, a barely visible swatch from a shop's cluttered entry pile. I approach to dissect the misplaced specimen. I can see the shopkeeper watching at a distance so I camouflage my interest in case it really is what I think it might be. Distracted by the magical call of possibility, I don't notice that the propped open shop door happens to be a bright glossy blue. I recess back into the jambalaya of nondescript rows of chaotically assembled myriad. The second row from the back consists of a long line of old bookcases, covered with sundry objects, some treasure but mostly pedestrian crap.

Moving my hand casually over a few of the visibly interesting items, occasionally taking one in hand to test it for authenticity, my outlier hand stops of its own volition on a randomly placed oddity to which I wouldn't normally pay heed: a bright crystal orb, which quickly enlists the aid of my other hand, as it heavily gives way to settle into my fanned-out fingers. Heavier than it seemed, its reflective surface is in surprisingly pristine condition. Not a single scratch despite being unprotected on a conspicuously neglected shelf.

Taking it off the purple-indigo velvet pillow it nestles on, I brush-off the dust to examine it closer. I ponder what it is I've found and more pressingly why it's of any interest to me at all. It's unlikely to be anything but a simple tabletop ornament of no real value except for the brilliance of its reflective sheen, which is what grabbed me.

Oddly, the orb isn't as cold to the touch as a glass surface might be. Its clarity is unique to anything comparable I'd seen. This crystal has a distinctive look and feel. Though I'd absolutely no idea as to why, I insisted on engaging with the mysterious object. Just like puppy love, this kind of reaction makes no real sense.

When in Turkey, you need to know that a merchant's offering of a price isn't a suggestion but rather only a place from which to begin a longer exchange about perceived value, and never real value. In this land of have and have not, there's only something like perceived value. There's no expectation if a price is offered other than it's expected you won't agree to it or anything close to it. So, I unassumingly countered at one fourth his suggestion and the shopkeeper instantly agreed. In all my years here, this has never happened. Not once. I reasoned that, with it being so late in the day, perhaps he was as tired as I am and also like me, he has somewhere more important to be.

Proceeding to casually check out the shy carpet still beckoning, I was amazed it wasn't on more worthy display. Realizing the shopkeeper had no idea what he had hiding among nondescript kilims, I saw how large it was and the beautifully colored curved design of its weave. I knew it was exactly what I thought it was. I asked the shopkeeper, who today happened to be the nephew of the owner, what he'd sell it for right now. You see, in the market, everything is present tense and today is not tomorrow yet.

He offered me prices in a run of incomprehensible persiflage, until that fine moment when we came upon a landing that stuck. Not quite believing my good fortune, I made arrangements to ship the authentic Hereke carpet and the bitty mystery orb home to my loft in Soho. Normally, I'd route purchases to specific jobs, or to my warehouse, but because these were capricious buys, somehow post-Athena, I wanted them home with me.

I left the shop in haste, physically passing again through the blue door unaware, with less than an hour left before I needed to be flush in front of *The Nejad*. I quickly turned to snap a rushed photo of the shop with my phone, only as a routine business marker. It wasn't until later that I saw that the shop door was bright blue.

A pure silk Hereke carpet is considered fine art and wouldn't likely be caught gracing a floor. It's more likely to be found on a mansion wall. The artistic technique dates back to 400 AD with well over 500 hand tied double knots per square inch (KPSI). The average Turkish carpet has only 150 KPSI, so the craftsmanship involved in making this rug is a lost art and it's why the Hereke rug graces the palaces of Sultans. Hand-crafted with natural pigments from earth's bounty, the likes of saffron and walnuts, these masterpieces represent the highest form of the art of weaving. It's all in the combination of the density and the quality of the silk, the intricate, non-geometric designs, and the exquisite and intricate colorations, known to alter with reflected light on the surfaces of the silk.

Buoyed by my triumph of acquiring the Hereke, I proceeded to the art auction, Lady Luck riding my shoulder. But as soon as I entered the auction house I saw the blue Yankee baseball cap perched on the head of Pete Heller who was seated in the front row, and I knew I wasn't going to buy *The Nejad*. As strong as my client for it was, Heller wouldn't have been there without permission to buy it at any price. I usually would have stayed and bid the price up to make Heller turn around and recognize who his rival for the painting was, but I was too tired to do it with the poker-faced aplomb required to look back at him without blinking. I also knew that Heller would go out of his way to pay me back for gaming him and so I blew it all off for another day. It was a fine painting, though I couldn't put my finger on why. Matisse said he thought that the only real thing in a painting is the thing that cannot be explained. Perhaps it's this letting go of understanding that we need to know in order to be free. Perhaps it was the coup of the Hereke that had me spellbound enough – the inspirational win of unforeseeable possibility.

I didn't think about my magic finds until much later, when the orb and carpet were inside my home. As further proof that every head on this planet provides its own reality; it's only when I was securely tucked in for the night that I realized I'd taken baby steps at incorporating a bit of the personal into the mixmaster of my usual grind. I fell asleep wanting to also disbelieve that nothing in this world is wired to stand itself long enough to risk ever being real.

11 Stitch

New York

Rest assured that what we literally and figuratively set ourselves upon matters.

In design, it's easy to minimize the impact of the underfoot canvas in a space. But, taking the underfoot into account is essential to achieving a well-balanced vision. Having a well-primed canvas beneath your stance, just like a luscious lawn for bare feet, sets the stage for what's creatively possible when you're upon it. Plus, feet don't lie. Anyone who's walked upon breathtaking creations understands the fundamentals that are necessary to make the glorious panorama happen. Just as it is in The Villa dei Papiri, where alternating triangles of Numidian yellow and Africano with dark grey Lucullan marble create the artful floor on which one enters, none who place a foot upon it can ever forget the power of a first impression. Atop such intricate designs, Italians like to say that it's simply *"mozzafiato,"* it literally takes one's breath away.

And so it was the fatidic day the large crate from Istanbul found its way into my home's foyer, (marked H.C. or *hors commerce*, which in French means do not sell); the energy which it contained was palpable.

I'd been in a state of client deadline tizzy, on account of scheduling crap at the tail end of a testy celebrity travail that I'd let sit too long without attention. I just got home from wrapping-up a boot-kickin' grand ranch installation outside Dallas. While the owner of the ranch treated me like the artist I know myself to be—unlike a certain pop star -- the contrast between the Lone Star dynamic and my loft was a bit disorienting, to put it mildly. My French friends would say I was irrationally immersed in an *"ajustement hissy"* (hissy fit). Yesterday I'd been in the company of bulls, and now alone at home, I had to make room in my cramped psyche to take in the beauty of the personal purchases before me.

I have two other pieces at the warehouse that I'm holding for placement that once briefly circulated through my abode, breaching the wall I've emotionally constructed to insulate home from work, but in all my years, not ever before have I shipped a crate of personal finds directly to my home. The astonishing beauty of my Hereke steal called for a perfect placement. It's too elegant a work of timeless art to set foot upon; and though I'd love to keep the Hereke, it's doubtful I can do it justice in my petite urban abode.

By contrast, the orb can be plopped anywhere, the irony of its presence but a casual reminder meant to convey its mysterious nature. I had to laugh. This could be the closest thing possible to my having my very own crystal ball. And doesn't everyone need one in order to catch a glimpse of a compelling tomorrow? What better means than a crystal ball to help with the anxiety that the uncertainty of life brings? Oops, I'm shirking my Grecian instructions again. I must also ring Jonathon tomorrow to impart my thanks for his insight.

The crate sat neglected for over a week before I made a point of asking Terry, my P.A., to tackle it. Closing out the five-day set of eighteen-hour days in Texas, with the work dust still clinging to my psyche's boots, I set my digits onto the inside security pad, resolutely thrilled about shutting myself inside my sanctorum, questioning why most days there's too much beautiful crap to attend to 'out there'.

Wearily, I make myself a well-deserved Friday night libatio, my eye catching the framed e.e. cummings ditty placed strategically just above my bar—bars being second only to bathrooms as places to install profundities. *"When man determined to destroy himself he picked the was of shall and finding only why smashed it into because."* I'm reminded of the fear I secretly harbor. And this is pretty much the summing up of the universal road map of exactly how it's done.

Disarmed, I let my heavy bones fall atop the soft art of magic stitches, to nestle yogi style upon the uncased outstretched Hereke. Peripherally present, the crystal orb sits shyly by in a less prestigious zip code. Like a good Italian, I sip my VOGA on the rocks, before settling into a horizontally configured diapause, the kind that comes from being ideally situated in a moment of authentic quality down time. If only I could hold this magical sensation for a minute more. The crystal sphere catches a shard of light from the nearly risen full moon. Outside the pane of my terrace window, I see the white glowing orb in the sky steadily climbing in the night as if on a ladder, like me en route to something higher.

Terry thoughtfully left me a sealed envelope atop the empty crate, his little way of blunting the trauma of our week from hell. *"M, glad to see you've finally brought something home to roost! Let's see if you can keep it there. What a magnificent textile, but heavens, where does it end? Wherever. Enjoy the magic carpet ride. T"*

With all ten of my road-worn piggies nestled into the weave of this magic carpet, I wonder if perhaps indeed, like they say in Texas, I may be fixin' to change my ways. But to Terry's larger point, where does any kind of exploration ever really end? After all, everything is a treasure hunt. But I'm not too dog-tired to experience the relief of Italy's most instructive ideal, *"dolce far niente"* or the art of doing nothing. Some of one's most creative ideas are born in moments of sweet idleness. The ancestral voice inside my dull skull rumbles like a ghosted self. I hear it speak my namesake, *"O' San Buona Ventura; how good it is deep down to feel things in Italian."* Though every culture has its own magic, mine, so familiar, not just by aesthetic alignment but via my circulating DNA, shares an ancient comfort.

In sharp contrast to the Italian sensibility on the matter, the German inclination of *funktionlust* is a worshipped deity. Elevating activity for activity sake provides its own theology in the fast paced world of antiquities and treasure hunting; and I too am tied to the task of providing the wealthy with many a splendored thing.

As I run my hands across the Hereke silken threads, the sheer resonance of its tactile composition is like a Platonic ideal. Camel hair on cotton, silk on silk and silk on cotton, mixed with abundant gold and silver strands, showcase a grand design which once may have graced the Sultan's Dolmabahce Palace in the Besiktas district of Istanbul. Great thoughts for all the ages have fallen like magic spells atop a majestic *tappetto magico.* I turn over a corner of the rectangle to better admire the painstaking stitching that makes this creation one for all time. It's simply glorious, and all because the detailing serves as divine testament for the hallowed human touch in the skillful minds of ancient masters in the long ago Ottoman Empire. Rumi himself provides a philosophic summation of my lucky acquisition: *"No amount of searching will find this. A perfect falcon for no reason has landed on your shoulder and has become yours."*

In the design realm, textiles are the peacemakers of spaces. They're the harmony bearers that tie things together and spaces are never whole without them. I can add to this repository tonight. There's no better way to trust in the future than when at rest upon the artistic pride of Hereke masters.

Enlisting talent to be able to creatively house collections is imperative for anyone set upon making a house, mansion or palace a home. Greatly loved things require perfect placement. You just don't put something you love anywhere. I ponder how Edith Wharton got it so wrong, *"To touch the past with one's hands is realized only in dreams."* Pinch me but I'm fully awake right here upon this Hereke. Though to be the artist is a sacred calling, the role of audience is divinely inspired too; for admiration perpetuates the cycle of creation through the abiding act of seeing. Both roles are intertwined; purposely delivering a mutual awareness; a devoted symbiosis, a perfectly poised pairing of reciprocal guardianship, each to each.

With the VOGA kicked-in, I sense that I might be expecting that dependable little itch to show itself without overt invitation. It's been known to come for me in moments like this, until I greet it with a little scratch. It's never as far away as I think it is. Tonight, my magic carpet causes me to question myself about what it is that my own stitching says about me.

What holds my fragile soul together? I wish for double knots, but like all of humanity, always hanging by a thread, I get by with less. If I were to turn over a large corner of myself and peer intently at my exposed underside, of what am I comprised? Like this lovely carpet, will I pass the test of time, in the most spiritual sense, or are my stitches too randomly placed without the measured workmanship required or the purposefulness of lasting vision? Will love find me the way I found this Hereke? The magic of happenstance made real?

I ask myself why it is that I am still alone in this translucent splendor, on yet another chilly night, in the resident ripeness of some lost Eden. In an attempt to syncretize it, for me the Big Apple has become a crystal ball-like stage set where a poignantly posed but unsettling metaphor continues to play itself out; one in which I am but the Actor with still no perceived devoted Watcher in sight.

12 Glitch

New York

In the midst of any endeavor, when does that nemesis known as the proverbial glitch not manage to present itself center stage in full regalia? The glitch's severity is known to rise with the amount of money or passion at stake; and so too with design glitches. Initially insignificant, they can quickly escalate out of hand.

Merriam Webster defines a glitch as an unexpected minor problem that causes a temporary setback, but in my business, the words unexpected, minor, and temporary are harbingers of much, much, bigger problems. Experience teaches one to expect glitches as a natural part of things, but the nomenclature of minor remains a matter of degree, and I've seen something called temporary run on for years.

Inside the confines of my testy design procurement world, the glitch can result from one of the following scenarios: an entitled egomaniacal client who can't be satisfied without engaging in recurring fits of lackluster drama; an impossibly tight international delivery schedule; a lost container; an incompetent design resource; a client who starts divorce proceedings or files a chapter 11 midway through the project, one who has a traumatic death in the family, or one who goes MIA for some undisclosed reason, causing a ripple effect you wouldn't think possible.

The first glitch showed itself at sunrise. The client who's headlining today's ordeal is a prominent A-list actress. Obviously she chose the right profession because she can't seem to get enough of the drama. In her homestead production, we're providing everything but the script which, unfortunately, she has complete control over. She insists on placing a MacGuffin in every scene; something we're fated to chase, leading only to more inconsequential things.

She's become newly spellbound by a Hollywood Regency style for her great room which has since morphed, for the third time, to become instead an ultra-urban contemporary fantasy. Mind you, this in no way is the best use of the natural space. Plus, a particular problem with the ultra-modern style is if you don't mix in historically interesting artifacts and furnishings, the space becomes so industrialized there's no human comfort in it. I tell her that souls need space too, but then I remember she doesn't have one.

Despite this reality, no one wants a sterile showcase. Clients are all different, but everyone wants a little something incorporated that's special to them. So, when it's said and done, every client insists on at least a twinkle of warmth and grace. Even the devil has a comfy chair. I know this because he once was a client of mine, and I still design for many of his blood relatives.

Regardless, a home should be a vessel for our memories. But true nesting spaces are only born of trust and the aesthetic pairing of personal visions and select elements that hold real meaning. Currently, the options I have at hand thanks to her interference, don't reflect this aspirational dynamic. Instead, I must plead to the design gods for favor.

Immersed in the rip current of surfing the glitch, Terry has my entire team engaged in a feeding frenzy, hoping to meet an impossible deadline with new inventory that I don't have yet. Some of it is delayed, and some of it I haven't even found. I'm chasing so many tails I'm starting to feel like I have one. My team is well versed in the art of glitch deconstruction, but still it's only our endurance that matters because all glitch moves are exhausting for anyone in range.

Glitches never come solo. They only come in pairs. The second one today happens to be of a completely different and weightier character, and it provides a no less emotionally daunting interruption of caustic flow. This glitch happens to involve a Middle Eastern Crown Prince who's also a good friend of mine. The prince has just become overly preoccupied with locating a certain "something" which he refuses to explicitly name for me. It involves a mysterious item which he has intimate knowledge of but has been unable to find for himself.

Prince, which is the moniker he was tagged with among only familiars at Princeton because he worshipped the music of the Minneapolis Potentate, is focused on solving a grand mystery. And he isn't at all focused on finding anything like the kinds of things he would typically be predisposed to acquire. This unnamed artifact has somehow captured all of his waking attention, and now he's requesting it should capture all of mine.

Prince is a package of fascinating contradictions. His highly confidential conveyance about this mysterious artifact is unexpected because it's completely out of character for him to be so irrationally preoccupied. And we all know where things like this are wont to go. Aptly, a rabbit hole comes to mind.

We met over ten years ago at a prestigious summer lecture series my godfather, Gio was giving at Princeton on the Alhambra, holy grail of Moorish architecture in southern Spain. Our tastes and ideas cross-pollinated, and we became fast friends. With millions of petrol dollars at his disposal, he soon became a client and connector for me for many high end finds. Over many years now, Prince, Gio and I have become Three Musketeers, with Prince calling Gio his uncle as well. Client aside, as a good friend, there was absolutely no way I could say no.

After a series of obtuse calls, I learned that Prince had received word through one of his royal confidants that there's been a sudden and unexpected disappearance of an ancient crystal ball with royal ties and alleged powers. The ball was accidentally released by a royal family that had it in their possession for over one hundred years. Due to the death of the sole possessor and the secrecy with which knowledge of the object was held within certain royal courts, there's no trace of where it's gone.

Prince wants to desperately find it and he's convinced it's within reach. Prince has asked me to take this matter on as my own, with what he calls high seriousness. This request inherently implies expectation. He has asked that I literally spare nothing and should prepare to locate any trace of it, anywhere. He emphatically states that he will generously provide anything I need whilst engaged on his royal behalf. Needless to say, it's implied by the nature of my trade that if I'm successful in locating this magic ball, there are millions in it for me.

International goose chases are an official glitch point, that very minute when the best laid plan goes to hell, and then decides to come back just to torture earthlings a little more. I've experienced this chthonic glitch moment firsthand and often. I can feel the exact second in a design project in which it occurs. In the fragile creative process, unless the client can be influenced, literally, to let go—as in, to actually surrender and turn the reins back over to the professional creatives—the space, or in Prince's case the lost item, the end goal cannot be realized. Without that essential—the letting go point coming into play—only the process continues but never the hoped for resolution.

'Tis the very nature of the glitch to swiftly become larger than its dictionary-provided definition. I wrestle with the voice in my head as to whether a treasure like the one Prince seeks could even actually exist—and if it does, how far am I willing to go to find it? Besides, the dynamic between an old friendship and the managing of complex expectations gives me pause. I also wonder if the crucible of my own mind is stalwart enough to hold the heat that I know comes with this search. After all, a magic ball, if there really is such a thing, could pose serious issues to any seeker. I'm certainly not immune to superstition or the fodder of legends but finding it could come with unintended gifts or curses.

It's precisely in these moments that I emotionally flee to a coping mechanism I learned from Prince. When in doubt about how to frame something, turn to a literary reference to ameliorate your temporary loss of means. There's temporary solace in making as if you're part of something that others have known before you. His affectionate name for this pastime is "Make Room for Rumi".

Our shared affection for the Persian poet and Sufi mystic is well deserved, as this fellow had the uncanny knowhow to slice an esoteric piece of contemporary mindfulness right down the middle, leaving no detectable crumbs. Rumi's 13th century perspective demonstrates that when it comes to dealing with the unseen, or the elusiveness of earthly glitching, not much, if anything has changed.

"Water, stories, the body, all the things we do are rare mediums that hide and show what's hidden. Study them and enjoy this being washed with a secret we sometimes know, and then not."

Rumi's idea of combating glitch matters likely would have been addressed in his day with a spiritual ritual called Sama, the incessant spinning on one's left foot in concentric circles to music, singing, or instrumentation. Tight and rapidly contrived revolutions, up to forty times per minute, performed by enthusiastic spiritualists who are referred to as whirling dervishes. Groups of spinners, revolving together inside a circle of dancers, become one with God, thereby experiencing a sort of spiritual drunkenness that is transportive and otherworldly.

By example, this is also the point at which you can remedy unresolved issues by spinning, while leaving the bigger esoteric moves to the higher dervishes. I tell myself by moving through emotionally charged circles, hopefully I too will be enabled to pass through a dervish doorway. Although a morsel of madness may await, even matters which may be mortally marked as glitched might still be unwound.

Then again, sometimes all a guy can really do is stand back and wonder.

13 Bewitch

New York

Years ago, I had the pleasure of working with a Japanese architect, Shigeru Ban. I became familiar with the Japanese concept of *takumi* which means that whenever you behold real beauty, your soul innately knows to honor it, begins to vibrate to it, matching its vibration with the energy of your own tended awe.

The inner beauty that's realized when a creation is imbued with beauty from on high, cascades into a reverence that swells inside you. When the details are borne of honorable craftsmanship and a transformational vision, the creation sings as testament to the spirit in us that is godlike. Whether you're sipping a *Hibiki* whiskey or viewing a *Tomioka Tessai* canvas, the beholding enables otherworldly magic to reach into your heart, gracefully taking the beating vessel into its trusty hand to remind you that you too are made of stardust.

Likewise, another Japanese tradition knows just how to apply its unique kind of *takumi* in a liquid medium. The therapeutic benefits of Japanese deep soaking, specifically in a Hinoki tub are incomputable. I became such an intent fan of the *ofuro* (wooden) soaking method that I had to have one of my own. Whenever I'm at my wit's end, this artisan vessel is my go-to refuge. Many a matter surfaces differently after soaking Hinoki-style.

The Japanese have a way of understanding the details within ethereal things that the rest of us dismiss as insignificant. They have a knack for making impossible things seem within our grasp. Whether it's the art of bathing in natural elements, or artfully creating a sushi delicacy from raw fish, or elevating the art of entertainment to the geisha aesthetic or taking an abstract medical concept to describe a type of cardiomyopathy poetically referred to as *takosubo,* or broken heart syndrome; the Japanese know exactly how to befriend *takumi* to reach the illusively ethereal.

In Hinoki, you allow the clear medium of hot water to literally and symbolically wash away your inability to cope. It's about clearing the debris in order to take it all in. This bathing ritual and its curative effects stimulate circulation and decongest the lymphatic system. Hinoki tubs are made with a reverence for wood, believing that wood and water provide a relaxing natural elixir for physical rejuvenation and energy adjustment. The green harvested woods are first grade and contain natural bacterial agents.

Unlike Western tubs, these are deep soaking tubs, where you're immersed in hot water past your shoulders. Though the tubs are custom made from a variety of woods like red cedar or teak, I love most the prized Japanese Cypress, the Emperor of Woods. This sacred wood revered for centuries for its beauty, strength and fragrance is the wood of archer's arrows and Shinto temples.

As I soak immersed within the rising steam, inside the hovering lemon ginger scented fog, the only guests permitted entry are the thoughts inside my weary skull. The only means by which to claim identification of my personage is the soaked leather strap and the threaded *dzi,* a rare stone, faithfully sitting atop my sternum. This intimate talisman stares back at me with twelve eyes, poised near to my beating heart. Ironically, it reveals to me that perhaps the crystal ball is no different than the idea behind this ancient Japanese belief. Since the start of humanity's earthly rigmarole, man has looked to protective amulets and sacred instruments to wrestle with his relationship to the beyond— the life force, El Shaddai, Chi, Mount Olympus, Jesus, Mohammad, Buddha, Krishna, Ganesh, the universe, the spirit world, the divine, the godhead, the divine soul. No matter where we roam, no matter how circuitously we travel, all roads lead us here.

The word *dzi* in Tibetan means shine and splendor. It's believed to be heaven's bead for many cultures in Tibet, Bhutan, Nepal, ancient India, as well as parts of Asia. The beads are in high demand among the global elite because they have a reputation for attracting protective positive energy and sometimes also deities and ancestors. Though I obtained mine from a shaman in Bhutan, I've known other owners of the stones who required a sacred ceremony in order to rid a bead of its previous negative energy. Because of their powers, the beads are traditionally passed on and kept in families for generations.

My *dzi* is authentic natural agate and is extrinsically valuable because of its plentiful eyes. Though admittedly for me, its value is its emotional significance because of my respect for its genesis, grounded by seers in ancient belief. Difficult to obtain, by request, I've purchased similar stones for three of my clients, including one for a legendary English gent who goes by one name and is an inspirational musical talent across generations.

There's a robust history in the belief in a magically infused object, no matter what the culture. So I ask myself, then why not rare magical balls of crystal that have unexplained powers?

If a talisman like my *dzi* or an energy device like the crystal ball enables spiritual transport back to our Source, then so be it. For we are all engaged inside a complex process of finding ourselves, and like Dorothy, hoping to eventually end up Home. My ritual with this tub or with this *dzi* is no different than the medicine man's ritual in the deep jungle of the stone's origin. We long to liberate ourselves from the chains of not knowing.

All the myths from all time speak to the very same things. Though much of it may be forgotten, our roots in it are as deep as our DNA. Every religion has magical beliefs and tales anchoring its past origins and there's no spiritual quest that doesn't tell us to search for ourselves outside the visible lands where we dwell because our soul's real estate dwells only in the invisible realms.

Though I brought home a simple crystal sphere from Istanbul that I'm temporarily infatuated with, for no known reason, I'm not at all likely to think that it's a functional device capable of telling the future. Though the possibility permeates my consciousness drop by drop, the healing waters in this ancient wooden bath are too busy transforming my present.

That being said, my newfound curiosity has me reading all I can about the ancient art of crystal gazing—or the many names by which it's known like crystalmancy, hydromancy, and spheromancy. I learned that as the medium changes, so do the types of visions one receives in the tranced feedback loop that's created from meditative gazing. The various names for the practice speak of the same thing, a form of divination, a gazing into the crystal void which thereby gives one the ability to go into an interim state of awareness and see things that aren't otherwise physically observable.

To my surprise, the gazing exercise isn't about seeing a concrete future because the future isn't static; it's a moving reality, colored and influenced by passersby. The gazing is more about enacting the ritual so that the mind might clear for certain insights to be disclosed. These insights might help us navigate a tricky path or foretell of obstacles in our way.

I didn't realize at first that the ball itself doesn't show images but rather enables one to go into a trance-like state where the seeker sees revelations from one's own subconscious and imagination. The observational state is a sort of penumbra, or a state of partial illumination, between the shadow and the light of revelation.

I also didn't know that certain hard rules apply to the practice. For example, an authentic crystal ball should only be used by one person and should be kept in a special place of honor in that designated person's private space or niche. When not in use, others shouldn't be permitted to handle it. Just as a ball would receive a fingerprint, the psyche of the user is said to leave an occult imprint upon the crystal. Each crystal ball has an energy legacy which intensifies through the years based on the owner's energies.

Additionally, I understand the ball should be covered with a black velvet cloth whenever it's not being used so that it isn't exposed to the light unnecessarily. Importantly, the owner should also plan on naming the ball. But the naming may take some time, as it's supposed to be intuitively conveyed to the owner from the ball itself as one becomes familiar working with it. Lastly, the crystal requires regular cleansing to preserve its reflective qualities. This is best done on the night of a full moon.

The scrying technique for using the crystal instrument calls for sitting quietly in low lighting so the crystal can be seen as almost backlit while the rest of the room remains dark. The gazer should slowly begin gazing into the ball for access to inspirational and spiritual visions that come from within the gazer. This scrying practice has been used worldwide for centuries by many cultures and belief systems. It's customary to also use pools of water, mirrors, stones or even fire.

In ancient pre-Islamic Persia in the tenth century, an epic speaks of the Cup of Jamshid, used by wizards to observe the seven layers of the universe. The cup was believed to contain the elixir of immortality. Nostradamus in the sixteenth century used a bowl of water to see the future when he was in a trance from which he wrote his famous quatrains. In the 1820s, the founder of the Mormon religion, Joseph Smith, reported that he received miraculous reflections from using divination stones. Even the faerie tale of Snow White cites this seeing technique where the mean queen consults a magic mirror for the answer to her pressing issue of who's the fairest of them all. As I realize how diverse the practice is, I begin to shed my initial perplexity over relating to it. More so, I've a pressing awareness that all of the enlightened ones throughout centuries and cultures, speak of one thing: the idea that magic is never easy.

Though I don't understand the art or science, I know that light is one of the four fundamental forces in physics and that light is electromagnetic energy. Most simply, light is bent around stars that hold everything, including all that we cannot visibly see. The way things look is all because of light. If we control the way it bounces off something, the whole look of it will alter. If the presence of light makes what we see more relative, then it's implied that seeing via a crystal sphered instrument that uniquely refracts light could open further possibilities.

Having soaked to my full capacity this evening, I marvel that pondering my *dzi* and my humble crystal ball produce the same possibilities. Though I'm reluctant to attempt to use my orb, I hope eventually to osmose something merely from its presence as symbol. But first I must find a black velvet cloth to cover it for proper percolation before its first real cleaning, as I wait patiently for the magical light of the next full moon.

14 Hitch

New York

The Garden of Eden storyline is about knowing, how what we know or don't know is what determines our fate.

The big cosmic hitch I'm facing is that I'm not sure what I know anymore. As a grown man, I know less about what I know and what it is that I'm willing to let myself know. Perhaps thinking that I know is the biggest delusion of my adulthood.

My godfather warned me that doubt grows with knowledge but nothing's prepared me for reaching the point at which I must confront my beliefs. Because of my recent predicament and the resulting denial, I must answer the fundamental, dark question directly: Do I, or don't I, believe in magic? Not answering by way of a simple yes or no, but by standing behind a definitive answer to enact the power of my chosen belief is paramount to my overarching life.

You see, this issue, which appears to be frivolous on the surface, is of great consequence. It forms a foundational pillar of sorts, a premise which shapes a much larger perspective. I want to believe in magic, but I waiver because it's another matter entirely for me to put my trust in that belief. I'm stuck in place; painfully aware that any confusion of the real with the ideal never goes unpunished.

One of the hardest things in my life is when I'm squarely at a point where I just have to choose. And knowing that simply choosing between two things leads to two completely different experiences doesn't help me one iota with deciding. In fact, this is the point which seems to prompt me into not choosing. But, magic is pressing in hard and it's time for me to pick a horse in this race. If I wasn't pressed to make such a choice, I know I wouldn't come to terms with it. Either I accept divine magic as being a real part of my life, or I deny its feasibility and move the hell on.

The pressing question is really about my relationship to my future, but that could also be a deceptive distractor. You see, first it was the sudden appearance of a random crystal ball that surprisingly attracted me and now sits inside my home. It innocently presents in a Pandora's Box kind of way; it teases me to acknowledge it further. Next, it was Prince's intersection with the idea of a missing magic ball; and then Athena's forecast of a looming Papagena to my Papageno. The weighty sortilege of this trifecta is psychologically unsettling in untold ways.

Add to this that I'm still feeling the discombobulation of M's obnoxious pronouncement and it seems as if I'm looking at my life through a blurry lens. Rest assured, I'm not taking this convergence of happenstances lightly. I know just enough about the classic spiritual quests that ironically I realize my relationship with magic may turn out to be the most determining factor in the life path unfolding before me.

However, wanting and needing to do something and being able to actually 'do the do' are imperfectly connected things. Blasé Pascal warned about such crossroads. *"The heart has reasons, reason does not know."* I now stand in an admitted juxtaposition to myself, that is, knowing what I want to believe, while staying firmly planted on the marker of not knowing. All my efforts to search for perspective fall short. If I play this out honestly, it could be a blessing; but if I forfeit a choice, I could become one of those sad, old men Athena foretold who looks back with regret. We all know how the nature of regret is largely encased by a series of cowardly forfeitures. I pray that I will not be among them.

I believe in the power of the will and the existence of an enlightened plane where there's such a thing as mind over matter, though I'm not the least bit proficient in manifesting anything close for myself in the here and now. I also believe, as the Bible says, that faith can move mountains, though I've yet to witness it happening, nor do I understand how it works. Despite that I've failed to make either phenomenon happen for myself, I still relish the idea and imperfectly attempt it metaphorically every chance I get.

The cosmic hitch I'm facing is compounded by my personal relationship with Prince and his obstinate obsession with a lost magic ball; complicated by the not to mention remote possibility, that my little crystal ball could be the magic one Prince is seeking. I realize it's best for me not to assume anything ridiculous, but rather to just get my ass out there to find the real one. After all, there can't be only one of these magical orbs in all the world.

Truth is, I haven't got a clue about any of this, nor have I thoroughly digested that any of this is even real or happening to me. Abraham Lincoln said, *"When arguing with a fool, make sure the opponent isn't doing the same thing."* Since I'm arguing with myself, I'm the fool either way. Normally I'd call Prince as a friend, but I'm not comfortable raising the issues of my concern about a magic ball with a man who's insanely obsessed with magic balls right now. Likewise, my peers would surmise I've likely lost my marbles from too much work, which isn't a good look in any business, monkey or otherwise.

I try to talk myself down from all these bizarre possibilities. I'm reminded that historical legend says there are two Arks of the Covenant. Don't mega-artifacts of special power naturally come in twos, or with a backup? Surely, just as the godhead shares many aspects of himself, it seems likely there could be more than one of pretty much everything. But the additionally troubling possibility is that the magic may have very little to do with the object itself and instead, everything to do with the seeker.

Meantime on the more practical side, while facing my day job concerns, I'm smack dab in the middle of extremely challenging matters that require a lot less psychological distraction, and I've nothing close to a surplus of free time. Prince likes to joke that if you want something done properly you need to give it to a busy person. However, never once is it in the nature of any royal prince, anywhere, to attempt to do anything at all by themselves. For most royals, busy is a but hobby and nothing close to a past time.

When expanding forces like I'm facing come a knocking, it's well-documented that a man is weakened where he's most not fit to take it. In my case, this convergence is exposing something about my life that I can no longer deny or ignore. That is, that I have no intimate sidekick—Papagena—whom I can fully entrust to share the weight of it; one who might intellectually and spiritually assist me in syncretizing it and one who would prioritize me and my wellbeing unselfishly in the process.

Perhaps I'm not that different because many a man doesn't have a fully capable and trustworthy, intimate confidante. Some might appear as if they do, but when push comes to shove, how many mortals have an aligned so-called wingman? If you're a fortunate who does, you should hold them close because this kind of unconditional blessing won't come for most of us unless we own a dog.

Simultaneously I'm also thrust into other tricky business at hand. A testy remodel in which I'm immersed has me off balance. In design like in life, a lack of balance leads to progressively awful outcomes. So, to find a glimmer of temperance, I set out to itemize a handy list of what needs to happen, what to when. List making is nothing but an exercise that aids in settling my nerves, affording me the illusion of having some control, as my mind races over the odds of this actual accomplishment.

Truth be told, I'm feeling scrambled like an egg, I know it's best to loop Terry into my broadening plight. Though one-way roads are built for speed and two-way roads slow things down some, they tend to make traffic flow more habitable. Still, you must choose your own way to go. I'm just about to authorize shipping two of the brothers' statues to a California garden estate. Terry will check in on my sanity and ensure there won't be a hitch with the delivery and placement.

Now I must prioritize hunting for the real crystal ball for Prince. Despite my trepidation, I remind myself, my efforts will be rewarded, and beyond undoubtedly interesting. Though I realize open roads tend to hold the answers to many a spiritual puzzle, I wish I was already home with someone I love who loves me.

15 Fitch

New York

In the early morning on my way to Brooklyn, I'm meeting an expert restorer and old friend who I rely on for rehabilitating the worn pieces I ship back to the States for estate placements. As it is with all art forms, rehab is a necessary component of the desired evolution. Because I've been solely out and about combing for world-worn wares, my *tete a tete* rendezvous with the infamous Genevieve is overdue.

Though we've worked together for over a decade, our respective businesses do so much volume, we rarely have time to visit. I welcome our visits as her French accent can trick me into believing I'm back overseas, just as it seems like her hefty fees are lessened when I'm handed the bill by her in person.

"Bonjour Monsieur Bonaventura," she greets me at the door, poised with an oversized fitch in her pale and dainty right hand.

"Morning Glory. Look at you, bright and early, a Parisian dream with your trusty brush in hand. It says what an authentic and hardworking artist is right here before me. I swear though, this has to be a first."

"What on earth do you mean?" she playfully questioned.

"I've never seen you without an inventory list in your hand, Gen, let alone, with an actual instrument of your dark art. All you need is a raspberry beret to complete your most memorable entrance yet."

Giving her a little squeeze, I asked, *"Alors, quoi de neuf?"*

"What's up is that it's appropriate I meet you today with this particular brush in tow because just like you, *mon cher,* it has these uniquely tapered bristles. They are specially made for painting only the very finest of lines, and we both know"—she pressed my chest with a

96

playful poke with the wooden end of the brush handle—"just how much you love to cross all of them. Yes, those very fine lines you always figure out a way to *circonvenir*."

I countered, "Better that than mentioning the collection of fine lines I've recently been sporting on my face." I waited for her to contradict my self-deprecating assessment, but she didn't. Honesty, thy name is an uninterested woman. Unable to impress with my beauty, I tried banter. "Gen, I know that particular type of brush happens to be made from the hair of the notorious weasel or what you Mademoiselles call *la belette* (a pole cat). So, don't give me any of your *la muse bouche*."

"Ah, you of course, of all people, somehow recognize *la belette*. *On prend a se connaitre*. (takes one to know one.) Mitch, you know when you speak French that you don't fool me one bit?"

"Then perhaps, I should only accept your invoices in English from now on?"

"French, English, it's all the same when it comes to invoices. It differs only when it comes to matters of the heart, Mitch."

"Yes, and we know who has the *soi-disant* upper hand in that arena, don't we?"

As we walked through the center aisle of her abundantly packed warehouse, filled with interesting contents with the silent potential of rehabbed treasure, Gen teased, floating gracefully past a table of morning refreshments, "Would you fancy a croissant? They're very fresh, just like you."

"Have you become a fully equipped French café with eatable props, nestled among the ambience of priceless statement pieces?"

"Oh Mitch, the cappuccino machine's ancient and you of all people know, there's absolutely no such thing as priceless. Not in this world. *Manger*. Otherwise, with only coffee in you, I won't be able to secure a good price today."

As she led the way to clearer passage, I understood why we've worked together so long. Despite the affection we have for one another, it's the kind that spans the test of time because it's the non-sexual, friendship variety; so, we can quickly bridge back to the business at hand.

Putting her fitch down atop a cluttered table of assorted paints and stains, Gen pointed, amidst our persiflage, to a demarcated area billeting a recognizable stash of several of my back-logged treasures. From just across the way, I eyed a deep row of Chinoiseries paneling, the Herve vander Straeten table lamps I bought last year, and the memorably petit escritoire where Abigail Adams is said to have penned her famous letters to John. We moseyed past a Chinese lacquer cartonnier that I've yet to place, a favorite ormolu clock, a set of Takura Kuwata gilded ceramic bowls which were chipped in last spring's transit. We stop as we pass a real favorite find of mine: a rare 15th century Italian, hand-painted cassone from the Renaissance. "Yes Mitch, I'm touching up the gilding, so you know."

"Sometimes, I just like walking through your spaces and seeing so many random treasures huddled in raw form, like old friends after a card game that lasted centuries."

"Yes, *mon amour*, it's because we both share an unending affinity for interesting stuff. You know, just like our esteemed Baudelaire said, though I may not have it exactly right, *'It's the unexpected, the irregular, the surprise, that are an essential part of beauty'*."

"And Gen, does this artistic tolerance also apply to people?"

"That goes without saying. But you know what?"

"I can't imagine what."

"You Mitch, remind me of the notorious *Lombarde*. You know of it. The northeasterly wind that dominates our border from the high alps out of Lombardy, right?"

"What's your point?" I ask, knowing full well what was coming.

"Well, it's mostly a gentle wind along the Riviera, but in winter it becomes blustery and cold and causes snowdrifts in the mountain valleys, if you get my drift."

"You are a dangerous woman, Gen."

We continued walking through the dense hodgepodge, with Gen dosing me with more reality.

"You know I'm working on at least four dozen pieces of yours and that's only as of sunrise today. Where have you been? To the land of misfit toys? Those crates over there are also yours but haven't been logged yet. Tell me, are you planning to clone yourself anytime soon?"

"No, I can't even keep up with the bastard that's here before you."

"So, it is you who admittedly is the real *bilette* here.

"I assure you, Terry and I have all our projects under complete control, that is, except for all the damn doors. Everyone loves a good portal, Gen."

"Mitch, why are portals notoriously such a pain in the ass, and I don't mean only as metaphor."

"My nemesis appears to be niches and yours, doors."

"How many doors are in your shop for us?"

"Seven sets with hard deadlines that I know of for sure but there's more in the queue. I swear, when so many doors are off their hinges, it's the worst, and more so than the people who own the places where they hang."

"You only confess that to me because I'm your favorite client."

"Regardless, they're not supposed to come unhinged any more than we are."

"Yes, we're all just happiest hanging together with our special purpose in tow," I added, hoping to be reassuring about the volume of work still at hand. "How about getting all the doors finished, first. Let's say, before Bastille Day? We're on an American timeline, my petit Parisian tart, and I literally don't have a minute to waste getting the sevens sets out."

"Truthfully, six yes, seven only possibly, my Italian Casanova. There are issues. You see, I absolutely must have your early eye on the large Middle eastern set because of a technicality. I'm going for an extremely unique, weathered authenticity with a fragile color wash blend. I think it works perfectly with your South Beach palate. It won't be anything ordinary, mind you. I need to make sure you're okay with my going outside the delicate fitch lines, and I won't have them ready for you to see until earliest, maybe next Thursday. I'll send photos to your cell but hear me now, Michello. You will need to get back to me pronto.

Do you promise? If I wait too long between the series of coats, I run the risk of inconsistent coloration and, you know I'll make you eat that. I want it to look organic, not staged, so don't mess around on this. If you screw with my art, you know that it is you who is going to pay through the nose."

"I promise. But I also need to talk with you about something. It's about the stone statues and it's a bit of a weird, off-beat little detail. Nonetheless, I need to make you aware of it. Tell me, how much work do you think they need? In order to be optimally presented that is."

"So, by that you mean, perfect?"

"We communicate so well, Gen."

"Only because I stay one step ahead of all your exotic dance moves. First, Baudelaire, I don't think you want them to look either A, worn, or B, perfect. Neither option will do them justice. We all need our eye candy to lie somewhere in between the fates—that is, in interstice, no? Get the right words out of your *bouche*, or I might go a whole different way with any one of your precious things. I am an artist and the stuff you say to me matters, you adorable, pompous weasel."

I had to suppress a twinge of discomfort at Gen's certainty about her thaumaturgy. I wish I could be this certain about how I feel about magic. That certainty is attractive in any context and in sharp contrast, uncertainty continues to be a lackluster bedfellow.

"Gen, let's find all six of the statues and talk when they're in front of us. That way, I'll find the best way to explain my point, before I turn you loose with them."

"I think it's that you Mitch just prefer having a larger audience. Why do I dread the coming of a fateful denouement?"

After her workers assembled the sixsome, she said, "Okay, here's all six of the feisty royals, nestled in a little throne room all their own; the statuesque icons are safe, awaiting their new digs. I trust they'll be well placed on grand grounds, adjacently guarding yet another wealthy bastard's portico?" Inspecting each, Gen mused, "I don't know how much you paid to find an assembly in such good shape. They're not museum quality, but good job, Mitch. They seem to be Apsaras, maybe from the 9ᵗʰ century. I'm baffled because they're so well preserved."

"Do you think they're images of gods or do you think they're the Hindu angels?"

"You know Mitch, maybe three look like Asparas. But then, Asparas tend to have more graceful garments and more stature, and also breasts. They tend to look like they could comfortably sit atop a cloud. Also, Apsaras never have wings, yet they're the Hindu or Buddhist version of what we know to be angels. And, yes, miraculously, they can fly, though their wings aren't visible."

"Invisible wings?

"Yes, but it doesn't mean they're not there. Whatever these are Mitch, I really, really like them. They certainly have immortal genes. They look like they know more than they're letting on."

"I know. I felt the same way when I saw them."

"It should be a requirement of all our friends, don't you agree? Despite the lack of factual context, they have soul. Should I have Alex research them further for you?"

"That would be great. I need to nail the period down for the invoice; plus, depending on who they are, they could have a secret or two to share. You know, before we let them fly away."

"A secret?"

"Oh, you know, just a secret something, maybe about companionship or immortality."

"Then I hope it's the latter. I think I have the first one mostly covered by now. Though mind you, *monsieur*, you are still lacking in this regard. However, with the second, in the very best of cases, secrets would never apply anyway."

"So, it's settled then? You're rooting for immortality?"

"Yes, I'm afraid it's the case for women since the beginning of time. Plus, if we get a good finding, I can invoice you forever. Perhaps then I could take a real vacation, instead of going to Paris where I rely entirely too much on Dr. Sebagh. A girl's got to do what a girl's got to do, you know, to extend her shelf life, so a shortcut or secret is always most welcome."

"So, all total, you're more or less hoping for an Einstein-Rosen bridge to get you there?"

"Every wormhole needs a short cut, right? But you fool, I still would need to get back. Sadly, you sound like such an American man, all about the one-way ticket."

I was too distracted to parlay. "Hey Gen, look. See this? What happened here to this one?"

"Her little tootsie is busted. I think it's the equivalent of an angel stubbing a celestial toe. I'm assuming it happened in transit as the paperwork didn't identify anything amiss upon crating. No worries though, the tootsie is intact so we can work it back into place and make the imperfection less delineated."

"What's the fix?"

"Well, New York has no shortage of podiatrists, Mitch. For God's sake, can't you just go already and leave me to my work?"

Gen was only a little incensed so I knew we had some more bandwidth before she would shove me out of the studio.

"Oh, by the way, Mitch, be happy it's on one of the females. With her bare bosom revealed, a man's eyes won't ever make it down to her feet anyway. We'll take her right over there, to the land of misfits, to Carlo's trusty bunker. He'll make it like it never happened, you know, just like magic."

"Speaking of magic, Gen, since you brought it up."

"Well, of course it is always relevant among such ancient treasures. It's quite likely that magic is merely asserting herself again through the ancient energies. They may be somewhat displaced or forgotten, but they're not dead or gone. Divination is immortal, no?

"Um, Gen, there's something important for you to note when you work on the angelic six pack. I need you to not separate them. That is, I would rather that you just keep them together. Not all of them, though. Not all six; specifically; just keep them in pairs of two, you know, coupled."

"Wait, what do you mean?"

"Don't separate them or keep any one of them alone. That's

really all I'm saying." I clarified as if I was sure I sounded perfectly lucid.

"You mean these statues have separation anxiety and cannot be left alone?"

"That's one way of putting it. When you take any one over there to Carlo's, just plan to send a partner over too. She or he just can't fly solo."

"But, what if only one of them needs the work?"

"Yeah, but they just need to be kept in pairs, in a set, that is or, you know, together."

"You're serious? The statues must be coupled? Even when they're in the same general area? You must be kidding."

"Look, I get it. I know it sounds ridiculous, but trust me, you mustn't separate them. That is, they need to be in twos, all the time, with no exceptions. Even though the genders aren't completely clear, you kind of see these three as the more feminine ones? Pair each of them with one of the other three. This was the very explicit instruction from the merchants who sold them to me. I'm just trying to honor their wishes is all. They gave me a great deal, plus, I don't want to take any chances."

"So you believe in the poppycock that some loopy merchants with interesting accents on the other side of the world sold you about these stone statues?"

"No, not exactly; that is, I don't think I believe any of it. But honestly, I don't know the answer to that. Meantime, until I figure it out, I just don't want to test it."

"Well, when you do know, be sure to fill me in. You, *mon amie*, are officially *tres* Daffy, like the Duck. You do know better than to think that any of this is real? Now, I'm a little worried about you. You're the most stable of the handsome Italian grown men I know. And I thought the French were a superstitious lot."

"Gen, look, I don't know that any one of us can honestly ever know better. I realize it sounds ridiculous, like hocus-pocus stuff, certainly outside of my range. So maybe we can revisit it together at another time? Meantime, all I'm saying is to please do keep them in pairs because why should we take a chance."

"But if you do believe in what you're implying, you must know something more about this that I don't."

"*Com si, com sa.* Maybe. I don't really know; so humor me, maybe because I'm your favorite client."

"Okay Mitch. But you sound like a Noah's Ark lunatic with this coupled perspective of yours. It's a bit exasperating. Are you sure there's not more to it?"

"Really Gen? Couldn't we literally say that's so about everything?"

"Okay, but when you get tired of keeping your big secret about your magic stone paramours, angels, gods, couples or whatever, do fill me in."

"It's a deal. But I'm not hiding anything from you. I don't know if it makes sense, but I've got so much going on right now, I can't stop to think about it clearly, let alone, know for sure. It's important that I not risk anything unnecessarily, you know?"

"And why does that sound familiar? God forbid, Mitch that you should ever take a big chance."

"So, what do we have left to cover this morning?"

"Well, you wanted two of the statues shipped out by the end of next week, right? So, the one with the broken foot and her paramour will stay here, until you advise where they go."

"You know what? Send Mademoiselle Footloose and her lover, Jean Pierre, to my loft and no rush, but whenever you have them ready, after her podiatry appointment."

"Sure, but tell me, are you going to keep them for yourself?"

"Possibly. I need to see how they look nestled in with the new lusher vegetation on my loggia. You know how hard it is to stage it suitably for four seasons? I want to make a statement, but I also need to make it cozy. Right now, it just needs some character."

"Well, I think these two characters will amply fill that void. But Mitch, make sure they're in proximity. You know, that is, not placed too far apart."

"You insist on mocking me?"

"Only because I'd hate to hear of yet another conscious uncoupling in your busy building. For a player, you sure seem to be acting darn domestic lately. After all, today I've caught you taking art home that doesn't go on someone else's wall. It's a rather unique experience for you, Mitchy-poo."

"Okay, who's being bitchy now? First, don't Mitchy-poo me. Second, I'm not a player, and third, I admit, I'm feeling more like a homey lately and yes, it is a new twist for me. You know, real friends, allow friends to change and to grow, don't they? In case you might want to give that a try."

"Hmm. My only question for you is, why now? Is there perhaps someone special in the picture?"

"No, not at all; but you know how I'm known to only hug the road? Well, lately, when I get home, I want to stay there. Home feels like a hot bath, perfectly ready for me to sink into and as a result I'm not getting out nearly as much as I did or should. Maybe I'm just tired. Or maybe it's the Hinoki."

"Or, Mitch, it could be your age, or that you're finally facing your own mortality. I will give you this, *monsieur*, you're juggling more projects than ever and for higher profile clients. It's a lot more than you're used to doing and only with the same staff. It's real pressure and I bet your staff is tired too."

"Yeh, but other than Terry they're on commission which, as you know, has a way of sensibly maintaining one's energy. I've got to be able to trust my crew implicitly; quality's way more important to me than quantity. I'm not set up to have more bodies on board willy-nilly. There's only so much letting go you can do. Ask Hermes, Gucci, or Martyn Lawrence Bullard."

Gen escorted me out of the maze of museum backstock to the front entrance of her expansive rehab hospital for artistically flawed collectables.

"Are these all spoken for?" I pointed, asking about a few eye-catching pieces.

"*Oui*, of course, or why would I be fuddling with them? I would be at the matinee instead or drinking Beaujolais. You know how I'm either making money or trying to play—but there's absolutely no in between for Little Genevieve. You totally get that too, I know you do."

"*Oui,* that I get. *Oiseaux d'une plume,* n'est ce pas?"

"*Oui,* but next time you get a minute, and I also get one—something which we'll need to seriously coordinate, because we both suck at finding time—when you have a few hours, and the weather is good, and you're not cranky or exhausted …"

"Gosh, you make me sound impossible, Gen."

"I'm just saying you're definitely not for everyone, is all."

"So, next to impossible, maybe?"

"So, I will introduce you to someone who I definitely think you should meet."

"For real? Who is she?"

"She is a friend of mine. I think she may be a good match for you."

"So how do you know her?"

"Well, you could say we have an affinity for the four Ys."

"Gen, do I want to know this?"

"Yoga, preferably Vinyasa; yogurt, frozen, Greek or French; Yves Saint Laurent; and of course, our pinstriped Yankees."

"Sounds like an enviable sisterhood of artistic selection. Should I take you both to a game?"

"No, I don't want to wait to see if you can hit a home run; a baseball game does not a first date make. And don't worry, Mitch, I know how you tend to overthink things, but she's not clingy. She's independent and travels nearly as much as you do. She speaks three languages, is super down to earth but also worldly and sexy smart. Look, I know your type, *monsieur.* Yours is the tall, California, easy-breezy girl on the surface, meets the Manhattan art critic, philosophical brainiac snob, but she's far deeper than that and comes wrapped in a lovely poetically assembled package. And yes, to answer your unasked male query, she's hot."

"You actually know this girl?"

"*Oui,* she exists, and actually but I'm also warning you, she's fitch brush fine."

"So, she's French?"

"Of course, she is, you silly boy. Would I work this hard, were she not one of my prized sisters?"

"French is good."

"Well, I've no doubt of that. Just don't forget, though I'm Parisian I'll never be as big a snob as you are on most days. But do not waste her time, Michello. I mean it. *Indemnite.* Now the conundrum is how shall I begin to describe you to her? Now go."

Just as I was about to scoot out of the studio's monstrous steel-framed door, I turned to ask Gen, "So, what's her name?"

"Her name is Chloe, but no more information for you or you'll never arrange the meeting. I'll text you her cell."

"Gen, you're a lethal combo. I did not see this coming, but I look forward to meeting her. You start my day with the fitch and a croissant. The flakey buttery crust of a quarter moon mixed with the unwelcome hair of a proverbially sly weasel. And we end with your matchmaking. Does it get any better than this?"

"I sincerely hope so. Go now, *Bientot.*"

As I slid the heavy metal factory door shut, I paused for an instant contemplating that stranger things have happened than mere coincidence. No doubt now, my forenamed curiosity was dashingly piqued by the mysterious mark of 'C'.

16 Enrich

New York

The discrete Old World Italian gem on the upper eastside, Parioli Romanissimo, is where the notion of the blind date took me like a tiger by the tail. Tucked away from the exposed banquettes, I sat at a table for two in the corner, in the exact place where—what was later to turn out to be a fateful rendezvous—a literal *coup de foudre*, was about to manifest.

Actually, no one has an idea of what will manifest into more or what will be just another tedious entry over days. But tonight, like a single star poised in a dark night sky, this evening had the potential of being distinctly luminescent.

Simply, I was about to engage in that inner terror of facing an emotional rollercoaster ride and with Genevieve's fabled friend and Athena's heeded namesake, a French sophisticate named Chloe.

I gazed, transfixed, at the foyer. Butterflies were beyond ludicrous at my age but trying to dispel them makes them flutter crazily. I was setting myself up for a grand mal seizure of disappointment. Nothing was likely to live up to a build-up that Genievieve gifted Chloe. As the minutes passed, I became more resigned to the empty anticipation of greeting that dullest of all possible dinner guests—regret in my mind, or in this case, possibly *a' regretter,* the apercu of all human tragedy.

There was an elegant stir in the entryway, and I felt the energy shift. The calm I felt moments before accelerated into physical panic, which abated only when I saw her.

Her honey blonde hair was mid-length casual with a soft wave that held its own in a relaxed way. There was clearly no false pretense to her gait as she entered with a classic, confident style. Tall and slim like a birch tree, deeply contrived on all levels, I liked her vibe straight off.

I reached out to her with my left hand, instinctively overlaying my right atop hers in a gesture of polite caress, "Bonjour Chloe, thank you for meeting me. I'm Mitch."

With ebullient flair she answered, "Yes, I figured as much from Gen's description, though you're taller than she indicated, which for me, is *tres bon*."

I felt the glow from what was clearly a lively concoction of energy, even from across the table where she seated herself without pretense in lovely grace.

"May I get you something?"

"Yes, a pinot noir, please."

I informed the waiter as I hoped he'd hastily leave us. "A bottle of Simboli Pinot Nero please."

I turned to Chloe, hoping I still had her uninterrupted attention. "I trust you're fine going with Italian vino tonight, even with a pinot?"

"Oh, most definitely" she said smiling slyly, "It's all aged in French oak barrels anyway."

"I'd love to know what it is you like about the pinot neros?"

"You know, on the surface that seems like an easy question, but I can see, you're a very smart fellow, so Mitch, I'm going to approach my answer rather thoughtfully, okay?" She didn't wait for my approval. "Well, you see, I like that they're translucent in color and paler than most reds. I like that their flavor is subtle. I like that they love their home or their French oak barrel. It's teamwork at its best. I suppose they're not as rich or as big, but to me, they're more noble, not to mention, challenging to harvest and therefore also rarer. So, might that tell you anything important about me, Michello?"

"Yes, delightfully so."

Then, breaking the ice with a more robust inquiry, she cut to the chase. "So, what did Gen tell you about me? I'd like to have the opportunity to tell you if it's all that or not."

"I assure you, absolutely nothing in detail. She only insisted that we meet."

As the vino was poured, we continued to check each other out discretely, so as not to appear blatant or impolitely stirred.

Raising my glass, I offered a first toast, "Here's to us both, listening to our mutual friend, Gen."

"Yes, I wholeheartedly agree."

"So, then, the next toast must be yours," I said, wanting to know exactly how she would choose to frame the evening at that precise point, a little later in the second act. "You must propose it in French of course," I cajoled.

"My, you're advocating for my proposal so soon? I see you're already making demands?" she quipped. "I'll let you know when I begin to take either of those seriously."

Amazed that her humor was so akin to mine, I liked her sense of disclosure and also for whatever it was she was holding back.

Later for our second toast, Chloe confidently presented an appropriately latent sentiment in a mesmerizing French repertoire which did not disappoint. "*Voici a la magie d'une vie pleine.*" which she aptly translated, "Here's to the magic of a full life."

I offered a semi-boasting retort, "Well, you know I do speak French but not as a native. It's most useful when I'm not in France, because you know how any attempt there tends to be so remarkably unappreciated."

"*Oui*, mercy isn't exactly a boasted French trait. But we do make up for our inadequacies with other virtues, you know?"

"I think I'm experiencing that firsthand this evening."

I yearned to know more about her. "Running prestigious galleries must have its challenges, especially with an international clientele as well-versed as yours? The array of tastes to which you must cater must be a daunting task; not to mention handling the size of your operations both here in New York and in Paris."

"Yes, for sure, and we've recently added a third, Belgian gallery.

But I'm not the *faineant* type. Sometimes I wish I were much more so, you know, intellectually idle? The work keeps me on pointe, dancing most days faster than I'd like, and some days more than I honestly can muster. There's such a fine line between being challenged and being happy. I struggle with that balance and not very successfully, mind you. I guess you could say, I have a problem. Gen alluded that we may have this in common."

I obliged. *"Ah oui, je crois que nous pouvons etre des oiseaux d'une plume."*

"But you, of all people Mitch, know in the art world how quickly things move? Despite its large, dramatic persona, which comically, outsiders only see as well paced and ever so civilized; you know very much as I do that the pace is anything but. When push comes to shove, it's about taste and catering to or understanding the nature of desire— though, that's a pressing demand, isn't it? The desire and the demand never rest for the unquenchable client. It's the nature of the beast, but sometimes it borders on insane."

I was impressed with her sensibility and how it aligned with my own take on the design world. And more so, and perhaps even more critically, how our foodie tastes were so comfortably compatible. I especially liked that she was smart but not stuffy, educated but not arrogant. It was apparent as we shared an intimately arranged table, it was as if we'd known each other much longer. This included our mutual gastronomical amazement at the old-world flavors of the lemon risotto with lobster and the Chianina beef with porcini mushrooms. I was thrilled that despite her runway frame, she was open to sharing dessert. The zabaglione with raspberries topped a memorably *perfetto* moment in real life.

"Chloe," I said raising my glass again, "Here's to our mutual understanding and what appears to be—and I hope it is so, a *folie a deux.*"

She generously obliged the sentiment, of which I've always been particularly fond. "Yes, the idea of being mad by oneself is absolutely of no consolation. But my preferred, more literal French translation of 'double madness' may indeed, have many more intriguing advantages."

For me, because of who I am, what I do exactly and the nature of the pursuit of "desired things," my own reality can be quite disappointing or, at least, unfulfilling. But tonight was living proof in a more classical belief I'd shelved, that of desiderata. I marveled that suddenly, almost as quickly as a rogue wave can appear at sea, what I wanted and more importantly, needed, was suddenly sitting right before me in magnificent candlelit view.

I decided to try to see behind the curtain. "So now, because of your elegant French toast, I must ask you something else, which may be rather personal."

"Of course, *je suis un* open book," she smiled.

"Chloe, tell me; what do you know about magic?"

Without hesitating she shared. "Obviously not enough. But, for heaven's sake, why do you ask?"

"Well, I think it's important I get your perspective on it. I have the distinct feeling we should be frank with each other when it comes to - invisible forces."

As she swirled her pinot counterclockwise in the stemmed Reidel that was still branded by the memory of her Chanel rouge lipstick, she hesitated. "I certainly believe in what it stands for, if that's what you mean. That is to say, assuming that whatever it really is, what we call magic is all around us—all the time. Just because we can't explain it doesn't diminish it or mean that it doesn't exist. To me, God is indeed the master and his ways seem like magic to me in my limited perception." She took another sip. "You know, this thing that is our life is already akin to magic too. The good, and even the bad of it—all of it, especially in retrospect, after illumination, is like some magical poetry. Just because we expect it to always rhyme doesn't make it any less. We give to it what we can and it takes from us what it can. It's all an actual dance; a flowing poem completely made of something called magic. So, really, magic to me is what we call everything that we can't see or explain or understand. If you're asking me bluntly, whether I believe in magic or not; then yes, I do believe. But why? What do you know of it, magic I mean?"

"Chloe, I'm so pleased to hear your lovely answer to such a

loaded question. Though I couldn't have put it nearly so well, I do wholeheartedly share your perspective."

Her eyes sparkled in the candlelight, and I had to put mental brakes on my emotions. It seemed impossible that the stars were aligning so perfectly over us.

"You see, Chloe, I do have an agenda in asking. You know on first dates, the tendency is to inquire about the facts of a person? That is, asking what's real with them by way of practical questions, in order to determine who they are, what they like to do, etc.

"Yes, of course,"

"Well, I think I've probably found out the hard way, over so many single years that these compatibility of perspective matters are what's most powerful and they're either mutually there or not."

I continued, "Now that I'm older and less puerile, I think for me, it's better that I begin with the esoteric. One's perspective on these matters says a lot more about who it is we really are, you know, on the inside. And truth be told, I already know that I absolutely need to be with someone who believes in magic."

She took a small sip of her wine and said softly, "Me too. Mitch, I happen to be convinced that what we think of as only perception is the most fateful harbinger; more than we realize, though; and that the way we choose to live is the purest reflection of that same perception but put into practice. So, why on earth would I want to deny myself the miracle of perceiving more magic? I'm up for it. Magic, that is, if that's what you most wanted to know."

"Chloe, your thinking is more intoxicating to me than the wine."

"And you're sure it's not my accent influencing you, *un peu*?"

"It's a very welcome bonus."

We talked and laughed at the small, corner table until almost midnight. There wasn't enough left of the evening to begin to cover the romance of compatibility and the physical and intellectual chemistry between us. Still, I had to ask it. "So, in your daily pursuits, are you more a tortoise or a hare?"

"I suppose by nature I'm a hare; though that's largely influenced by the business I'm in and the demands of my schedule. I also know the tortoise won the race but I'm racing my race, not someone else's. But I must confess to you personally, I'm itching to become a blend of the two."

"Do tell me more about this curious ideal of yours."

"You can make light of it of course because I suppose it's silly. But the Swedes have this word I like. You know how different languages capture such intricacies?"

"Go on, please."

"It's *solkatt* for when the sun reflects off your watch. It's lovely that they make a point of calling it out, you know; but it seems like both a good and bad thing for me day to day. That is, I like the idea of illuminating time, but for me, it always implies some pressing deadline. It just reminds me of the push-pull between the tortoise and the hare, you know?"

"I so get that. So, what's your name for the merging of the tortoise and the hare?"

"Oh, I just coined it. *Tortue Lapine,* to remind me of where I want to eventually be."

I toasted her ideal. "So, here's to turtle bunnies in all their resident glory."

"Hippity hop," she closed, laughing.

"You are a delightfully funny girl, Chloe Joubert."

"You know, Mitch, I happen to be a big believer in pursuing the satisfaction of an incomplete understanding. I trust that this becoming is such the process; you know, so arduous, so beautiful, and so full of stars."

"*Voici a la magie d'une vie pleine.*" I took her hand and kissed it.

"Count me in."

17 Quitch

Middle East

The world is chock full of the boundless energy of quitches.

Though no one's resistant to acting like a quitch occasionally, those who choose to stay resolutely in quitch mode, no matter the circumstance, are the steadfast offenders to common human decency. We all know them and some of us are related to them. These obnoxious, miserable life forms are like dutiful thorns, they stick, perpetually causing disruptive mayhem and sometimes pain.

The classic definition of quitch is a type of fast-growing grass with rapidly spreading stems, like a troublesome weed. The modern use of the word is more memorable depicting the male version of the word bitch. Whether the quitch is a weed in your garden or the masculine version of a bitch on testosterone energy or a resident termagant in your emotional flower bed, the meanings have definitively negative associations, depicting invasive qualities not sought after by discerning and thoughtful humans.

Unfortunately, quitches tend to live very long lives and make the rounds to affect a large number of people. What motivates a quitch is an evil inclination, a pathology that can't be contained. The amount of energy it takes for a quitch to stay in denigration mode is incomprehensible for self-aware people. It's regrettable that their Asperger-like focus can't be redirected toward a more fruitful pursuit, to demonstrably make this world a lighter, if not better place.

As I enter the bizarre world of Middle Eastern royalty, traversing through the Great Hall's main gate, inside there is one man of character and authentic goodness; offsetting the other with quitch-power, who discredits the human soul on many levels. For starters: denying women their human rights, their daughters just respect, abusing their senses in perversely indulgent acts beyond civilized standards of plausibility.

Here's the hard reality: both good men and quitches comprise my clientele. Though it's getting harder for me to serve the latter's whims.

It's a paradox that while most people aspire to great wealth, more than half of the wealthiest men are among the nastiest men you'll ever meet. By contrast, the other less than half are among the most generous. However, both kinds go to great lengths to exert their influence, as all men are concerned with pushing their own agendas. In my mind, what most separates them is simple. It comes down to the ideal they serve, either the betterment or the worsening of all.

Now, I am standing alone in the Great Hall of Prince's father, the King. In America, we use an expressive turn of phrase describing someone like him: SOB. But the son is not one and is related only by genetic association.

Thankfully, I'm neither a political envoi, nor healer, nor doctor, nor one who ministers souls; reminding myself also that my connoisseurship is a skill that's appreciated here. Still, it's important I compartmentalize what I do and why and not always evaluate for whom I'm doing it. The king is not officially my client. He's an adjacent purchaser of something I've got access to that he happens to want very badly.

I'm brokering Gustave Moreau's "Salome" masterpiece for the king. It's reputed to have a strange magic. The classic story based on the biblical accounts of John the Baptist's beheading eerily came about when Salome danced for her stepfather and received the granting of a wish from the lecherous King. Though this is a mesmerizing piece of art, this king's desire for it likely has more to do with something autobiographical. My proximity to him again now makes it clearer than ever that outside of our being the same species, and being the father of my dear friend, Prince, I would prefer not to know him at all.

But, back to his art collection, which is ravishing, beyond a rational dose of aesthetic understanding. These are not the things that mortal men can expect to surround themselves with. His opulent collections are trusted treasures by the standards of Athens and Rome and seem to be more suitable for a museum of the gods of Mount Olympus. Perhaps what Zeus would have showcased in his mythical palace is likely here. The prince's lair is also well stocked. I credit myself for having provided a positive influence, a less senseless style of ornamentation, including more actual objet d'art, interspersed in a somewhat more *au currant* composition.

My increased irritability while inside the king's walls is an allergic reaction to the sort of atavistic lavishness on display. It seems born from an aberrant nature of hoarding and the exercise of a greed-centric use of power, not from an honest appreciation of artistic beauty. Regardless, I imagine the dark heart of the acquirer within the preoccupation of abuse, taste or treasure.

There are basically two distinctly different paths of accumulation, as incompatible as the type of clients who claim them. In order to do what I need to do well, I must remain detached from both modi-operandi. While resolutely poised with either type, inevitably I must boldly ask them the inescapable question: Are you sure that you want everything you can afford? As usual, Rumi has the perfect insight for this precarious point. *"Every object, every being, is a jar full of delight. Be a connoisseur and taste with caution."*

I soothe myself that even though I cannot have everything I fancy, I do have access to something that the king will never be able to claim for himself. And at least I have a shot at this, though I'm not there yet. Einstein wrote in a Tokyo hotel in 1922 that *'a calm and modest life brings more happiness than the pursuit of success when combined with constant restlessness.'*

Like all great gifts that pose something besides what they seem; this gift too appears to be compiled of lesser-thans. But nothing is further from the truth for the more-thans lie just beneath the lackluster surface for each of us to access with some re-invention. Though I'm clearly doubting myself in stride, the possibility of re-invention still exists for me. Knowing I'm but a broker to the king's desire du jour, I remind myself that as I can morph to heed Einstein's counsel, I too can find the real buried treasure.

Though I want to believe that it's character that ultimately determines what we become, I want to face this reality squarely. Not all of us have that option. Sadly, there are plenty of characters among us who lack character.

18 Which

Middle East

Deep into the doldrums of my Middle Eastern overnight, I'm bunked in a south wing suite chock-full to its vaulted ceiling with priceless artifacts; a suite that's usually reserved for visiting dictators. The excessive display of artifacts in this wing resembles that of a museum. This isn't objectively good or bad, but it either jives with your sensibility or it doesn't. It's hard for me to sleep because it's overly stimulating in the most unfavorable way. Tomorrow, I'll have to talk to Prince about getting my old room.

Be that as it may, despite the distraction, the primary reason I'm here, is to dampen Prince's persistent preoccupation about my finding him the lost, magic ball. And the grand irony isn't lost on me, God forbid, that the magic orb I'm to search for may be sitting on a shelf in Soho. But since I don't really believe that, I've got other issues top of mind. This is a strange and uncharted type of friendship intersection that I've been thrust into. I know exactly how easily things get lost in the sands here, suddenly buried, never to be seen of again.

The Prince busted into my suite addressing me volubly before his man closed the doors behind him.

"Mitch, I'm sorry that my father's covetous ways discomfit you. You know I do not condone them. He's an old man. It's too late to hope for any change."

"So, you've settled to opt for tolerance?"

"It's more like distant vituperation."

"Much more appropriate."

"I guess my respect for him as my father and king takes precedence. It's not like your ten commandments don't cover this kind of thing. I feel I must honor his past to some extent; where it is he's been, what he's seen; his generation's cultural reality. What he's been part of historically that makes him as he is today. Until the Brits departed in '67 we were royal in name only, you know."

"It's one thing to know what he is in the abstract and completely another for me to stand in front of it in the flesh."

"Of course. But the understanding must cut both ways, which is the only real kind of understanding. Look, I see what you see as the hard reality here, but it will take generations to change things in the slightest in my world. Character doesn't have the same cache here that it does in your hood. Oscar Wilde isn't seen as charming here like he is in your world. It's a bitch to admit, but you know that where it is that we are born matters. It's delusional to think one can ever completely slough that off. It's a part of me no matter what I choose to take from it or not. That was why I insisted my father allow my going to school in the States. I wanted to learn more than what I only had access to here, for my one life experience, at least this go round. And he acceded, as you know, only after I threatened to go anyway. Just your seasons alone were miraculous to me. I feel the chill and the beauty of them sometimes when I'm seated on a camel at some vassal's oasis. We're supposed to be striving to be a vital part of a much bigger picture, but it isn't going to happen here for a long time, and you can't stop by and wish it so. When the old geezers like my father see even a slight shift, they dig in their heels and poof, progress is securely locked into mere rhetoric. Not much different from your swamp in DC, though, is it?"

"True, but sometimes your world triggers me."

"I have to co-exist with it. While you're here, you have to, also."

"I'll take solace in the fact that I'm leaving shortly."

"Enough! It's a waste of our time together to go on about things we can't impact. Instead, tell me what you know about the magic ball."

"You mean the ball that's secretly thought to exist; that cannot be described except that it's round and formed of crystal; that may or may not be capable of doing something magical? You mean that ball, Prince?"

"Mitch, it's not like I can overtly be the one who's out there looking for it."

"P, you just need to understand that this search is a lot like looking for something so elusive, it's like searching for a little piece of God."

"That should make it easy to find, because after all he is everywhere."

"Very funny. I trust that you likewise are still pursuing the leads you might have? I mean, you do have some, don't you?"

"Yes, but I told you, my original trail went cold very fast, which told me I must have been very close."

"And how do you know this?"

"I just know. Last I traced it, it was said to be kept by a neighboring king. He suddenly dies and the ball is gone without a trace? Trusted harem hearsay—stop smirking!—trusted harem hearsay says one of his innumerable wives told another wife that it was sent anonymously to a relative in Turkey so that no one in the family would know of it or ever be able to possess it after the king died. Apparently, it left with a large shipment of nondescript things that the king's son wasn't fond of keeping. His father's body wasn't cold, and he was busy culling the palace goodies. I would imagine there were a few treasures among them, but the ball was just an ornament likely thrown into the mix unknowingly as insignificant."

"Why would the king not have left this prized piece, if it had magical powers, in the care of someone like his brother or a trusted son?"

"His brother's a greedy bastard and his sons are all jerks. The entire family's unimaginative and corrupt. Not one good apple in the entire bunch. They probably hated him and dumped his goods for a stash of postmortem cash. You know how ignorance and hubris keep blind people from ever really seeing."

"Every single day of my working life."

"Cold trails are lonely roads but often make for exciting endings.

I feel, I believe, a destination's close at hand. As a treasure hunter, you've told me how intuition and timing are critical to every great find. Things that matter most can only be known from inside, in here." Prince pointed to his heart then gestured to his head to bookend his point. "What's up here is quite limited, but not so here. It sounds cliché but it's true."

"I understand it to also always be the case."

"You say that you do. But it seems that you don't really trust that you do."

"I'm just working through a lot right now, Prince."

"That is ridiculous. You are always working on a lot of things. You are also always dodging committing to something like this."

"And what is this exactly, P?"

"Why, only the biggest and most consequential search of your life."

"I think you overstate the significance."

"Look Michello, cut the crap. You were reared on this stuff. Maybe you just lost your way and need to get back to it."

"Very well could be the case."

"You see, you have to think of it like this. If you were that king with the magic ball, and you too legitimately did not have anyone to fully trust, what would you do?"

"I have a hard time thinking that not a single one of those wives could be trusted."

"I have yet to test one of those for myself, but I assume trust would be the whole reason for taking one of them on in the first place."

"Just so you know, it's not just your dad making me wobbly. I'm thinking about taking on one of those for myself. First time the thought's even entered my mind, you know."

"A wife? You? Are you in love?"

"Pretty sure I am. But to stay on point, you're saying a king wouldn't leave something that powerful to a woman ever? "I honestly don't know how you take it, ensconced in such resolute backwardness."

"Some days it's hard but having anything I want makes it more tolerable. Plus, I can escape whenever I want since I'm still basically ceremonial; but I don't expect anyone who's not from here to understand this life, not even you. If there are two things they burned into my brain in university, it's that geography matters and so does the relativity of literally everything. I suppose I should begin to look for a real wife. But, you know, concubines are plentiful and I'm one of those weirdos who secretly would prefer to have one really great wife, rather than thirty strangers like my father. But stop making me think too much. I know the game you play when you're trying to throw me off track. Let's get back to my favorite ball. Apparently, that blabbering wife I mentioned, who couldn't keep a secret, tried to use the sphere herself without the king's knowledge once before he died. Not knowing what it was, other than a source of some power the king coveted, she quickly grew weary and dismissed it."

"Or, maybe negated its potential?"

"She must have suspected that he was up to something with it but had no idea that it could be anything specifically powerful. There's another story about it too; that she abandoned it because when she did peer into it and saw her death reflected back at her, she was terrified. I tried to find her to better trace the story, but sadly I found out that she died."

"Prince, wait. Does everyone who touches that damn magic ball die?"

"You're going to find out, aren't you? Both of us are."

"You're saying the king died, the paramour died, and the ball's disappeared. That's all you've got for me to go on?"

"That's all I've got. I want you, my trusted, savvy pal to pursue the lead in Turkey because to me it feels viable."

"Oh, that really narrows it down."

"Seriously, Mitch, what if you as the pursuer begin to think as the crystal ball would? Listen, please. I swear it on my mother's grave, don't laugh, all of the magic I've encountered in my life is well versed in how to play possum, to lay low for centuries. Magic always waits for the magician to appear. It comes only if you are ready for it. And Mitch, I know that I am ready for it. You know what I'm saying. Magic is no stranger to you. I feel strongly that our little magic sphere is not very far away at all. We have the advantage because we know of its existence and its capabilities. Wherever it is today, no one with access to it is likely to know what it really is. Treasures are dismissed all the time because people don't see what they are. They hide in plain sight all the time."

"And what if the ball doesn't want to be found?"

"That's impossible. Discovery is a universal principle in life. Everything that exists wants to be found."

"That's why this search unsettles me. There are things it's better not to know."

Prince was pacing in widening circles, his soul enraptured with possibility. He grabbed hold of the curtains to keep from falling off the balcony.

"Why Mitch, the ball could turn up in a marketplace. It could be sitting propped on someone's desk and they have no idea what it is."

" So you really believe there's a ball with true magic powers?"

"I absolutely know there is, and for some reason you won't admit you do, too. The ball of which I speak is magical. Our ignorance about it doesn't make any iota of it disappear. Someone not believing in Allah doesn't make God nonexistent. The eternal things get caught in our throats, and we either swallow or spit them out to our detriment."

"I think you're suffering from a bout of belief."

"And you, with a bout of disbelief which is a far worse matter, my friend. How can you know what's true if you don't know what you believe, down deep? You're surprising me. The Mitch I'm fond of wouldn't be scared by the specter of elusiveness. It's much easier to go about your days pretending it's not real, while knowing magic exists and is always there somewhere, despite your inability to see it. Elusiveness is totally undervalued, but I remain a faithful fan."

"Elusiveness? You're not in philosophy class anymore."

"Are you crazy? We live permanently in philosophy class. Since the moment you emailed you were coming. Just think on it; you dislike it here so much, but you didn't ask me to meet you in Beirut or Granada. Why?"

"I'm listening. Go on."

"So how is it that we are uncannily here together, and each at such a unique point, where our paths should not readily be crossing. Admit there is more to it than we can see."

"Food for thought then P, think back to philosophy class. Toynbee pointed out that when one is spiritually uncertain, one is prone to turn to magical chimeras to not have to deal with the uncertainty common reality presents."

"Oh, so you think I may be turning to the ball and to magic as a way to delude myself from having to face my reality?"

"Possibly. At some level. Your father outlived his usefulness to your realm a long time ago. For reasons actuarial, you're soon going to be king of this mystic desert."

"That's true, but that's another issue completely. For some reason, you're turning your back on knowing or worse, standing up for what you believe you know. All this could be something calling to you for an unknown reason that you could deeply benefit from addressing."

"And you're being rhetorical not practical. If the supposed magic ball's out there somewhere in the hubbub, how the hell without a warm trail to follow do I go about finding it?"

"You're the treasure hunter. I've never known you not to have some sort of a soft lead within reach. Not when you're sincerely searching for something. Look, I've seen you in action. I know when you want something, you know how to go for it; that is, if you believe in it."

"Hmm. Well, I've a few, perhaps, but nothing to hang my hat on."

"Then don't wear a hat."

"Desk-top ornamental crystal balls are common in the markets of Istanbul, Paris, London, the US and Canada. Round things have universal appeal, so they tend to be around. But, come on, Prince, you know this is a wild goose chase at best."

"The fact that it's a hard search doesn't mean it's impossible. At some point, you just must agree to go for it or not. It always takes time to see, if one can really see or not. The magic may also recognize us. We may not have to find it at all. It may find us first. Can you concede that something reciprocal could be at work here?"

"Or at play."

"Let's just not overthink things, okay?"

"Oh, like that's never happened between us."

"Mitch, I say, we just go for it. Plain and simple. No more nor less. Boom. Done. All I need is a wing man in this adventure. You know I cannot fly alone. All magic requires two. Are you in or are you out? You decide."

"You're actually suggesting that I set out to buy-up all the crystal balls I can find, any and all balls that fit the basic description, and ship them to you for your gaggle of seers to decipher exactly which is the magic one? It seems pretty ridiculous, not to mention extraordinarily time consuming with not much potential benefit."

"Mitch, I think you mean feasible benefit not potential benefit. You of all people know that I do not care one iota about feasibility. And I'm telling you that the potential benefit is worth the world to me."

"If I agree to do this for you, and underline, for you, which is the only reason I would even consider such a ludicrous proposition; how will you ever know which ball among all of the balls is the real one? You may never know even if it's sitting right in front of you in your ball museum."

"Honestly, I don't know that I will know. I'm itching to know, of course. I hope I'll be able to know. But knowing and seeing take some time. So, I can wait. All I can say is I trust in the possibility. I also trust in your ability to find it. Besides, tell me what is the harm? Unlike you, I have nowhere I'm expected. I'll collect them as a pastime and keep all the balls in my palace, hoping that at some point I can discover which one is the real magic ball. Anyway, why does it matter to you? You're a treasure hunter, for God's sake. Go do what you do."

"Wait, P."

"For what?"

"For me to contemplate all the work involved in what you're demanding of me."

"Let's cut to the chase then. You are a businessman and I am a ready buyer. I'll pay you so handsomely that if you find the ball, you'll be willing to part with it and give it to me."

"My dear P, there's another dilemma here. We're good friends. This hunt we're about to embark on violates the rule that you should never go into business of any kind with a friend."

"Then, let's make a deal between us right now that you can't resist. Does ten million sound appropriate? Let's get this over with so we can spend the afternoon at my stables. You're a lover of beauty. Wait till you see my Arabian stallion. I've named him Salmon, as peaceful protector."

"Well, I think you should pay me handsomely for every ball regardless if it's a magic ball or not. And on the honor system between us, if the magic ball announces itself to you, ten million would be applicable over and above whatever else you've paid up to that point, until such a time when you tell me that you no longer want me to continue pursuing the hunt. Mind you, I will be anxiously awaiting the day when you tell me that you are duly sick of crystal balls. And next Tuesday won't be soon enough. But Prince, until then, your hobby will be my hobby. This will last as long as it lasts, which will be entirely up to you."

"Hobby? This isn't a hobby to me. I feel my future depends on it. We've talked long enough this morning for you to know how I feel about this. Put the terms you've mentioned on paper and provide them to my usual administrative stream, as I feel talking money with a friend is demeaning to us both."

"Okay, but I'm omitting any reference in writing about our sourcing an actual magic ball, one that may be black magic for all we know."

"Of course, the details are only ours. Know that I'm not deterred about believing in the existence of magic of any kind. But know I am not personally going to be pursuing the black variety. Standing for what we believe in is always a good thing."

Then Prince took on a lighter energy and laughed, patting me on the shoulder. "This arrangement of ours will let me know that while

I won't always be at the tippy-top of your mind in your travels, you'll at least have me somewhere on your radar."

"As your friend, I need you to tell me exactly why it is that you want this ball so badly."

"Oh, come off it. Every man wants to see the future and know what it holds. That goes especially for me as the successor to the throne. I don't want anyone else to have it. If its magic is black, it could fall into the hands of an enemy."

"There's a reason why such things are only meant for the hands of sorcerers or magi."

"Why? Because historically it's been so? That sounds like an argument only my father would make."

"We're talking about powers that most men can't begin to fathom, let alone handle."

"That doesn't scare me one bit. The only thing that scares me, my friend, is that you're scared. I have courage and you have less of it than I thought you had."

"You're the second person to point this out to me lately."

"Honestly, I don't get it. To me, you embark on an adventure precisely because you don't know how it will turn out or what price you might pay."

"Easy for you to say. There's no price you can't afford."

My insistent friend led me out of the room into a small private dining room off the hall, where a table was generously set with dates, lamb, delicacies and a bottle of Montrachet Grand Cru.

"Now Mitch, we are going to have some fun today if it kills you, and I want to hear all about this love of yours. You are the oldest man I know who has not been in love, so I am quite stirred by this news.

"Well, I am doing my best to keep it together, I hope you know."

"And all I know about you is that I like that finally you cannot keep it together when it pertains to love. So this does sound promising, I admit."

Prince apologized for changing into riding gear, or rather being changed by his valet into riding gear, as we ate. But then it was my turn.

After a long afternoon of riding, followed by an equally exhausting late-night banquet accompanied by oud and percussion players, I called it a wrap in order to turn in to fly out first thing.

As we meandered back through the main hall, I realized this is the last chance I'll have to thwart my ball-obsessed royal friend in person.

"Prince, let's stop right here for a minute. I want to breathe in the spirit of this trumeau. Isn't it interesting how just one piece in a giant space can determine the spirit of the entire expanse?"

"Yes, it's very interesting to me that you paused right here. I find myself stopping in this exact spot whenever I come through, just as you did for no apparent reason."

"It's like that spot where Frost stopped in the woods on a snowy evening, isn't it?"

"Ah, yes, *The woods are lovely, dark and deep, But I have promises to keep.*"

"*And miles to go before I sleep.*"

"*And miles to go before I sleep.* You are a dear friend to me, Mitch. You can annoy the hell out of me, but thank you for being frank. Around here only one opinion on everything is taken as word. Too often it's mine."

"You're relentless, Prince. You win. Okay. On a completely unrelated note, tell me if your father might be inclined to accept a small gift from me."

"I suppose, if it isn't too small."

'Perhaps it will help matters between us, too. He's just purchased a priceless treasure that frankly was a huge challenge to sell. There are only a handful of men in the world who can afford such a thing. I'd like to, you know, extend some kindness and to keep our trade channel open, as they say."

"I'm sure he would be accepting of your gesture, but I can't promise you that he'll like your gift or tell you where he will put it, as in a closet perhaps. Truth is, he hardly likes anything anymore, save beautiful young girls. Most days I cannot understand any of it. Besides, he is excellent at keeping secrets. He hasn't given me even a hint of advice on how to rule."

"Probably because he doesn't believe in his own mortality. Kings never do, not even on their deathbeds. The gift I want to give him is more like a gesture of thanks for completing a seamless transaction and because I'm so fond of his son."

"Do as you wish."

"I'll be sending two eighth century stone figures directly to him, with a formal note of thanks. He can place them outside in one of his twelve gardens. They're not Islamic but then neither is half his collection. And one does have exceptionally large breasts."

"Thank you for hearing me out today, Mitch. This was a good visit for us both, I think."

"Let's hope for only the best."

"Yes, Mitch, always. I appreciate this more than you know. Safe travel tomorrow and a restful night. And do practice that French of yours a little more. It sounds like you're going to need it. By the way, you can have the wedding here if you wish, though I'm not holding my breath that you won't find a way to mess this up.

Gesturing with his hand to his heart, Prince turned away. I walked down the long corridor to my suite wondering how my friend in the midst of such opulence can shoulder the burden of a power he feels such ambiguity about. I texted Terry about sending the two statues at Genevieve's to the king; with a note to accompany the dynamic duo, along with the enclosure of detailed description about their historical origin.

Your Royal Highness,
With special thanks for closing the deal so promptly. May the road between us be paved only with life's true treasures. Enjoy this royal pairing in your gardens.
Best wishes,
Mitch Bonaventura

A bit later, I received a text from Terry inquiring further about the merchant's original directive.

M,

Just checking. Outside of the pairing caveat, do you want to mention anything about the mysterious need for keeping them, you know, close together?

T

I promptly replied:

T,

No need. I mentioned they're a pairing. Besides, I've had to deal with pressing issues here that made me decide that the pairing caveat was probably a con to get me to buy all six. Please tell Gen I've come to my senses in order to remain in my number one spot among her clients. The King has plenty of hectares that may benefit from the presence of these ancient guardians of something or other. For sure, I don't want their supposed mojo on my terrace. All's good to go, No worries.

M

19 Sitch

Middle East

Truth is a part of every last sticky situation. It sits by only to jump out and yell boo. The ever-dazzling jokester carries irony in its back pocket as another means to torment. Trouble is we must live a long time with the punch line as aftermath. Though lamentable in design as well as in life, freedom is the first casualty when it comes to creating anything. There's just no way around it. You have to know, going in that you've got to be willing to let go or surrender your freedom first in order to get to the disciplined vision. It seems counterintuitive but if I could only get inside this one principle, I too might be surprised at what's possible. And whether you're designing a space or a life, this misunderstood principle requires you to protect the ideal behind the creation—the one that's in there—itching to become. Though I know it's true, I need to be reminded.

Upon preparing my departure, I contemplate what my heart seems to be telling me. I'm falling in love, so unlike Prince I'm not obsessed with the possibility of some obscure and hidden magic. But I also realize that the way I prefer my magic is for it to present itself as a slow organic revelation that doesn't demand everything from me up front, rather than an in-your-face realization.

Prince and I, obsessed over different particulars, are existentially joined at the hip. While I'm caught up in clarifying my perspective about the nature of magic and my relationship to it, Prince's interest is in magic's utility—being able to see and foretell the future. We're like spelunkers in adjacent caves where invisible things like magic are said to burrow. Since there's no hope of deterring Prince from his preoccupation, I figure, meantime, there's no harm in my doing what I'm going to be doing, which in this case involves the relentless sourcing of crystal balls. I'm not going to abandon my search to know more about what magic is; rather, I'm hoping to temporarily straddle a fence. Limbo is stressful, but when you don't know the question you're waiting to answer, it seems a reasonable perch; though unfortunate for me it tends to be a go-to that doesn't always get me where I need to go.

The incomparable Rumi tells us, '*Sell your questioning talents and buy bewildering surrender.*'

Understanding Prince's delight in his compulsion does help me see what I've been blocking in my own mind—not surrendering is holding me back from something I've always needed, an at-ease state of sheer bewilderment. Sounds a lot like love, I admit, which is also a step in a new direction for me.

Funny thing but I no longer must worry what it is I would do if I had the real magic crystal ball because it's quite possible I already have it. I think I finally feel ready to risk everything, come what may.

20 Flitch

Italy

The faeries have had a hold on my fate. They've been riding me lately to prioritize visiting my godfather in Italy. Upon reunion, Gio acts as if I'd never left, but we both miss each other in ways I can't explain. It's as if he needs me as a vessel of his treasures as much as I need to receive them.

My spirited godfather and virtuoso mentor, Giovanni Cristoferetti, taught me as a boy that we're fortunate if most of our life is spent in the company of water and wood. Perhaps it's why I so love the Hinoki tub, an apt provider of both in artful unison. When I was in my single digit years, Gio shared, with a sense of imagination and seriousness which I vividly recall, that only the faeries of the woods and streams know this secret and it is why magic chooses to live there. He would say, "Ah, we must be thankful we have friends that we cannot see."

Though I believed him at the time, I didn't know where to find such a thing near as flighty as a bit of real magic, let alone a real faerie to enact it. So, I pushed it aside, leaving it for tomorrow, when I might see. Only today do I realize that I drifted far away from the ideal of the simple magic of the water and the wood; caught in the currents of career, finding success and romance in world travel and fulfilling desires of the rich and famous.

But, I have the sacred seeds Gio planted within my heart long ago and it is only now that I anticipate the fruits of his lessons. Gio had a natural affinity for magic which he nurtured through his Masonic heritage and a familial affiliation with the Grand Orient of Italy, using their vocabularies to share mystifying insights about unexplainable surrealities. Without preamble, he would let gems escape casually as though mystical truths were part of pedestrian conversation. At the time, I didn't comprehend nuance, and always thought Gio's secrets would be there waiting for me, like faeries in the distant woods, I had yet to realize. Thankfully some of it stuck, because now my soul yearns for more, despite my fear that I didn't inherit his easy access to secret sources.

I'm reminded that aging builders like my dear Gio have something in common with what is known in construction as the flitch beam. The flitch is a longitudinal cut of a log reinforced by a steal plate, providing a sturdy, long lasting constructional advantage. But with advantage comes disadvantage. Since the flitch requires fabrication, it's more expensive and because of its steel reinforcement it's also heavier. Once a ubiquitous and reliable foundational staple, today it has decreased viability. Though the function of the flitch isn't disputed, builders are less likely to rely on it.

Gio's access to art via magic is overlooked because there are more easily accessible strategies. But I find that *il mio Padrino* continues to teach me incredibly beautiful things, forgotten things that I too have displaced.

"Michello, you cannot ever forget that The Great See is always, always, hidden in plain sight. *Momento mori,* we all die. Smart men study philosophy all their lives to prepare for death. Do you see? We each have our day, but eventually we all outlive our usefulness. Oh, and don't feel badly about it either. What you can accept cannot hurt you. But what you fight against will surely kill you."

"But, uncle, you know I believe that the soul is immortal."

"Then what else is there to know? Everything else pales in comparison to this, no?
Momento mori. Everyone who knows anything about life knows how to gracefully accept this. I taught you better, but you go off to America where it's easy to forget that you won't live forever. This knowing is the difference between concrete and a tree. Whatever you do, do not chase

that bird, son. It always ends badly."

"Gio, I know, like the steady flitch, it doesn't mean we're not good enough any longer; only that there are other good things in plentiful supply, as our own performance may simply show signs of wear."

"And tear. It is not the wear that gets us, Michello, the tear is what does us in. Better that I remind you about this again. It is a natural process; one of those universal rites designed especially for us in this realm. Round and round we go, and it goes on with or without us. But if like me you don't believe in death, except in the physical form, then it is nothing but another passage. It's all good, only different. The journey continues after we die."

"But death makes people sad."

"It is only the young ones left behind who think mortality is sad or something other than what it is. *Verita.* Michello. Ah, but I must confess. It is lonely."

I had a dark foreshadowing of my life without Gio in it. I couldn't help the physical manifestation of that foreshadowing. Tears choked my eyes.

Gio would have none of it. "It's not me that you will miss," he said. "It's the dynamic incompletion. Just as de Kooning lamented."

I was familiar with de Kooning's lament. He constantly re-worked his paintings. He always felt that there was more to be done, and that it was the nature of art to be unfinished. Is this what we miss about the people we love who have died? That the nature of life is it's an unfinished work?

"Oh Gio, you don't have to be stoic with me about any of it. Those not directly involved in witnessing the passage of time pay it no mind, but when time's finite ticking becomes louder, it gets personal."

"*Basta!* You, my boy, are missing the bigger point. You must see above and beyond, Michello, always look there. Otherwise, we only do our part to perpetually lower the bar here for each other. This is not a good thing. We have set the bar far too low already. If anything, the bar needs intense spiritual lifting. Life is not to be lived this way, with no time to think. Don't settle for being busy, chasing your own tail."

"I would weep at the thought of my ever letting you down." I said, internally doubting the strength of my actual performance.

"What is your biggest issue right now, Cello?"

"I guess that everything is complicated."

"But you know what complication means, son? It only means that a decision isn't being made. Complication is a means of stalling. Trust me. If you make your decision, the complication vaporizes. When you know what you believe and you put your action there, it's just not that complicated anymore."

"You think I'm putting off something that I need to greet?"

"If it's complicated, yes I do. Follow your heart and put your energies there, and everything becomes simple."

Of course, Gio had hit the nail on the head for me even though I knew I had to take an action I hadn't yet. The fear must have shown in my face.

"Cello, everyone will also tell you that God is complicated, but I know that he is not. God works simply by way of right and wrong, light and dark, good and evil. He is quite clear over millennia. But we are the ones who blur the lines and pretend not to know what we all deep down already know; the part we all know is coming. Once we face God's inherent simplicity and take a position relative to it, the complications we entangle ourselves in will disappear."

"Easier said than done."

"Not true, Cello. This cliché is a misnomer. It's far easier to make the change and do something than it is to postpone it, or to make it complicated and live with the nagging uncertainty, rather than to just bring it on, face the music and dance. You have been bamboozled by the modern grind, personified, if you will, by the so-called Big Apple of yours.

What Gio was saying hit home and applied to love, but I was still unable to act with certainty, unbravely as Athena warned.

"Oh, and Cello, absolutely do not do what that Dylan Thomas fellow said you should do either: 'Rage, rage against the dying of the light.' No. The British, or in his case the Welsh, had this wrong. It is best to listen to the Greeks and the Italians. In matters of life and death, art and love, they are the real A-team. Rage against the dying of the light? Nothing's worse than the ridiculousness of raging energy. Rage only showcases underlying fear. Rage doesn't even make for very good drama." It occurred to me that I had never seen Gio angry, even when he had cause. His equanimity was another thing that made him so compelling.

"I am counting on you, my godson. You are my immortality. You carry on a sacred tradition, the authentic appreciation of beauty. And Dante was right. *'Beauty cannot be separated from the Eternal.'* My Jewish friends who teach Kabballah say it's *Tiphereth,* the force that balances beauty and spirituality. I coached you on beauty as a bambino. It is something we artisans will share forever on our journey, all through life and through death. Besides love, what else works like this? We can take with us what we create while we are here."

"So, I take it the baggage clerks must be very strict up there?"

"Yes, but I am hoping some of them are artisans, like us; gatekeepers who know the holy imperative for creating and honoring good design. Art is the greatest expression of our humanity. Other than love, of course."

"I understand that love is the greatest art of all; that is intellectually I do. But I have yet to enact my belief for myself."

"I have something to tell you."

"What is it, Cello?"

"I'm afraid. I'm very afraid."

"Of what, dear godson?"

"I've met someone remarkable. She is waiting for me to declare I'm in love with her. I know I can't keep her waiting much longer. She isn't the type to endlessly wait around for me. Our talk today makes me see why I'm holding back. Art is eternal. We are mortal. Love isn't. I'm terrified of losing a person I might come to love as much as I love you, *Padrino.* Please don't leave me yet." I threw my arms around Gio and wept.

Gio hugged me tightly then held me at arm's length. We were

outside enjoying the sweet smells of his garden. I took them in with a shudder of relief. I'd been holding my mental breath.

Taking a long breath himself, Gio said, "Without the soulful spirit of love, our anima cannot travel the last passage to the sweet side, let alone take along the few things for the next leg of the journey. We must learn as much as we can here because certain things are capable of going with us. Hindus have this right, I think. Probably because they have been at it longer than us. Love is the art of life. There's no contradiction, my boy, and I am not dying. I am completing my journey. I will come back to tell you more if I can. You know I will."

"What if you can't?"

"Michello, if for any reason I cannot reach out to you directly, then know that I will come to you in dreams. If there is not an opportunity for direct communication, you will need to pay attention to signs and mystical insights that I provide to you indirectly. Cello, you know me. If there is a way, you know I am creative enough to find it. I am counting on you to be creative enough to recognize it. Otherwise, you will know that I am either very busy with important matters that await you, or it will be that you already know what it is I would share."

Despite the brilliant sunset, I felt the cloak of darkness fall around us. For we were talking about my beloved godfather's demise. It occurred to me how much I would miss Gio's physical presence, with all his warmth and familiarity, and his formidable intellect. They seemed like the same thing to me.

"I will forever miss you, *Padrino*. There is a hole in my soul that only you can fill."

"The whole love thing is intricately connected from here to there, Cello, magic to reality, life to death; all of it. This is the essence of God, and it alone reveals our best. Trust this is the very point where God abides. Trust the longing. Trust the love. Trust the magic. Trust your own heart to know what is right."

"I am trying uncle, but you know this is my first time to seriously do so."

"Just do it son. Doing counts; trying not as much. Fear not,

Cello."

Then he went on. "I will tell you something you do not know. I have loved and I have lost, and I am 80, so more than once. One, a Lebanese poet, was killed in a crossfire on a street in Beirut. Another, a Milanese fashionista, left me for an American, can you believe it? I have doubted love's worth, like you are doubting, but I have never for a moment denied it. I'm remembering. Remembering is idealization. It's an art all artists practice."

His housekeeper, an ancient mariner who ironically was mute, brought out some limoncello and butter cookies and set them on the small table between us.

"La Dolce Vita," Gio said aloud with a sparkle in his eyes. "Lest we forget to enjoy the sweetness of life even as we anticipate death. You know, there is no culture that understands the nature of beauty and love better than we Italians. It's as if the angels who are the divine protectors of art are all fluent in Italian. Art knows where it is most welcome. Like love, art fills all the empty spaces here."

We finished our refreshment and walked through the backyard to the street and strolled past an old church, as Gio pointed out architectural details that he knew firsthand. "There is a road from the eye to the heart that does not go through the intellect, Michello. Those are Chesterton's words, not mine. He was speaking of a different kind of love than we are at the moment, but his words are applicable, aren't they? And any decent architect understands this before he envisions anything. I know you understand this, or you would not be such a great designer. You might use this idea though a bit more in your personal life."

We walked on, exchanging inner understandings that always begged to be revisited whenever I was in the presence of this magical man.

"Do not forget that when you were but a bambino I would smother you with kisses then just watch you play. Ah, watching in silence is a dying art. You would ask me why, uncle? What was I hoping to see and I said, only you, little one. I was watching the beauty of creation unfold right before my eyes. The point of both love and art is to make the invisible visible."

"I remember that you told me to ask myself every single day what it is that I love. And then you would say, You are the only one in the whole world who can answer that question for yourself."

" Michello, do you remember my telling you about the part of the brain that manages the visual memory?"

'The lingual gyrus?"

"*Si, si,* it was because I knew you had a good one. Not everyone gets such a gift. You and I got the artistic talent, so we must relish the visual splendors, as we are able to create the same beauty in our everyday lives. But listen, son, you must stick with where it takes you. The holy gyrus provides that we are never disappointed in life. Michello, you must make a real point to befriend it. Promise me, you will not lose it or drown it out with the world's nonsense. Your life is up to you. The way you love is up to you. Whatever you are facing is always only the half of it. If you understand this, it is much harder to be fooled."

We walked in silence for a while. "You know the Latin word *velum,* I think," Gio said. "Though it refers to a botanical covering it can also refer to a line between what we see and what we don't; what we perceive and what we ignore; what we are and what we think we are. What we have here is but a mysterious and passing thing; none of it is actually secure or real in the sense of having perpetuity, eternal meaning, or lasting value. Everything in this world is on loan to us, we must embrace it but not insecurely cling too tightly to it. It is not ours to own."

"Gio, as odd as it is, I have some pressing questions for you."

"Of course, you do."

"I'm struggling with that imperative known as editing. As a builder, what was the hardest part of it for you?"

"Most definitely the editing itself. And this pertains to editing life as well as editing blueprints, renderings, jobs, scripts, art, friends, lovers. However, whenever you can enlist an artful edit, to minimize life's clutter or senseless excess, is when you realize how instrumental a process it is. It's the continual refinement that enables the very best result. But tell me, why do you have an issue with editing now?"

"Not just now. Always. The editing exasperates me and makes me weary. I love creation, but editing is simply exhausting. It's the part of the process that haunts me most and causes me the most duress. Sometimes, I feel as if it's going to eat me alive before I'm done with it. I was hoping to learn from you how to better endure it."

"I can tell you what worked for me. Just accept it and let it do its thing until it's done."

"And how do I know when that is?"

"Either when you come to know it is enough or when you just can't stand it anymore. And maybe stop trying to manage it so tightly. Don't fight the need to do it, or deny its role, or you won't enjoy the win when it comes. God edits constantly and so does Mother Nature. It's not a negative thing. But all editors get belittled when they are literally indispensable forces in any creation."

"Uncle, so next, here's a crazy one for you."

"My favorites all tend to be a little crazy, like me."

"Seriously, I must have a straight answer to this one. Have you ever really seen a faerie?"

"Oh, this one is easy. But you sound as if you may have also seen one."

"I need to know if they are real."

"Most definitely, I assure you, they are completely real but in ways you may not yet understand. But I promise you this, if or when you do meet one, you will know it. Do you know what Einstein said about such things?"

"I don't."

'If you want your children to be intelligent, read them faerietales. If you want them to be more intelligent, read them more faerietales.'

"About the faeries, you cannot readily see them because their reason for being here isn't anything we can comprehend. This is true of many entities however, not only faeries. Nature has its own language. It happens to be a symbolic one so we can't interpret it intellectually. Faeries do exist but completely outside of our understanding, similar to the way that God or love does. You must personally experience it. The arc of majesty in certain creations is simply beyond our mortal competence. Also, the faeries are both constantly in a state of here and not here, but they're mainly set in schemata for purposes of natural balance, one could say. The most practical way for me to explain them to you is that they were never meant to be the visible leads in this earthly drama. They function more as a supporting cast, like a behind the scenes troupe for things we cannot yet realize here. They function similarly to the way bees do, or like a Greek chorus in an ancient drama."

"I think I see."

"There is just so much going on behind the scenes here; so much that we cannot see. Most of us cannot even keep up with the small parts that we can see. We have no earthly idea about how it all fits together, and this is just how it is with the bees. Most only know of the buzz, the sting, or the honey. And the sting and the honey are ever so conjoined, aren't they?"

"I suppose."

"But Cello, trust that the faeries are important to the order and balance, much like the wind. Just try telling a faerie that they don't exist and you will feel sadness immediately. They know we only believe in things that we pretend to understand. But know that as our understanding develops, things we do not see can, do, and will become more visible to us. Unfortunately, except in earliest childhood, this tends not to happen again until we are in our end game years."

"Give me a practical example of something they might do here, you know, regularly."

"Okay, but just one. There are too many for me to explain. The thing with faeries is that the more you tell about them, the more there is to explain. This is why so many invisible beings stay unseen. There's not enough time in the day to deal with all this openly. Eventually, it's all too much for the human sensibility to absorb, which is largely why faeries have been relegated to the land of make-believe. You know how angels accompany the human soul in the deathly transition to the other side?"

"You've told me it's so."

"The faeries are like the angels for the animals. When an animal passes, they make the voyage over with them. It is a different journey for animals than it is for us, but they are still part of the kingdom. Enough for now, okay? You are tiring me out. Let's go back to the garden and breathe. You must remind yourself about all the things you already know but simply might have accidentally forgotten."

"Or possibly, mismanaged," I laugh.

"You seem to me to be struggling right now from a world-closed mind."

"Tell me, Gio. Is the future fluid or is it fated? I'm about to embark on a project for our beloved friend, Prince who desperately wants to know his future ahead of schedule."

"Oddly, the future is both set and not set. Parts of it are stable and parts are fluid. Prince should not focus on trying to understand it. Tell him plainly from me. If he's minding the store, the rent will take care of itself. It is only your actions in the present that are the source of anything and everything that is yet to come for you. Relinquishing your present power is never a wise choice. This is a loaded gun. Is Prince assuming that the future can be predicted?"

"Yes."

"The reason it cannot be is that it is not written yet. An outline of it exists, but nothing is fully determined about it. The actions you take is what manifests into what is to be. Your intention is the magic ingredient that brings it into the present. But then it is no longer the future, is it? I believe dwelling on it is a waste of precious time, but everyone struggles with this to some degree."

"And me maybe more so these days."

"Then it is only because you are choosing instead to be stuck. The fear of the unknown will do its very damnedest to keep you stuck. If you wait to understand it to make your move, you are in danger of missing out! If you tell yourself you can wait but you know down deep that you cannot; you will lose out. And you will ultimately regret it when you are old. No. You must act. Play a card from your heart. Do something. If you do not play the card, you cannot win. Every action causes a reaction, but standing still does not count for much, if at all. One day, you will look back from where you are, and you will not believe that this was your life. It will seem surreal in every way. If you take care of today, you literally have no idea what winds will blow in for you from seemingly nowhere and swoop you up into an awaited magical reality."

"Gio, if you had a magic ball and could see the future, would you want to?"

"It is not a worthy pursuit for any of us to try to predict the future. It's always only about you. I hope you realize this. Another great misnomer is that character determines fate. More specifically, character determines action, and your actions determine your path. What we believe and what we love Cello, determines absolutely everything, in our life and in our death."

"Oh, you are my dearest Padrino and I am so blessed by you."

"I want to meet this remarkable woman you've spoken of. Tell me her name?"

"Chloe."

"Ah, a lovely French girl? Where is she right now?"

"Paris, I think."

"I want to meet her."

"She's waiting for me to commit to her."

"Do you want to?"

"She's magic, Padrino."

"Then what are you waiting for? Man spends his life hunting for magic, trying to find it or claim it for himself. Even those who say they don't believe in it are still obsessed with trying to find it. If I could, I would give mine to you, but you have to find your own. The miracle of it is that once you find it, no one can ever take it from you. Your only job is to find and claim your magic. This is the whole point of your life, son."

We walked along in companionable silence. The sun had set and I knew the housekeeper had a supper prepared for Gio.

"Oh, but wait, Cello. I know you are ready to leave but there's a bit more you should know. The magic within us is the only real power we have within our reach here. It is elusive, and it takes real courage to

145

look for it and to claim it. But the magic we carry allows us something else, something less celebrated except by those who know."

"Pray tell, Padrino."

"The magic within us is the true divine power source and it's only limited by us and our capacity. It's like an electronic grid, propelling the energies that reflect our perspective constantly, sending beams out into the universe, back and forth, reciprocally. Divine magic, if we enlist it, allows us to perpetually re-invent ourselves. Just like alchemy, it affords us what we need to continually create, re-create, and connect to our evolving hopes and dreams, and to make the life that we are envisioning actually happen. It's a big thing to swallow, this resurrection potential and the responsibility we have because of it. Michello, we are the creators of our tale."

"Everything you've told me today is proof that it's time I should undertake a massive re-design of the most personal kind."

"That is always a very worthy plan. Never doubt that."

"I'm not doubting, godfather; just preparing myself."

"Do try to meet your magic more than halfway. You don't want to make it walk too far to find you. Without divine magic, Michello, we only have reality. Reality is the real illusion but that is for another day."

We embraced, the old Flitch and his apprentice. Just as I was departing, he stopped me at the door. "Cello, there is something I want to leave you with but I admit it's a tricky one."

"So, you're opting for a sphinx-like riddle to test me further after I've left?"

"Of course. You need to know this one and to remember it forever, promise? You should also share it with our good Prince."

"Why do I feel that you will leave me spellbound tonight?"

Gio looked at me squarely now with high seriousness. "The magic that is real isn't considered real, but the magic that is considered real, that can actually be done, is not real magic."

"So, I understand; you're saying that real magic that is true magic is not considered real by most; while magic that can be done that most think of as real, is not real magic?" "Yes, son. The real magic is missed by most. Don't settle for being among them."

Bedecked with nothing but blessed possibility, I spoke my farewell. "Then let us prepare to be amazed."

21 Sandwich

England

I boarded the plane to London the next morning because of an oddly contrived clandestine ultra-private invitation I surprisingly received from a distant relative of none other than the Queen. The details were such that I sensed there was an unexpected treasure awaiting. Despite my piqued interest, I had no idea what I was about to see, but I knew they wanted to liquidate it promptly. Besides, though my body was enthusiastically on board the plane by sunrise, the rest of me seemed to lag far behind.

My sage uncle had left me feeling as if I'd managed to miss half the world around me. I had an increased sense of peace from his words though I still needed to enact the lessons. I knew I had to employ the gifted magic of our visit, but I was transfixed by the pile of pressing work before me, and my mind robotically shifted to address the kerfuffles of my day job. The full court press left me sandwiched, straddling two incompatible worlds once again. And so the saga continued, my solace interrupted, as I rationalized making the jump from the nurturing spirit world of Gio's counsel to fix a mess created by a tech mogul client and his irrationally compromised vision. But because nothing is ever really coincidence, the particular fix required, happened to serendipitously involve an architecturally derived symbol that until today, would not have been on my radar.

I can't help but to see the parallels boldly unfolding, taking me along for the ride, once again. I know how cultural crossroads can be gateways to revelations, but sometimes we can only see the meaning when we experience something through different languages and cultural sensibilities. No matter how far you roam, though styles of expression vary, the lesson is always remarkably the same.

And so is my life's unfolding; so much so that I can't keep up with what I'm emotionally processing. I wonder if I were to keep going, if I would eventually have a nervous breakdown, but I realize I don't have time for it and would have to ask Terry to schedule it for me. Whether I'm searching for meaning or hiding from its painful and inconvenient revelations, the learning beckons me as the itching intrudes on my sanity; by means I can't seem to anticipate.

Back at a time in history when what is known as the Mughal fascade came into being, the idea of the passageway was manifested in a massive and weighty rendition. The Mughal period began in northern India in 1556 when they united their realms under the rule of Akbar the Great. This ushered in a period of peaceful coexistence and prosperity that created a cultural renaissance for architecture and art. Gio knows far more about this than I, so I can't wait to tell him what I've serendipitously stumbled upon today.

These artistically configured doorway specimens are massive works of art and extremely rare. By chance now, somehow I'm encountering two such priceless creations, which are also available for expedited private purchase. The ornate facades are typical of the Taj Majal and were known to only grace royal tombs, prayer gardens, mausoleums and temples. The style is marked by Jali, a latticed-work in stone for an elaborately carved decoration technique called *pietra dura,* where fine stones are inlaid into marble. When you're in the presence of such an exquisitely designed marvel, the breath trapped in your chest ceases to make room for your eyes to take in the dancing intricacies. They're massive, strong and bold but simultaneously ethereal and very fragile structures. Standing before them, I realize I'm beholding a visual symbol that tells of the vast mysteries of this strange universe and secrets that reside between life and death.

It's a tricky revelation before me because though the facades appear to be of wood, they're actually comprised of sandstone. They weigh more than the modern mind can sensibly imagine feasible, with crafted detail worthy of the holiest angels and the best of good kings. As Terry and I painstakingly communicate from London to prepare to complete this transaction, the enormity of the preparation details required for shipping alone is daunting. Gen must ready to receive these mega works because of the space required to hold them. She would also need a week's time built in, just to amply stare at them awestruck. We must prepare for 160 custom crates to safely contain the facades by sections and then consequentially arrange for an even more contrived hosting once shored and later assembled.

The tech mogul will want these for certain. They are that incredible and don't seem to be made from human hands. But the timing and the coincidence involved in this viewing isn't lost on me. Ironically, the structural support required to securely hold these façades in place requires an even more lavish functional configuration. You see, it needs to be braced in order to attain the strength of fifty flitch beams. Yes, the flitch makes itself known again.

After my heartwarming visit with Gio, this Mughal façade is but a further symbol to me about the complexity of the mysteries in which we humans must flow; when attempting to apply ourselves to the magic that's possible in the midst of such exquisite beauty. Thankfully I realize, the unnecessary facades we erect for our personas need not be as lasting. Despite the quake of awareness when these eureka moments come, the convergences are not accidental, nor are they about to stop coming for me.

22 Snitch

Middle East

Our subconscious is the closest thing to God-like essence in our human composition. Unseen, the mysterious subconscious mind, the tenant residing in the penthouse, many floors above our practical consciousness, is eager to reveal itself; eager to hold-up a mirror to our endeavors and assume the dramatic role of Snitch. Nothing can be hidden from this god-like entity and our subconscious would like you to know it.

Before we can begin to think about what's hidden and what's not, we must consider what Kant said about the distinction between the *noumenon*— the essence of a thing as it is in itself —and the *phenomenon*— the thing as it appears to our senses. Kant being a champion of the latter because to him the essence of everything lies beyond our grasp, try as we may to get a hold of it.

Despite our religious divide and difference in age, Prince and I were both college-reared (same college, different decade) to respect the Kantian bias, which is itching to lure me in today and claim my loyalty, because when a matter prompts the admonishment of the snitch, it demands that I wrestle with what might be its *noumenon*. What's true matters, even if we can't explain it.

And so it was, a few months after I had the two stone statues shipped to the king that I went to the ontological mat. I'd basically jettisoned my belief that the statues must be kept together for fear of some unknown spell.

I rationalized that the whole story didn't hold water. I'd also mentioned the pairing, without sounding like I might be completely insane, if I ventured in to the abyss further. Plus I knew this particular king never listened to anyone anyway. It wasn't until recently that I'd been admonished by my resident Snitch to examine my decision. Was my honest intention to assuage the relationship with my friend's father by way of this gift, or sub-consciously was I hoping to inflict some serious shade on the Grand Poobah Quitch? I'd absolved myself of guilt on this matter and dismissed it as an innocent oversight, but the Snitch wasn't buying.

Added to this guilt-triggering buffet were umpteen work distractions. I was burdened, like a load bearing wall, by the increasing weight of client deadlines. Objectively speaking, I was unable to keep pace and somewhere along the way I'd lost sight of the entire matter with the king and the ridiculous narrative of the two statues.

It was at this same time that I, zombie-like, crossed more working lines. I began accepting design delays willy-nilly into project timelines, and, worse, I rationalized that it was okay to do. After all, most high-profile designers did this. Perhaps my trying to stay above the norm was what was causing me so much angst. I knew that the super wealthy were expert practitioners in the art of delay to the extent that most seemed to expect it, at least with customized work. And so it was that the slight series of inept moves unfolded like a bolt of mulberry silk on a Huzhou showroom floor.

I see now, though, just how it is that one tiny thing leads to the next less tiny thing, paving the way to more. I grew accustomed to feeding a beast I didn't realize I'd begun serving, so entrenched in my delusion that even my subconscious snitch was weary of providing the necessary clues.

The unsettling nature of everything around me was in extreme contrast to what I'd hoped I could enact for myself. The more I tried, the further away from the ideal I got. As I landed at the Sultanate's airport, Prince's full entourage greeted me as if I were a big mahoff from a neighboring kingdom. And as I made my way to the armored fleet,

Prince himself was seated inside.

"You're getting out more than usual," I greeted my friend.

"Yes, I was excited for your arrival. Some days, a drive-about is salutary."

In the Arab world, the word *wasta* loosely translates to clout or entitlement based on who one knows. In the Middle East embracing *wasta* is key, lest you deny something that was fated to be. And once among Prince's preposterously opulent entourage, I saw how my visit could be attributed to *wasta*.

"You know that you and I are actually both prisoners?" Prince started in, blowing air kisses at both my cheeks. "You, a mule chained to your work and the demands of spoiled clients and me, imprisoned by the velvet ropes of life inside a palace I had no say in building."

"So, P, is our respective bondage the official agenda today?"

"Things are not the best of circumstances for me lately, Mitch."

"What's going on?"

"I'm plagued by a period of heavy personal angst. I feel something looming, like I've been exposed to a virus I cannot identify that is taking hold of me."

"It's not contagious I hope."

"No worries. It's all me. It's like I'm waiting for the other sandal to drop. I cannot seem to shake feeling stilted and stymied."

"Welcome to the non-royal world the rest of us chickpeas inhabit, Prince. You'll have to be more specific for me to offer any insight, if that's why you insisted I come."

"Mitch, I bet you don't realize I now have over seven hundred crystal balls. It's important to me that we stop to really see them all together. I mean, you and me and them."

"I had no idea we'd amassed that many. I stopped tallying after the first three hundred. But this is why you asked me here, just to see all those damn balls again."

"Guilty as charged, Mitch."

"You mean I'm really here to look at what I've sourced and already sent to you?"

"Mitch, my friend, I mean well by this invitation. A grand gesture revelation awaits your tandem presence."

"But you know that I've seen all of them already."

"Yes. But seeing them in collective composition will be a very different thing for you. I promise that you have no idea what they are like when they are all combined."

"P, with all due respect, you're out of your sand-swept mind."

"You could maybe humor me a little, you know? Perhaps a bit of your sense of irony would be helpful."

"You know full well that I don't care at all for this obsessive hobby of yours that I've been feeding. Not only is it time consuming, but it's caused me some infringing personal duress."

"In what way?"

"I can't explain it but things have been happening; you know, incessantly converging. I'm overbooked, and I mean in every way, including philosophically. And you know what a pain in the ass that always ends up being. The impact of a charade like this can overlap in untold ways for us both. Honestly, I think you may have just gone too far with your ridiculous sideshow."

"Trust me. This is not a sideshow I've invited you to, Mitch. When you see it you will know what I mean. I promise."

"Prince, you are my dear friend, so why don't you just tell what your real problem is? These balls are nothing but a big distraction for you when I know it's much more about something else. You must see it's time for me to stop sending you balls now that you've enough of them to put on a full-blown spectacle."

"But this last shipment you sent was a game changer. *Alhamdulillah,* but where did you find so many unusual specimens? I once again must bow to your infinite sourcing ability."

"Knock it off already. "

"What?"

"It's what I do for a living, that's all this is and you know it. We each have our roles. You run things, and I run around looking for more things for you. Here I am, trying to deal with overwhelming business deadlines, and here you are, choosing to chase after the remote possibility of finding some doorway to the future. I don't have the luxury of that kind of spare time. The disparity isn't lost on me, but it apparently is on you."

"But I am not playing with you, Mitch. I am dead serious. I am telling you significantly that this last grouping seems to be of a most different sort."

"You mean, magical? Please!"

"The jury is still out on that, but this last batch has a certain *duende*. I think you'll see something rare in their luminescence when you look again. I cannot explain it, but they feel charged in an inexplicably odd way. I need to see what you think."

"I'm here, aren't I?"

"And I must ask, had you been saving them up for a while, you know, collecting one or two, before sending them over in one batch, or did you buy them all together? You see, somehow upon receiving them, they affected me. This last covey did something to reset my inner awareness. I felt like a boy on your Christmas morning, getting a gift he'd given up getting.

"Merry Christmas, your Royal Craziness."

"Mitch, I'm serious. It was a great gift of reprieve. One that I badly needed. When you find real solace you must be thankful for it. Suddenly, I was delighted at our progress, as if we arrived at some artful plateau in the process. I would like to honor this idea, you see?"

P was into his royal aggrandizing. I'd seen it before, and I knew that a grand gesture was at hand. I smiled, encouraging him to continue. He nodded back appreciatively as his face lit up describing what he'd envisioned.

"So, you see, I arrived at this idea of arranging a little celebration for us, a supernatural show of sorts. Something to warm our tortured hearts. Having to live day by day without feeling magic, well, it makes you stop and take note when it glimmers from the recesses. You know what I'm saying?"

Phenomenon! But I needed to bring us back to Noumenon.

"Okay, P, so here's some background for you about where this last grouping originated. They were all from a single source, in Lichtenstein."

"What? Such a teeny place to contain so many beautiful shining crystal balls. They must have crowded the land from end to end. You know, there must be something peaceful about overseeing such a pristine and orderly little kingdom."

"Such a prosperous kingdom too, P. Less than 70 miles and only second to Monaco in per capita income."

P went on in a recharged fashion. "And so few people to have to rule over. Did I ever tell you that in 2000 my father rented Liechtenstein for a night?"

"For real?"

"Yes, it was a pittance, he said. Only $70,000 USD for the night and it included use of the Vaduz Castle. He knew the king, you know, in *wasta.*"

"Of course."

"He took an entourage to party in his newest jet, but he ended-up not liking the restrictive vibe, or need I also say, likely the women there. Of course, he brought his own bevy along and made it through the night but returned late the next day complaining about how cold it was. For some reason, what stuck with me at the time was that he said they didn't let women vote there until 1986. He saw it as a marker of social demise. But shortly thereafter he became obsessed with the bikini and set out sailing the Caribbean. He has a mid-life crisis monthly.

"You should know, P, that I've done some design work for the royal family of Liachtaschta, as its citizens refer to the sweet little fruit tart of Liechtenstein."

"Did you like it there?"

"My favorite thing was their daily mid-day break for two hours. You dare not impose on it. And yet, it doesn't affect their prosperity one bit. I hope someday to embrace this idea more fully myself."

Prince was luring me into good humor. I felt my advantage of pique slipping away.

"You know, Mitch, I am quite infatuated with the idea of this little principality. I bet you didn't know that they are the world's largest manufacturer of false teeth."

"Well, let me sink my teeth into that strange fact."

"I know, right? I mean like 60 million sets a year due to their tight relationship with Bollywood dentists, supposedly. I guess I like that they seem a little big kooky."

"And you, P, are more than a little bit kooky. But, let me fill you in further. As you know, with all worthy artifacts there's always a hearty back story."

"How good it is to get the scoop, as you say. I would never have gotten this without your being here."

"The affluent source I stumbled on had been married to a famous clairvoyant. What I sent you was from her personal collection. Madame Gisella Myerscough. She died, and on the third anniversary of her demise, he put them up for sale as a pocket listing with an infamous Swiss art broker. When I heard of it, I pounced quickly. I told Terry that there must be at least one magic ball in the bunch. After all, she was a coveted messenger of some sort of sortilege. She ran seances for kings and queens worldwide. What were the odds that there weren't several high energy specimens in her very own private collection?"

"Mitch, that explains how it is that one of the balls is engraved along its base, with a hint of that."

"I missed that. What does it say?"

"Look best by pair, to see."

Pairs again. Can I not escape this advisement? I began to perspire, and we were in an airconditioned Mercedes.

"What's the matter? Prince asked.

"Your bizarre crystalmania gives me repeated bouts of agita. It's only because I know how intelligent you are that I don't doubt you completely."

"You should learn to trust more than you do, you know."

As we turned into the palace gates, Prince said, "And now for the rest of the surprise I have for you. I've invited some noteworthy readers to the palace tonight. I thought we would see how these psychic talents behave in the presence of the spherical energies. Tonight is a full moon."

"Of course it is."

We wended our way through various groves of plantings and covered arched corridors, and once again I was overwhelmed by the idea that one man, the King, could harness so much opulence. There was nothing like it, not the Vanderbilts, not Bezos, not Elon.

"Prince," I said, "I still don't fully fathom why you are so blinded by the crystal ideal of the future."

"Mitch, you know that everything is just one big, unexplainable journey. Why do you insist on explanation? As a royal, I have the luxury of taking any path I choose. Why would I not exercise that privilege as fully as I can? You take it too seriously, my friend. Lighten up. I'm fascinated by this opportunity. I feel like a college boy again. You know, you would make a very lackluster prince."

"You claim it's the journey that interests you, but it's arriving at possibility's destination that you're obsessed with."

"Well, we shall see. Both of us. Maybe the future will take off her veil tonight."

We passed through the last winding hallway and came upon a large ballroom. The dimly lit expanse had about twenty over-sized exquisite crystal chandeliers arranged at varying heights, artfully set around the sprawling, prism-kissed room. The coziness of the crystal lights in contrast to the interspersed darkness from deep toned velvet textiles and plush draperies brought a faerieland quality to the presentation. The entrancing symphony of sight bestowed a transcendent mood of twinkling possibility upon everything in its reach, including me. Clearly, I'd underestimated the genius of Prince's imagination.

"Prince, it seems you're destined to become who you choose to be. You were right. Something is shifting my perspective, too."

"Spellbinding, isn't it?"

"It really is magical. It's just as fantastical as you envisioned." Captivated, I stood emotionally suspended in transcendent awe, just trying to take it all in.

"Tell me, who is translating your design ideas so elegantly?"

"Do you mean why not you? You doubted is why. It's mostly all me. But the few questionable additions are my father's recent meddling. He gifted me a *longuer* of supposed creative dabblers who altered some of my ideas. He's finished or so he says, over on his side of the palace, ten times now and he's too old to undertake a project, so he tends to wander over to dabble to edit mine. Of course, his harem of prom queens are always traipsing behind but I pay them no mind."

"Thankfully, your apple fell far from that tree."

"And critical for me too is that my apple fell first, ahead of the six rotten ones from other mothers; three of them supposed brothers who will, of course, challenge my inheritance. I have no idea what my father has willed them, but as for the kingdom, well let's just say, I already have plans for dealing with them if they so much as bark. I have always thought you to be lucky that you're an only. Siblings are an overrated consideration in most cases. You know, I hired an actual taster recently because they've been lurking about the palace kitchens."

I began to appreciate why Prince wanted to be able to see his future ahead of schedule. As we rounded another bend inside the all-aglow ball room, we approached a grander vantage point. One end of the ballroom was dramatically set with draped round tables. Each table was lushly accessorized so that the balls themselves were surrounded by shining crystal shards spread upon velvet cloth. Each was perched at a varying height, some on silk pillow poofs, some on ornately jeweled gold and silver cradles.

"Voila, Mitch. See why I insisted on surprising you with this visual feast? It is all right here, my friend, magnificently here for us to take in. But you must breathe it in, and you must look at it in order to really see it with your heart and your mind. Will you marvel with me? I mean really see it. It is an exquisite creation, is it not?"

"I had no idea they could be so resonant when all together like this. You certainly have mastered the power of assembly. Presented this way they're truly magical. You've hit one out of the ballpark, P."

"Mitch, you taught me in design that the art only happens in the magic of assembly. It's orchestrated presentation that allows us to see things for what they are."

"Well said, P. Well done."

"And to think I learned it from you. But look, we must also prepare for the parade of chosen seers to assemble shortly. Each one will investigate twenty plus balls this evening. I have no idea if they are gifted seers, but they do come recommended."

"Has dear old dad recommended any? This is out of his Islamic comfort zone."

"Despite how he's compromised his power, he does understand it's human to pursue opportunities for divine communication. Everyone does it to some degree, even when they don't admit it. Who would argue this?"

"Just most of the people you know."

"So, then we won't tell them. Fortunately, uncensored confidentialities here are punishable by death. But listen, soon, the real fun will begin, once all the witches are poised. Who knows what we will find? Are you as excited as I am to wind our way among them, tossing out random inquiries or just observing their practice?

"Ah, now I see. As we stroll about, you hope to pose all kinds of intimate probes; likely also about me and the status of my life."

"What life? You don't have one. You only work."

"I was kidding, P. I really am mystified and astonished at what you've done here. Your vision and your fortitude to bring it to light is exemplary. I'm really glad you brought me here. I never would have imagined this kind of beauty emanating from the crystals. And to see you among them, and so delighted by whatever it is that they hold for you, means a great deal to me. It's splendid already without the readings."

"Mitch, listen to me please. Tonight is proof that we shouldn't underestimate our curiosity about what is possible. Probing what's possible is an art. You know that. I think I needed this concentrated spectacle to snap me out of my fear and complacency. This amazing assembly of crystalline light makes me feel justified in collecting every last one of these orbs. Among them I feel like a poet. I feel like anything can happen."

"You're younger than me and you recognize, I'm further entrenched in my ways."

"Come off it, Mitch. Gio taught you better than that. Anything can happen at any time, if you're not afraid to be open, if you make room for it to happen. If you do something about it."

"Here's to you, my friend. Uncle Gio would applaud you."

"This is our work tonight, Mitch, not just mine. It was a tandem effort and I embrace you for making it possible. Dark days have a way of locking up perspective. I've had my share of more than usual lately."

"Maybe to further de-funk yourself you should come visit me in New York. Anonymously of course. It's been far too long."

"Yes, I can cut my hair, get rid of this beard, wear Western boots, gorge on spaghetti, wearing a bib in public. My handle will be Ray, since I seem to thrive in reflective light. We can do the spas. We can see flicks. I would like to be in the audience of a live tv show. We'll find venues to celebrate my balls into the wee hours, and not these crystal ones. David Bowie. Young Americans. You know I love him second to Rumi. It's been too long. But alas, not right now, not yet. I'll share more with you after our celebration tonight, during our visit tomorrow. I want this to stand alone and not diminish one bit by association."

As seers entered and began engaging with the spheres I remembered what Rumi had to say about what was happening right in front of our eyes. *'There is a law about revealing what's hidden. If you are not friends with the vast nothing inside, why would you always be casting your net into it, and waiting so patiently?'*

I felt both happy and sad for my friend, conflicted as he was by his educated Western head. Upon first visiting his native land, I realized what an alien life he led between here and his time in the States. There was no way for me to know the burden of his fate.

"Since you're the official Rumi enthusiast, P, here's one you may not know that may be most perfect for this particular evening: *Father Reason says, No need to announce the future. This now is it. This. Your deepest need and desire is satisfied by the moment's energy here in your hand.'*

"Easy for Rumi to say. My father will be leaving me with a mess to clean up when he finally goes. Unfortunately, I think there are some lessons only grief can teach."

23 Switch

Middle East

Research shows that by the close of elementary school the path we take can be largely predicted. We may not know that we're going to be a biologist yet, but we know if we're good at science and if we like it. We also know personality-wise what our temperament is suited to and whether we have introverted or extroverted inclinations. Yet we pay almost no attention to knowing about our natures. It seems that not knowing who we are or what motivates us is locked in a subjective closet.

Self-awareness apparently doesn't self-start. Futures unfold with or without a crystal ball, and unforeseen forces happen without our consent. The illusion of control explains the cause of pain for our souls, and yet we persist in placing our faith in mirages. Most of us choose to move forward without a clue of what's behind what we're doing.

Assuming somewhere along the way that we get caught up in the race we're running, stuff happens to lure and attract us into other lanes. And once in a groove, contemplating any change can be interpreted as our losing valuable time relative to some self-imposed grander scheme of things. Yet, nothing could be further from the truth because there is no grander scheme of things.

For those contemplating a change, the good news is that change is inevitable and it's designed to wait for us to catch up to its unfolding opportunity. The even better news is that by grand design our creative souls yearn for change. Simply put, Rumi got it right again, *'The entrance door to the sanctuary is inside you.'*

Not listening to a naysayer, me, Prince persisted in tending to his itch and found more than he knew was there. Sometimes taking the misplaced journey is exactly what gets us to where we need to be. No one else may be able to see it at the time, and the journey may be lonely, but nothing is as significant.

Prince's journey with the crystal balls was not mine. Yet by partaking in it, I unknowingly set out on a journey of my own. His path is about winning out over the frustration that comes from not knowing, when so much of what he'll be responsible for is at stake. Prince's grand showcase is a literal light in the darkness inside his own backward kingdom, to better inspire and illuminate his destiny as a ruler.

Was there a real magic orbuculum in the ballroom or are all the balls magical because of what Prince brings to them? We may never know what forces remain suspended in Prince's magic room. Or we may find that a magic ball is only awaiting the right thaumaturgist to release its power.

What's important to me is that I enable myself to switch from the singular track of my own way to make room for his way. This is the only graceful means by which men can ever become true brothers. What could be more fraternal than to give genuine support to another along his personally perplexing journey? Though we're fooled into thinking that only those who believe what we believe and see what we see are worthy partners, it's quite the opposite. It's only by making room for another searcher that we find the space to become our higher self. Parents of little children may understand this best. Though we come in and go out of this world by the rule of one, we can only find our magic here by the rule of two.

When I left the glittering showcase, I realized that the inspiration from the experience took place sans any notion of reality. Some of the seer prognostications had resonance. Some fell flat. Instead, the evening's magic was about the yearning we all have to search and find ourselves. It had nothing whatsoever to do with outcomes; rather it was about visual experience and the promise of creative possibility.

As I switch my vantage point—altering my capacity to see—it dawns on me that my journey too is unfolding anew, just as Athena forewarned. Already underway to some extent without me, it's disclosing itself whether I'm ready or not. Like Dorothy in Oz, I'm no longer standing on familiar ground. As Athena counseled, by placing one foot in front of the other, a new way on many levels is creating itself, if only I will agree to get the hell out of my own way. The artist inside me already knows the way. It's only the other fellow he lives with who pays the bills and books appointments and showings, who thinks not having a clue about what's going to happen next is a waste of time.

It's detailed in ancient texts that when the compelling itch stirs, embracing the obscured way is a beneficent call from on high. Instead, we mostly treat the itch like a virus, enlisting an army of antibodies to make it go away. Athena preaches it's the sole reason why we're here and that the road not taken only ends in regret.

As to whether I believe in magic or not, it's not what I believe that makes my life magical but living what I believe that makes for a magical life. As Joseph Campbell put it: '*We must let go of the life we have planned so as to accept the life that is waiting for us.*'

Part III

Beauty will save the world.

Dostoevsky

24 Tyche

Italy

I was like a pirate inside the treasure trove of a private gallery in Gardone Riviera the day I got the call. I was attending a famous curator's secret stash of antiquities that were being discreetly liquidated due to his abrupt heart attack. The famed curator of this divine stash was to his good fortune born with a gifted eye for the beautiful and the means dedicated to such palpable scrutiny. It's a shame that his health was too fragile for him to continue the concert of creation, but then we're all vulnerable to the oncoming attacks of both heart and art.

I was already dumbfounded by the collection when my phone startled me. I heard Prince's voice mixed with the weight of unmistakable foreboding.

"Mitch, I am very sorry about this short notice, but I need you to come back as soon as you can. I think I really need your help."

"P, what is it? Tell me you're okay."

"I am okay, but you really need to come as soon as you can. I cannot say more about it until we are in person."

Knowing this request wasn't his norm, I booked my departure out of Rome that evening, a direct flight to be at the palacio pronto. I started to make my way toward the door, but I couldn't get there. Seventeen of the Italian curator's masterpieces were among the rarest I'd ever seen in a decade, let alone assembled in one purview. The collector's vision enabled a metaphoric time travel from the spiritual hands of artists of the Middle Ages to the appreciative hands of contemporary admirers. I wandered in distraction through my favorite kind of maze, the arcade of sheer amazement and awe.

A sub-rosa understanding was in play. Security guards were at the door. Not on the invitation list? Then no admittance, no matter your cachet. It was specified in the curator's will that these gems were not to go into the Vatican's or the Mafiosa's greedy collections. These were not the kinds of artifacts that merely oblige the acquired tastes of private admirers. These were authentic manifestations of hidden centuries in the flesh; ancient and creviced creations, secretly holding their own through the centuries like well-placed wrinkles upon an exquisitely beautiful face. A tenacious heart continued to beat at a fundamental level where truth and beauty cross together like predestined wires of a divinely inspired circuitry. A stash of treasure from the ancient gods. If you can afford it, you simply want it. End of story.

Like Knights Templar, the dozen of us fortunates present were on a mission to harness our proximity to these holy relics for years to come; each of us hellbent to own the ancient art that manifested such an inspiring display of human creation. If one had prioritized becoming sufficiently learned, one might, now and then, have the great good fortune to put one's gloved hand on something truly eternal.

I had time, I thought to myself. I would leave in an hour.

I have a small global cadre of clients that care far less about the look and feel of their digs and far more about the indisputable treasures they can procure for a legacy of generational proliferation. And I had several in mind as I wandered through this Eden of Beauty. But then, there it was, something ridiculously misplaced that captured my fancy. A Nobel speech in draft which Aleksandr Solzhenitsyn had hand-penned to receive the award for literature in 1970. I was always moved that he was unable to accept the Nobel Prize until 1974 after he'd left the Soviet Union. Like the ancient histories that captivate our imaginations, I felt that I must possess this manuscript; that it would speak to me in untold ways for what was yet to come.

In my trade, one can get lost in valuation, but it's the actual magic which artifacts can hold that can really tell us who we are and why we're here. Though it's worth quoting all of it—so much in it we need to remember—I'll paraphrase what captured me in the here and now of my being. In my heart I knew the moment I saw it that it was meant to be mine.

'Just as that puzzled savage who has picked up a strange cast-up from the ocean, something unearthed from the sands, an obscure object fallen from the sky; intricate in curves, it gleams first dully and then with a bright thrust of light. Just as he turns it this way and that, turns it over, trying to discover what to do with it, trying to discover some mundane function within his own grasp, never dreaming of its higher function.

So also, we hold great art in our hands, considering ourselves to be its masters; boldly we believe that we direct it as we entertain ourselves by way of it. We renew, reform, and manifest it; we sell it for money; we use it to please those in power; we turn to it at one moment for amusement—right down to popular songs and nightclubs -- and at another, grabbing the nearest sword or cudgel. We fail to honor it. But art is not defiled by our efforts, neither does it depart from its true nature, but instead, it trustingly on each occasion and in each application gives us a glimpse of its secret inner light.

Like that little looking-glass from a faerie tale, seek the art in it and you will see— not yourself—but for one second, the Inaccessible, whither no man can ride, no man fly. And the soul gives a groan. For a work of art bears within itself its own verification. Misconceptions if devised or stretched do not stand being portrayed in images, rather the artless comes crashing down, appearing sickly or pale, convincing no one. But works of art which have scooped up the truth are capable of presenting it back to us as a living force – their energy takes hold and compels us, and nobody ever, not even in all the ages yet to come, can refute them.

So perhaps that ancient trinity of Truth, Goodness and Beauty is not simply an empty or tarnished formula as we thought in the days of our self-confident materialistic youth? If the tops of these three trees converge, as the scholars maintain, but the too direct stems of Truth and Goodness are crushed, cut down, not allowed through - then perhaps the fantastic, unpredictable, unexpected stems of Beauty will push through and soar to that very same place, and in so doing will fulfil the work of all three.'

I felt humbled. Amidst the aura of so many ancient manuscripts, sketchbooks and etchings of Italian masters like Boccaccio and Dante, I stood, literally, with goose bumps. An original manuscript of John Milton's; a Greek and Latin original translation that once belonged to

Cosimo de' Medici; a 12th century text used by European alchemists not burned in the Inquisition; early works of Nicola Pisano, Benedetto Antelami and Stefano di Giovanni; a lone creation from the very hand of Petrarch; a Madonna and Child painting from the 1400s by Carlo Crivelli; a late sketch by Michelangelo di Lodovico Buonarotti Simoni from 1561, which I'd previously surmised was just an old art myth; but clearly it lived, just as does his Sistine.

One trembles at the thought of such treasures, let alone being in the presence of such works in one sighting. The round of breath inside my lungs was seized. I became *verklempt,* unable to find my voice, except for the tiny whoopee inside my grateful heart.

The light of this moment said to me that despite our modern strides we're still creatures from the Middle Ages, struggling with old ideals we've tried to outrun. But also, many of us knock upon the ancient door for admittance, insisting on finding our way back to the comfort and terror of immortal truths.

As I held the parchment page of one of Leonardo's lesser-known journals in the white glove of my left hand, the surge of divinity from this Renaissance genius coursed through me. Like the Hermetic principle of transmutation, who can claim that the proximity to such treasure doesn't wire one for increased aspiration?

Suddenly, I froze in my tracks, stopped before something I clearly knew I must possess. An Athenian amphora from the fifth century BC, depicting in relief both Nemesis and Tyche. It's only in tandem that this matter of providence, chance, or fate can be seen for what it is - a roll of the dice. It's a delusion to view our lot in life from one fixed vantage point. For there's nothing in the universe so confining as our own perspective. Aptly in portrayals, Fortune, like Janus, has two faces, but unlike Justice, she's depicted without those notorious scales; instead with only her rudder to steer us, be it her infamous Wheel.

Fortune—whether Fortuna, Isis, or Tyche—is resolutely blind to the concept of justice. She's s the personification of luck and fate, a la Bonaventura as my Italian father would proclaim. Ovid claimed she was 'the goddess who admits by her unsteady wheel her own fickleness.' And fickle as she is, it is certain that nothing lasts forever, not even the overbearing reign of a Middle Eastern tyrant.

Reality bites back. I missed my flight.

25 Overpitch

Middle East

Once my plane touches down on the strip of vast desert, I'm whisked away by a more intense security detail than usual and taken directly into a suite in Prince's rear palace. No longer in residence in the more familiar portion of his estate, I'm told I should make myself comfortable but not to expect the prince until morning. I'm free to roam the estate and directed to find a plentiful buffet served in the ballroom until midnight, set for a flow of expected guests and dignitaries.

I ask my poker-faced guard. "What exactly is going on here?"

"Nothing that is usual," he offers as he turns his back and departs.

Circulating without accompaniment, I walk for what feels like a mile, in and out of balmy alcoves, atriums, peristyles and connected courtyards, surveying the grounds for a hint about what was at play.

Mind you, these courtyards are not welcoming expanses like Italian piazzas, where life bustles with humanistic possibility. Instead, the unending grounds seem like fortresses of mathematically compelled landscape. As I turn into a section which I faintly recognize, I realize I've ambled past Prince's boundary, entering the outlying King's commons. Here, lush vegetation in the desert is a feat of modern engineering and irrigation. This is near to be close to where I believe I last saw the two gifted statues posed.

Night falls. The heat is dense. The stars arrive slowly. With a pinprick of unease, I see that only one of the statues is where I last saw her abiding with her companion. My mind starts churning, where is the other statue? Why didn't I say more about the brothers' warning, even though I was sure it was a sham? I nervously searched the adjacent gardens to find the missing mate. It was nowhere to be found, so I went back to the sole stone figure, as if trying to reassure her about what I was doing on her behalf. I continued fitfully zigzagging through the expanse for her lost counterpart, but no trace.

An older guard who'd had his eye on me, motioned me aside. In makeshift English he asks if I've found what I was looking for. No, I reply and ask him about the statues. He explains they're being relocated to another enclave. I instruct him to get them back together quickly. He smiles at me assuringly, as if to appease me that they will be moved together as soon as ongoing priorities are tended.

"What priorities?" I question, but he puts his index finger to his lips and left me standing there continuing to wonder what is happening.

I retreated into the ballroom and arranged a plate for myself. Lamb kebob, pepper, rice, humus, and flat bread. I settled near a Turkish ambassador who tells me unprompted that the king isn't dead, though his death is imminent. He'd had a stroke. The lump in my throat became pronounced as I hoped this unexpected blow had nothing to do with the statues. Surely, this was a ridiculous notion.

The Turk went on with what he knew. " I believe it happened in the middle of the night. We simply must wait," he said matter-of-factly. "Shortly, we're expecting the official appointment of his successor, the Crown Prince.

"Are you here as a matter of political sympathy?" I asked.

"Yes, and you?"

"A friend of the family,"

"I'm very sorry," he said in the hushed tone that's used to connote sympathy in the presence of death.

Taking the last of my tea, I closed our encounter. "Have a restful evening. I'm sure I'll be seeing you again," I say in the same hushed manner.

My mind raced. When were the two statues separated? It was well past one in the morning when there was a soft knock on my door, and surprisingly it was none other than the dauphin himself. He closed the door quickly behind him as if he might be followed.

"Thank you so much for coming so quickly, Mitch," he said, unaware that I'd dawdled and missed my first flight.

"Of course, Prince. You must tell me what you need. I'm here for you."

"There is something," Prince said as he sat in the chair by the window with his chin resting against a clinched fist.

"My father's locked archive; the one to which I now have access because he is seriously infirm. Well, you see, inside his personal vault, there are some things that I don't fully understand. His vault is a hidden room, well disguised along the back wall of his office. Only one other person, my father's chief of staff, is allowed even in the vicinity of his office, but he's never had access to the vault, if he even knows about it, which I doubt. My father equipped entry for only his or my fingerprint, as well as via our retina scans."

"You're certain the chief of staff has absolutely no access?"

"Not without my eyeball and index finger which you see are both intact."

"And I presume your father's are as well."

"Yes but very soon, I will be declared king. Should my father recover, his continued reign would be next to impossible without my interference. Regardless the briefings have begun, and it's a massive hot mess. I can't begin to tell you the half of it. First, there's the looming possible loss of some of the autonomy of the kingdom itself – several predators I've been informed are sharpening their scimitars: the Israelis, too. Trust me when I say, there are heirs and people supposedly close to me whom I absolutely cannot trust. Slowly, if I am not careful, my lack of trust will all together turn me into a paranoid version of my father."

"Perish that thought."

"You understand that my making sense of this intellectually and emotionally are two very different things. I'm operating at a great loss of perspective. I think I'll need some serious American therapy by the time all the dust has settled. I am not joking."

"And you have proof that therapy's actually a worthwhile pursuit, do you? Look at what it's done for me thus far. Well, you get my point."

"You should know that we royals tend to secretly obsess over some very odd things."

"Like crystal balls perhaps?"

"I'm referring to something you will not understand also involving other rulers and regimes. You wouldn't believe how akin we all are. The similarities speak to me like psychic breadcrumbs. Most mortals don't have any experience with this bizarre stuff, or care, mind you, minus a tabloid titillation or two. I don't want to sound whiny or ungrateful, but in many ways we royals have a lonely road. There are only a few humans who know the plight of such weighted responsibility. For good or bad, regardless of where or when, it is still a weighty load upon very mortal shoulders.

"Enlighten me."

"Sometimes ruling can seem a lot like occupying a Mount Olympus post from what I can tell, and my vantage point has been only that of prince. It's all quite crazy, but frankly, it is more so the case than any one royal is free to publicly profess or to admit. It may sound self-entitled of me, but whenever rulers, both the good and the bad of them, leave this world, there is strangely, well, some sort of price to be paid."

"Go on."

"The ramifications ripple out across continents. I think the US knew of this when Lincoln died. And both Kennedys. And you see, it has nothing to do with the quality or the intentions of the leader. It gives me chills to think how much aftermath is going to follow from my father's death."

"Do you have any specifics on what this comeuppance entails?"

"Oh no, not at all. In fact, this matter is not about detail; rather it's about an energy of sorts that stirs and circles and tests and torments in random ways. Because it's so evasive a force, it can seem as if it isn't there or that survivors are imagining it. But trust me, this is very real, and it doesn't rest for quite some time."

"Prince, we've talked about this journey you're about to embark on before. It's only natural to have trepidation in your position. The anticipation is the worst part I'm sure. There's no way to know the outcome. You're afraid of things you absolutely can't control. It may not be easy, but I swear, you've got this. I know it."

"Mitch, you're thinking this is a mountain to be climbed. This is not that. This is a thing born of an elusive force that chills one's bones. What I'm referring to as aftermath, it lingers like a shadow and circles like the wind. It sets in motion strange and eerie occurrences that bring out the worst in everyone. I mean literally, the ensuing aftermath will linger, hovering about the palace, the court, rippling out by degrees, to everyone—wives, lovers, siblings, friends, enemies, confidantes, viceroys, soldiers, chamber maids. You see, this is why I wanted the magic ball so badly."

"You, Prince, will find the answers you need, and I know they aren't in a damn ball."

"Listen, Mitch. But you see, there is more."

"More?"

"Well, I mean, it actually is altogether different than what you may think or know about the balls. I have come upon a sort of gordian knot, and I know that only you can help me untie it."

"Now you've lost me."

"I'm in what the Brits who play cricket refer to as overpitch. You know, when the bowled ball is pitched too close to the wicket?"

"Something like a wild pitch in baseball?"

"Yes but hear me clearly now, please. The very ball we've been searching for has been in my father's private archive the whole time. When I knew he had a stroke, I entered the vault. I put my imprint on the pad, obtained entry and saw the crystal ball. The moment I saw it, I instinctively knew exactly what it was."

"Oh my God, Prince, how can this be?"

"Mitch, I'm completely stuck in my tracks. Plus, I'm exhausted. I felt palliative and tried to look at the ball objectively, but the damn ball stared back at me dismissively saying, so now what are you going to do? And boom! The weight of everything came crashing down upon my shoulders. That's why I called you. I was very afraid, something I cannot admit to anyone in this land of mine. I needed you to be here with me because I don't have the confidence right now to know the right thing to do. I don't trust myself."

Prince went on trying to explain his predicament. "My father left me a sealed letter on the shelf next to the ball. Mitch, I do not have the courage right now to open his letter by myself. I have no answers, but I can only conjecture that my father got the magic ball from my grandfather who was into the occult. Once the rumors began to circulate that a royal had a magic ball, my father must have panicked and fabricated a clever story about another king having it. And I latched on to that idea and ran with it as you know. Deflection is his signature move when in a bind. I've been its victim before, but this time, well, to use me like this. I'm his son, his heir, for God's sake."

"Tell me about the letter."

"I brought it with me. I will need you to read it with me. I'm more anxious than afraid; or maybe I'm more afraid than anxious. There is a part of me not sure if I want to know what it says."

Prince reached inside his left pocket. The ivory envelope had a large crimson wax seal with a thin grosgrain gold ribbon centered on the squared flap. Prince's hand shook as he unfurled the four pristine folded pages of handwritten cursive, consisting of the neatly arranged strokes of a dark blue fountain pen. Prince was shaking. I rose to hug my friend. A piece of us dies when a parent dies, regardless of the relationship.

"Prince, I think there's something else I may need to tell you. I may have messed up, but I honestly don't really know."

"Can't it wait?"

"Honestly, I don't know if it can or should."

"If you're not sure, then it can wait. Just look at me. I feel like a captain surveying a shipwreck. Did I mention that my security detail has doubled? I have people clinging to me, yet I'm more alone than ever before, holding a letter from a man whom I seemingly don't even know."

Prince held the pages open and began to slowly read, translating the words before him into English. Line by line, the sentiment revealed itself in the same way that the feathered cards of a fortune teller present themselves to unearth a hidden truth whose time has come.

My Letter to My First Born,

By the time you hold this letter in your hand, I will be dead.

Before I knew you, I knew that we would not be the same. Your way is not about the kind of power I believe in as supreme. However, as you are not willing to see how dark is the nature of man, you cannot see that our land cannot handle the freedom you so value.

I knew my time was near because I saw it in the crystal ball. Son, do not look into the ball of magic, for it is only the bearer of news that you cannot handle. The worst of it is, once you decide to look, you cannot turn away. It tells only of things too hard to know. I do not know why good did not come to me through it. I hope you will choose not to be as curious as I have been with the ball. Know it is comprised of an ancient magic from the sixth century. Unless you find a trusted seer who can authentically channel its power, do not ever probe it. Just as I could not see good in it, I could not find any one who could know it rightly. Now, it is you who must be careful.

There is something I have never told you. When you were born, a seer that your grandfather trusted, long before I knew anything about his having the ball, calculated a mathematical point from your natal chart. In ancient Roman culture, it was known as the Fortuna Primigenia and the prescient formula can only be applied to the first born. Though in our public culture such ideas are taboo, you will soon come to know how it is that rulers have access to other magical opportunities. This fact has been true for millennia.

Your chart, via the calculation, indicated you would become king at the age you are now. Also, in your natal chart it said you would rule for over a quarter century, or until the start of the last war. May your rule be blessed and may the painting give you some necessary solace as you embark on your kingly way. You must trust this. The only good magic inside my vault will come to you from the artful representation of the crystal ball from an artistic master, not the real round orb.

I leave this world trusting you will learn to forgive me my transgressions and agree not to reveal all my secrets. For I am only a man who happened to be king; but in the high heavens, I am just a man. We are each deeply flawed.

Fortune is a fickle mistress and not even a king is exempt from the Wheel of the World.

In sha'Allah,
Your Father

Prince's hands fumbled until I took the liberty of returning the folded pages securely back into the envelope.

"Prince, I'm dumbfounded that all the time you were insisting to me that the magic ball was close by, you were right, it was. It is too much for anyone to fathom let alone process. I can't imagine how you are feeling."

"No, you can't."

"P, I suppose we should learn what painting he's referring to in his letter."

"First, I need you to come with me."

"Where?"

"To the vault. There's something I need you to see with your own eyes, not mine."

"Now? It's three in the morning."

"Yes, now."

26 Britch

Middle East

We made our way to the ailing king's private office quarters through a hidden underground passageway. It was like being in Macbeth's castle. An ornately hand carved floor-to-ceiling wall stood as sure as a giant redwood. Prince pushed it in and a large section of forest moved to reveal a marble vestibule and a short series of stairs. By way of his finger and his eye, Prince closed the wall behind us so that nothing could be revealed from the office side of the entry. Beyond the stairs, the ceilings were tall and expansive with decorative crown molding. The king's family seal hung centered on the largest wall.

We moved through a narrow passageway into a deeper vault. This space was arranged like a panic room; along one wall a long navy-blue velvet sofa with ornate pillows, a small refrigeration unit, a glass cabinet with firearms inside. On the other wall were thick marble slab shelves. On a shelf furthest from the door, Prince removed a black velvet drape revealing the magic ball. Reflexively, I bowed my head to greet it. I had no idea why.

Prince smiled at seeing me do it as if we both understood something charmingly irrational. Then, he pushed a hidden button from under the ball's shelf and the back wall contracted silently to reveal a shrouded entity in veiled residence behind it.

"For god's sake, P, what now?"

Inside the niche was a large rectangular object with a thick black satin cloth draped over it. Bowing to me ceremonially, Prince took hold of the bottom corner of the cloth and pulled it to the floor, revealing a painting beneath.

"Mitch, my friend, tell me what we are looking at."

My heart dropped into my belly as I beheld what he'd uncovered. I was dizzy with disbelief.

"This can't be what I think it is."

"My father had it so well hidden that it's likely exactly what you think it is. But I need to know, now with you looking at it in the flesh, exactly what it is you believe it to be."

I walked closer to the painting, the Catholicism in me telling me to kneel and bow my head. "Prince, this is the apex of artistic creation. There is absolutely nothing like it in all the world."

"I felt what you are feeling the moment I saw it too, but I wasn't sure what I was looking at."

"Before you, my royal friend, is the *Salvatore Mundi,* the Savior of the World; what I consider the greatest work by the greatest artist of all time. Christies sold it for $450.3 million in 2017 to an unidentified buyer. I was at the auction just to see it happen. Mind you, despite common understanding, it was a bargain. How can you put a price on something priceless? Believing it was conceived by human hands is hard to fathom."

"Can you be sure it's Leonardo's?"

"I'd stake my life on it. No one on this earth paints like this. Come stand next to me. Feel Christ's hair with your eyes. Makes you want to dare to run your fingers through it, doesn't it? No one paints folds of fabric this way. No one's brush conjures such ethereal mastery with every stroke. It's as if his hand was guided by angels on high. It's quality is like an apparition. The form appears to alter before your eyes, but not the essence which doesn't alter in any way. It's painted on walnut which is consistent with Leonardo's work. Just to be standing here before it is inexpressible bliss for me."

"How is it that such a magnificent thing is accomplished?"

"The only feasible explanation for it, P is pure magic. There are motif likenesses; maybe a dozen by his apprentices, one by Crivelli and another by Titian. But this ethereal Christ is beyond every other master's rendition."

"You're absolutely sure about it?"

"If I had any doubt, I'd tell you. There's no doubting what we have here before us. I can't believe anyone can gaze into those eyes and not feel stirred and disoriented. To hear both of us not mouthing about its monetary value is pretty unique, isn't it? We should probably sit down. What we're feeling is called Florence Syndrome because there are so many accounts of visitors' blood pressure pulsing-up at the Palazzo Medici amidst all the artistic beauty. The term wasn't coined until the 19th century, but the medical term is hyperkulturemia and it comes with dizziness and hallucinations whenever one is exposed to something significant in art or nature. I'm sure Leonardo understood exactly how it works from the inside out because he studied esoteric phenomena all his life. His special genius was able to make it manifest so magnificently. Gazing at this art is all present tense, no past, no future, just divinely inspired energy that feels distinctly other worldly.

"Mitch, on some level this gives me hope. I don't know why, but somehow I don't feel so alone."

"It's like we're in the presence of God." I said confirming his sentiment.

"But what is this painting doing in my father's private vault?"

"Well, it's got royal karmic lineage. It resided in the palaces of Charles I and II, and later James II; it's thought to have been commissioned by Louis XII of France; there are a few rough sketches of it at Windsor Castle. It vanished for 200 years, and then suddenly it's rediscovered and your father anonymously buys the most pedigreed painting of Jesus ever painted and hides it. I'm stunned.

"Mohammad, *salla alayhi wa salaam*, recognized Jesus as lord, so I can make the leap about my father buying it. Jesus is the most cited personage in the Quran. He's referenced 25 times by name and 45 times in the third person. What I don't see is why he wouldn't have hung it among his other collections."

"Maybe he was afraid it would be stolen?"

"Afraid no. Once a servant took a small urn, and when he

confessed my father had him shot. This is quite the deterrent, you see."

"I have such a hard time with some of what you tell me, P."

"I'm not a Christian, Mitch, but this is a face I would follow. I'm completely drawn to it. It's mesmerizing. I could never admit that aloud in my country, but you know that I know that we are woven into different patterns but are of all the same cloth."

"Yes, and I believe this painting speaks to all mankind. The mystical quality of Christ's face. His piercingly wise expression. No matter who you believe him to be, you can see he is a personage of incredible spiritual substance. It's a haunting stare that goes right through you. Part of you wants to look away, but something else pulls you deeper in. The perfectly poised hand; the gentle way it cradles the orb; the three tiny specks inside the orb. I tell you, if I had enormous wealth I would impoverish myself to acquire it."

"Well, we know who bought it now, don't we. But I still can't believe it's right here, and it remains unaccountable to me that, despite the cruelty of his kingdom, my father had these two mystical treasures ensconced inside his only completely private space."

"In his letter your father instructs you, pleads really, that you not give credence to the crystal ball. I mean, it seems he secretly cared about your future. These two pieces could possibly have put your father in touch with his higher self."

"Or maybe he was entrapped by the power of the magic ball, not able to turn away from gazing into the future, and the painting was his way of countering the unholy force."

"I don't know what the king knew, but these two artifacts indicate that he knew something ethereal; or that he was an incredibly refined collector."

"Of course, I'd rather believe that too, but I prefer looking for the truth."

"Mitch, you must admit that it is most strange and uncanny that my father has either accidentally or deliberately captured both of the spheres. In all the world, he has placed them in here together.

"The implications are staggering. If your father awakens, maybe there's more he has to tell you."

"He isn't going to awaken, Mitch. It's likely over for him."

"You did make me think of something else but admittedly, it sounds rather ridiculous ."

"You must tell me anyway you know. "Prince cajoled.

Well, we know that truth often crosses at the corner of ridiculous, just north of unlikely, right? So what if the two pieces together are a kind of parallel."

"But a parallel of what?

"What if just maybe P, the ball could not be alone. Magic wasn't made to be a lone, nor was art. Both require watchers in their respective time-honored roles. The object of art and the voyeur become one in the process; the two seemingly alone in their entrusted bubble, apart from the goings-on of the outside world, but distanced and protected by the bond, reminiscent of some divine promise."

"Mitch, I like the idea very much but that sounds like your father, not mine."

"But what if my father was instructed by the ball to buy the painting? What if he saw the future and it compelled him to purchase the painting? We know of the ball's influence and what my father believed was possible because of it."

"Our conjecturing is good because eventually we'll come upon something that feels appropriate and we can best rest it there. But for now, we *have miles to go before we sleep,* my friend."

Prince began to reluctantly cover the painting, his hands still slightly trembling.

"We have to go now. My guards are probably searching for me. But we will be back."

27 Lich

Middle East

Not all truth is capable of being neatly packed into a portmanteau, available to us at a moment's notice to fill some blank requiring our attention. Truth rarely presents itself as the sunshine and roses bouquet we expect it to be after watching too many Hallmark tales with happy endings.

Truth is more like blood in the human circulatory system. It moves along at its own pace through the ins and outs of our veins and arteries. Until the destination reveals itself, the pathways appear as if they lead both nowhere and everywhere. Truth's twists and turns aren't something any of us are adept at navigating. But once the grand design is realized, the truth knows exactly how to get to where it's going, and how to flow forth in plain sight, forcing us to see it.

In this shadow world, everything is interim. The flower blooms, it dies, then spring returns. The cycle of loss and return follows like the setting sun at the end of the run of day. There is nothing which does not follow this choreography. No wonder we remain baffled by the interim, trying to make sense of tiny pieces of a grand design we cannot see.

"Mitch, I'm sure you know I'm going to have to begin to rule with some upset the apple cart actions."

"I trust they'll be the actions of good conscience."

"But that doesn't mean it will be any easier for me to accomplish. Fighting for the evolving soul of a people never is. I must simultaneously turn back the clock and set it ahead; find a way to forge a means forward without disrespecting the past and alienating the elders. It's inevitable that heads will have to roll. I plan to move the kingdom in a new direction, which could mean that my head rolls first. My initial announcement will be a minor departure and then the bigger things will follow abruptly. It's going to require a kind of magic to make any of it happen."

"So, P, if we strip it back more, your determination to find the magic ball was something you felt you absolutely needed. Why didn't you make it clearer to me?"

"That would have made it too easy for you to presume to understand, and I didn't know what I knew at the time. I believed the magic ball would help me find my way through the monumental task before me. I thought by having it I could have confidence in the acceptance of my moves."

"You owe your father a big thank you for warning you not to use the magic ball."

"Yes, because I would have."

"P, you've affirmed that your actions will be born of good conscience."

"That doesn't mean they'll end well."

"Shakespeare said that action is eloquence."

"Philosophically, I get that Mitch, but I want to make my rule worthwhile for all concerned, and I'm no saint. I have a small window to take full charge. There are many who secretly hope I fail. I wasn't ready for my father to die, and I didn't expect to feel afraid. I don't know exactly what I fear, but I know that I feel deeply afraid."

"You know, our Uncle once told me of a concept regarding the beginning of anything. He said that we're being readied our whole lives for what's coming, though we don't know it clearly at the time. You need to trust that for each action you take with a sure heart that a good wind will be at your back. It's only by doing that you'll find your right way. Honor this and it will guide you through it. I know it. I promise."

"I miss Gio, Mitch. A visit is long overdue. He really is a Merlin."

"I wonder, have you ever heard of the fictional concept of the lich?"

"Never."

"Liches are arcane non-divine spell casters who magically increase their lifespan to the point of becoming undead. In fantasy fiction, a lich is a type of immortal creature who's thrust into an undead state that results from some sort of self-induced personal transformation."

"Are they good or evil?"

"Just like kings, the good ones are rare."

"Anyway P, liches were once considered magi. They're capable of mesmerizing spells through their intuitive natures to facilitate their magic. Though I don't know enough about this creature or its abilities, I'm citing the idea behind them to you; that is, celebrating your innate ability to intuitively spell cast a new reality. This is a lich strategy of sorts, and how you can deal with whatever's ahead of you."

"And how do you know of this idea of the lich?"

"Ha! I stumbled across it from an old Dungeons and Dragons game. Voldemort in Harry Potter is also a sort of lich. Basically, it applies to anyone who defies death by magic. The ancient myths say we each have the power to alter our reality. Our limits are contrived by us to confine our potential. The lich sees through this illusion of implied restrictions and opts instead for the possibility of re-invention. Every man craves the opportunity to tap into the magic energy inside him. Of course, the lich is a fictional character, but what he shows us is that we're capable of enacting more from ourselves and that believing anything less about our potential is a lie."

Prince expounded. "So, we buy the lie rather than dig to find the part of ourselves that can soar."

"Exactly and the lie's a lot easier. I've bought into it too many times, as you well know."

"*My sun sets to rise again, the aim, if reached or not, makes great the life,*" quoted Prince.

"Browning, isn't it?"

"Admittedly, that damn liberal arts education I insisted on getting in your States sometimes does soothe my soul. Didn't our wise uncle say that our real job in life is to inspire ourselves?"

"You have no idea P, how relieved I am that you've opened this trusty door in your troubled head. You know you had me worried that you were going to tell me you were ready to summon the magic from your father's magic ball."

"I admit, it continues to lure me, but I'm going to take his advice and not go there. Last words are powerful things."

"Royal bravo to you P. Listen, Gio knew I was coming to see you and sent you a message. He said to tell you to remember, the soul is perfectly round."

"Wow. That's perfectly lovely. Do you think that Gio would believe that the orb wasn't representative of the world but rather our souls?"

"Soon you can ask him yourself. I told him how we were hoping to get together the three of us again, as soon as we could arrange it. But meantime, he asked me to give you something. He said he wanted to help you through some things he knew you would be wrestling. He said to give it to you at the right time. Of course, I have no idea when that is because I don't know what he said, but I'll have to trust my intuition that the Sacred Now will do. I have it with me. I handed Prince a bright white linen envelope.

"Oh, look Mitch, it's a quote from 'The Once and Future King'."

Your Royal Highness,

I will tell you something which may surprise you. It will not happen for hundreds of years, but both of us are to come back. This is all that you really need to understand. Knowing it will give you the perspective you need to face anything that comes your way. The cycle of possibility continues. Let it move you. Trust in it and trust in yourself. Ask yourself, 'How can you have boundaries if you fly?'

Forevermore,
Uncle Gio

28 Last Ditch

Middle East

On my last day sequestered with Prince inside the king's secret cloister, I was moved by the connectivity between the two mystically infused vessels. Both the exposed orbs entranced; one of ancient crystal and one of Renaissance brushstrokes. As if alive, both orbs were imbued with something conspicuously surreal which had us in their grip. But unlike when something sinister has you by the tail, in this case we couldn't get enough of whatever it was they whispered in an ancient language in which we'd been granted emotional fluency.

In their presence, we could reflect our potential. The more we were still, the more the steady impact of their creative force gave us comfort. Their company provided a sense of timelessness, as if the world were somehow round again. Gazing at these creations made us grateful to be two steadfast watchers in a secretly shared uni-dimensional awe.

"You know, your father saved you a lifetime of woe by warning you not to even think about addressing the magic ball, and he gave you a metaphoric astrolabe so you could know exactly where the holy magic is kept. It's in Leonardo's masterpiece. It's a treasure worth millions, more than the millions he paid for it."

"I know. I know. I'm still trying to kick the dichotomy of the father I knew and the man who wrote me the letter and left me these treasures. But it feels schizophrenic, as if moment by moment I must split myself emotionally between the *bete noire* I knew and the man I'll never understand. I alternate between despising him, empathizing with him, feeling regretful and then just plain angry.

"Gio told me something about the kind of predicament you're in. One day we were talking about the other side. He said that the way we look at accountability here happens to be irrelevant over there."

"We're still responsible for everything we do and don't do here; and there's a comeuppance that each of us must face, but the rules work differently over there."

"Perish the thought that the rules here should be wisest."

"Once you review your life, where you failed and the pain you inflicted on yourself and others, if you come to see it and if you're soulfully sorry, you're freed to prepare yourself to do it differently the next time around. Your newfound understanding is something you take into your soul, like water into a sponge, and it goes with you so you have the benefit of knowing better next time. You don't carry the exact details of your reconciliation upon re-entry. But you have the corrective knowledge, just not the details of what and to whom. You're not off the hook for being responsible for your deeds, but they're repositioned, as lessons."

"What we have here should come with a strict rule book. All we have is the suggestive truths of literature, though who knows what we originally had that we lost or spoiled."

"This deep-seated knowing, he said, accompanies your soul everywhere. You don't lose it into your next incarnation. The karma for the deeds remains wholly intact with your name on it, but the new knowing you gained accompanies you. Gio said it's a perfectly intact loop system from start to finish."

"It almost seems too scot-free."

"Gio's point is we can't only view it as it seems here. It operates from the premise that nothing here is really real. It's as if we're each doing our part inside our own play, as actors or watchers, based on our own construct of reality.

"I buy into it intellectually. I get that life here is theatre and it's only at the soul level where the tally is kept. But the whole thing is needlessly laborious versus just giving everyone the necessary intuitive knowledge up front."

"Gio says we lost the knowledge we once had. We fell from grace and stuck ourselves with the long way around."

"I guess if we were taught to pay homage to the immortality of our souls, we wouldn't see things so myopically."

"Tell me bluntly Mitch, how this applies to dealing with my idea of my father."

"The answer to that depends on who you want to be. All that's important is how you live your life. In a way your father's shortcomings are a resource. It's up to you if or how you use it. You're on stage in your own play now, Prince, not his. As for me now, in the presence of Leonardo's masterpiece, I feel like we have absolutely nothing to worry about except the footprints of our own souls."

"In its presence I feel hopeful I can work everything out too."

"Great art is a portal to greater reality. By the mesmerizing expression in Christ's eyes as he holds our round world in his hand, I see there's an unquestionable insight imparted to any seeker regardless of their faith."

P added, "I agree and there's the wonderful irony that Christ is a Middle Eastern Jew, holding a soothsayer symbol, painted by a left-handed Italian, sponsored by the Catholic Church, to this day is extolled by Muslims as a holy one and worshipped by Christians as the Son of God. Beyond incredible, no?"

"Beyond for sure."

"P, do you know about the idea of the Chintamani? The ancients refer to the crystal sphere the bodhisattvas hold in their hands as the Chintamani Stone."

"I only vaguely know of it Mitch, but I thought it was Hindu."

"Actually, it has an established esoteric legend in both cultures."

After I said it, all at once, it hit me hard, right between the eyes.

"Oh my God, P."

"What?"

"When I was in Greece, the witch read my tea leaves and there were letters in the leaves. The letters spelled C, H, I, N, T, A, M, A, N, I. The witch said it was for me to discover what they meant. She hadn't a clue. But now I realize those letters spelled Chintamani. I can't believe I am so blind. The leaves spoke indirectly of our seeking the legendary wish-fulfilling orb, as if everything's come full circle and we are where we need to be."

"Now wait a minute Mitch, you weren't getting a reading to learn your future though, were you?"

"No, you know I don't believe in calling out the future. A colleague made the appointment for me, only to glean some spiritual guidance and inspiration about my present, directionally. Yes, of course it was to reveal something romantically, as you would well know too."

"Tell me what else you know about the stone?"

"Apparently there isn't only one stone. Hitler, the Nazis and even Franklin Roosevelt were known to be in search of it. It's considered the treasure of the world, sent from the constellation Orion, holding the promise of the spiritual evolution of mankind. I've also heard that it's considered to be the seeding stone for resetting the magnetic charge of the planet. The 'lapis elixis' the missing piece of the Tetragrammaton, the hidden pillar of the temple of wisdom, the lost word of God or the hidden energy vibration form the Divine Name."[ii]

"Prince, I feel lightheaded and dizzy. This realization is too much for me. Thank God you're here with me."

"I can second that. I suppose we can think of everything up to this point as a warm-up. This speaks to me only of a Gateway."

"We may not need to be completely proficient in magic in order to be its beneficiary. For now, it's enough that we've been rewarded, not with the answers mind you, but with vital hints and guesses."

"Mitch, promise me, no matter what comes next that we will never settle for measuring out our lives in coffee spoons."[iii]

"Promise."

29 Smitch

Middle East

Despite our diligent vigil, the King did not awaken. Prince and I hadn't slept well since being in the vault. We met in the conservancy before sunrise, possibly hoping to find a single string to unravel the great mystery that awaited back inside the vault. It was no surprise that the fecund prince, nearly king, could be counted on for rhetorical flourishes and cosmic grandiosities, even when poised at a threatening personal crossroad. My friend did not cease from raising more issues for contemplation, well before the elaborate breakfast spread of healthy delicacies could be swallowed.

Our only consolation came after coffee when we took solace in the temporary distraction of exotic fruits stuffed inside sticky pastries. The irony of predicament didn't settle any, though I felt myself altering as a result of the entirety of experience, as if a new me was emerging from an old shell that it had outgrown; but hadn't made its way all the way out yet.

I could not rid myself of worrying about my friend, about his loss, his looming, the extraordinary challenges he faces and how he will be able to find peace with so much before him. Meantime, I too was burdened by being here, and not tending to the details and installations in my business, and my own life, to my newfound love, Chloe, and what I knew I needed to do to make things right between us again.

Ever since seeing the painting with Prince, I have a clarity and purposefulness I've not ever had before. Despite a residue of predictable ignorance, the reigning blessings of Fortuna have graced me with enough insight to find, or more aptly face a redesigned reality of newly applied perspective. Only through this uncanny experience have I learned that developing my awareness for my intuition is as important as developing a talent. With some internal excavation, I can trust that Prince and I will somehow both find our ways. As we intend to set foot upon a road of action, we'll see that the tiny things which we can lose sight of in the heat of day, are the very things that mean the most in the silence of the dark night. I am reminded that the holiest of mortal places is, indeed, the Sacred Now.

30 Clitch

Middle East

On my way out, I have appointments in New York that need attention. Despite the frenzy of re-entering reality, outside of the vault, I'm steadied by what I've witnessed and inspired by what I feel I can accomplish for my life as a result of the hard-won lessons. Prince walked me out of the compound and made a point of putting me in an armored car this time, as an extra precaution.

"If I've learned one thing from this entire escapade, it's that what we believe shapes us more than anything else ever can. Everything in this life pales in comparison to the forces that push us toward personal discovery."

"I agree," said Prince.

"Of late I think back on how I could I have been so out of touch with myself and not have known it. Somehow I chose to underestimate whatever wasn't part of my tangible success-based working reality. I convinced myself the mystical wasn't relevant to the practicalities of my work world. My understanding only came into focus because of my having to confront magic and that was really all because of your enveloping me in your obsession."

"So, you've come to know things that you didn't know before?"

"Well, meeting Chloe made me blink, but our collaboration made me unblinking about myself and what I need to do. Why it takes us so long to see what's in front of our eyes is disappointing."

"I too believed there were shortcuts I could find. The hunt for the magic ball was my attempt at a shortcut. The surge I received about possibility because of the finality of my father's departure has given me more clarity about what I think. This will make it easier for me to act, and I could swear that somehow my father's helping me."

"You realize how great that is, don't you?"

"I do, but my father and I were so estranged, it doesn't feel as natural to me as it would to you."

"I know for sure that the ties from here to there are real."

"I hope for my father's sake it's the case. Every soul deserves another shot if it's learned its lessons."

"So, then you might even see your part in your antagonistic relationship with papa. It takes two."

"We definitely have been well-taught on the power of two now. But more important to my well-being, those crystal balls you found for me give me more solace on dreary days than you can imagine."

"You know, saving all of those balls may actually be a good deterrent from anyone ever thinking that you might possess the real magic ball."

"That's true, like decoys. More important is my ballroom full of back-lit orbs coming alive at night, whispering to me of things I forgot I knew. They will remind me about the importance of emphasizing the journey without knowing how it ends. The visual experience in the ballroom gives me a euphoric sense of comfort. It's the energy in the room, or the collection. I don't have a clue but it's a place I can retreat to and engage in magical dreaming; my own private chapel and think tank. I know it sounds eccentric, but there it is. I couldn't read one of those balls if my life depended on it, and guess what, Mitch? I no longer care."

"You know, I've never been able to read a silly ball I have either, though I had an out of body experience with it one night. I have a little orb I brought home from Istanbul after meeting with that Greek witch I told you about. You hadn't even started thinking about your magic balls yet. This was just an odd little precursor."

"What happened?"

"One night I was home alone, and after seeing the moon was full

I took the ball down off the shelf. I was just reminiscing about my Grecian travels, you know, just futzing around, and suddenly I got a terrible premonition about Gio dying."

"Really, was it clear?"

"The premonition was. I called him right away and thankfully he was fine."

"Do you attribute your vision to the ball or just to your intuition because you're so close to him?"

"I'd like to think it was intuition, but I'd be lying if I said for certain."

"I think you should stay over tonight so you should see the full collection again, firsthand, in grand choral assembly. The collection is the only tangible evidence we have of our strange, shared journey. I think the highest goal that a man can achieve is amazement. Awe is the nectar of the gods. I'm amazed at how I feel I can go forward now despite the lack of a mapped path. It seems that somehow what we need is what will find us, even when we don't know that we need it."

"I applaud that P, but you know I really have to go."

31 Cross Stitch

New York

Inadvertently, Prince and I had become cross stitched, a pair of diagonal stitches of the same length, crossing each other in the middle to form an intersection. This potent design has since marked our respective cloths, mine a cotton-wool blend and his of purest silk. Despite our distinct inclinations, the pattern forced itself on our perspective of ourselves, of each other, and on the illusive energy of magic itself.

Prince and I were the only ones who knew and likely would ever know of the magic ball and Leonardo's masterpiece. We felt transformed from the inside out. I'm not sure if either of us would ever be able to explain what it felt like. For the three last days of my visit to the sultanate, we sat inside the secret vault for hours at a time just staring at the ball and the canvas. It felt akin to being in a barometric chamber. Sometimes we spoke, and sometimes we sat in silence, vibrating with the energy coming from both pieces, feeling it palpably entering our awareness through our pores.

The co-existence of these two conjoined creations was the closest thing Prince and I had ever come to feeling the 'deep knowing' Carlos Casteneda wrote of 50 years ago. There's a remarkable sense of peace in it, like putting on a cloak to shelter oneself from the harsh wind. If this is the cloak of knowing that Adam and Eve lost for us in the Garden, then that loss remains the greatest travesty for humanity for all time. Prince and I regretted not being able to stay in the vault 24/7. Leaving it exposed a void within me, but the intensity of it was also physically depleting, as reality beckoned us elsewhere. Possibly only Trappist monks are equipped to live without relief amidst such powerful creative forces.

You may wonder what Prince will do with the painting and the orb. But the inquiry is moot in the presence of such resonant magical possibility. The idea of functionality of the vessels never entered our minds. The king I left was content knowing just that they are; for the fact that they are is enough. Pure being attested is more magical than either of us could ever hope to explain.

32 Slip Stich

New York

Like the slip stitch, invisible from the outside, the threads that bind us are measured. When hemming is called for, as in the tucking-up of one's underside, the blind stitch, a type of slip stitch, does the inconspicuous trick so as not to disturb the look or integrity of the outer fabric.

As metaphor, the slip stitch is one we readily use to tend to loose ends, while maintaining the look and feel of maintaining a pristine surface. It's not exactly deceptive, though it does operate below the visible.

If I was forced to explain just how magic happens, I would tell of a very similar modus to the slip stitch. But unless you know how it works, you won't be able to see it for what it is at the time. It only shows itself on the underside, so one must know where to look.

In most minds, functional applications and magic don't go together. Magic never works on the surface. It operates in low light, under the radar, behind the veil, subconsciously. Many a lucky person has no explanation for how the winning lottery numbers came to them in their sleep.

I confess habitually feeling much the same. It's not that I haven't had to work hard or that I haven't consistently shown up on time for every practice. Still, the magic that graces me always gives much more than expected; enhancing everything in its path with the spirit of unforeseen possibility. If you doubt the magic, know that it intently calls you by name to enter into it. It pulls you in to a kind of reality tinged with stardust—the kind you secretly hoped was there all along. I realize now that I longed to be the target of this miraculous happenstance, magic and love both, though I was always too busy doubting their credibility, even as they were happening.

Let me expand on what I confessed to Prince on our last visit to the Leonardo and his father's magic orb. On a night when I was home alone, there was a full moon. Just before midnight, frazzled from a week of overwork, I took the crystal ball I'd been enigmatically drawn to in Turkey down from its shelf and started to clean it as I was wont to do on occasion. Thinking back on Prince's obsessive search for magical relevance, I gazed into the orb and casually said, what have you to share with me tonight? The ball clouded, gradually, just enough that I noticed. Still, because I was drowsy and distracted, I remained unmoved by the hazy alteration. I had left the inquiry in the ball's court, not mine.

Suddenly, untethered, I saw my Uncle Gio in a ceremonial procession with an angel poised just above him. I rubbed my eyes, looked at the ball, it was clear again. Regardless of what it was or from where it came, somehow I'd received a message. I realized that in only another hour I could call my early rising godfather in Italy to make sure he was okay. I paced atop the Hereke, watching the clock's hands, while sorting through what may have just happened. My heart raced as I pushed Gio's call button on my cell.

"Uncle Gio?"

"*Buongiorno* Michello. Good to hear you. Are you okay?"

"Are you?"

"Yes, why would I not be?"

"Thank God. I had a sort of dream and just needed to hear your voice."

"I haven't had my cappuccino yet, but I'm fine. Tell me, did I die or what?"

"Well…"

"So, I did die, and you were worried it was true?"

"I couldn't bear the thought of it, godfather."

"When you get to be my age, people expect you to just not show up one day. I appreciate your checking on me."

"I miss you, godfather."

"I always miss you. That goes without saying. You know that when I die I will be with you more than I can be these days. Of course, not in any weird necromancy way, but we certainly can stay united, and

I plan on helping you more then, too."

"I hope what you say is true but let's plan on spending a weekend together this month. We can go exploring, wherever you want."

"*Perfezionare.* I already have a good idea that I think will work well for us."

"Just say where and I'll book us."

"I think we should go visit Mont St-Michel. I have several things I want to tell you."

"I want you to tell me again how Mont St-Michel came to be."

"Edgar Cayce wrote about it in his book on angels. It's such an absurdity, which is how the best things come to be, you know, my boy? Let me get the book."

"Take your time, uncle. I'm all ears."

Gio returned promptly and he read the passage enthusiastically. "According to legend in the year 708, the Archangel Michael appeared in a dream to the Bishop Aubert of Avranches, instructing him to build a chapel on the Mont Tombe, one mile off the coast of Normandy. The absurdity of the request caused the bishop to ignore the archangel's command. It occurred a second time and still the bishop did nothing. Finally, the angel appeared in person and struck the bishop with a blazing angelic finger, which left a permanent indentation in Aubert's forehead. The bishop needed no further encouragement to begin his task and, finally, the chapel that would become Mont St-Michel, five hundred years later, was begun."

"I sometimes wish my inklings were as directed as Aubert's, uncle."

"Speaking of inklings, have you conquered your fear and cemented your relationship with your *bijou* of a girlfriend?"

"The cement isn't dry yet, but I'm going to seriously work on it."

"I have high hopes for this one, Cello, please do not tarry."

"I promise. I want you to know her."

"I already do. In many ways your life is about to begin yet again."

"That's heavy for so early in the day, uncle."

"If it wasn't weighty, there wouldn't be much there, would there be? It's part of the magic. You make the heavy load light once you find the courage to pick it up. Anyway, Cello, there is something I must tell you about when we meet in person."

"And I've a list for you as well uncle, but what if I can't wait to hear yours?"

"Well, remember when we were both last discussing how Heidegger's phenomenology relates to both sides of our work in architecture and design?"

"I do."

"I revisited Heidegger lately because I think it might be the best way to explain something happening to me personally by way of the ideas he posed on *phainesthai* and *deseins*."

"Yes, go on."

"I'm in a bit of a slump, Cello. I'm in a Heidegger-like *unheimlich*. Discussing art with you always snaps me out of it."

"I can't wait to see you. By then it will have shown itself more fully to you. But as far as the *deseins* goes, well, a sense of 'not-at-homeness' is the worst possible aesthetic state for an artist. None of your work speaks of this issue, so what's your concern?"

"This time, Cello, it's not about my studies or my work at all. This is about something else. I don't feel my grounded self. It has taken me by surprise and it's definitely an odd experience for me. Perhaps I have become lazy, as meaning can usually find me quite easily, but the older I get it seems that I must hunt harder for it. Suddenly things have become hazy. It may be because so many of my lifelong friends are dying. You know that I do not fear death. What is life without death? And mind you, I do not feel badly for those who've died either, but I do feel badly for me to be without them. I see that very soon I'll only be talking to myself. But don't be alarmed, Cello. I am resolutely healthy, so all I am really saying is that it will be so good to see you soonest. I need to give you a big hug. I think the crux of it is that I am simply missing only two things—you and more artistic connection."

"It's completely mutual, uncle. Everyone needs an accomplice in magic. By the way, Prince wants you to visit him when you can. So, we must plan a trip to see him this year."

"Ah, just what I need to shake off my cobwebs. Thank you for giving me that today, Michello. I will see you very soon."

"Uncle, but there's also something else."

"Of course, son. What is it that concerns you?"

"Well, I do worry about you some, you know?"

"Is it worry, or do you just miss me?"

"You already know that I miss you."

"Cello, some things will never change, and we should be glad of that, no? There is a part of you that has not changed since you were seven years old. Remember, we were on an adventure in the forest up north? You were trying to catch a bird because you wanted to touch their feathers and you wanted a feather to take home for your very own. And what happened?"

"I wore myself out getting close to the birds as they ate the seeds on the ground."

"And when you were disappointed that you didn't get to catch a feather, what did you learn?"

"Oh, I'll never forget this lesson. I've not mastered it yet, though. I said I wanted to hold a tiny bird in my hands. And you told me to meet the bird as it flies away, and the feather will come to me."

"Exactly. I told you that while you are trying to catch something to get what you want, if you let it go, it will give you what you seek. And isn't that what happened?"

"Yes, uncle. I took eight feathers home that day in my pocket."

Do I still look for feathers? Yes, and I have a metal urn on a shelf at home which holds hundreds of feathers I've randomly collected over many years. Not a single feather required that I grab the bird to get it.

On a slip-stitched level I was faced with something I didn't want to face. The premonition I'd received that night said life is a gift never fully in our grasp.

33 Backstitch

Italy

Our world is chock full of secrets. In the Italian piazza, secrets have a distinct way of whispering casually to passers-by. Needless to say, I'm briefly in Venice on a secretive mission, afloat in the ethereal Queen of the Adriatic. I think Truman Capote best described the surreal concoction here. *'Venice is like eating an entire box of chocolate liqueurs in one go.'* She is the one place in all the world that touches a lacuna in my aching heart, though I could not bear to routinely live in her midst.

A design theory from the architect, Juhani Pallasmaa, says *'The real measure of a city is whether one can imagine falling in love with it.'* For nearly three decades, with every visit, this water-worn parish still takes my breath away. Whether I'm here for business or rejuvenation, before I leave, I promise I will return to osmose more of her magical mystery.

For me, Venice exists at a Pallasmaa point, *'the horizon of emancipation and imagination.'* She's the perfect intersection of how design touches and emotionalizes experience, throwing you in to all of it the second you first set foot upon it. Venice is a most mystically assimilated crossroad because it makes absolutely no sense from any practical human perspective. It's as if ancient Italian faeries worked to create it from their collective imagination. Everything here is given the means to coalesce into something other-worldly and truly magical.

And speaking of a magical She, I've been following Chloe's doings on the net, and I've emailed and texted her hoping she'll join me at the Belmont Ciprianni on her way to Rome. My monogamous marriage to art has kept us too far apart. I realize dangerously so. We need to see each other in person. I haven't heard back from her yet.

Meantime, at The Procuratie—the three connected buildings on St. Mark's Square—were completed under Napoleon's occupation; I'm reminded of the oldness of the world, and that the oldness itself is the over-arching point. Everything passes away. Each life, each age, and us. We should travel regularly in order to remind ourselves that we are real for a short while and then we make room for others to come, including our future selves.

Venice, sinking beneath itself in Jungian context, conveys without word or sentiment all that art is meant to be - the embodiment of a sacred calling and the magic of something that human hands know to cherish. It is our conduit to the realm above and hints at what awaits us beyond. Quite simply, the underlying aesthetic of all art mimics the universe and like a dream it reveals a hidden aspirational dimension, *la dolce vita.* Once you see that the very magic you doubt exists, it creeps out to show itself slowly, coming seemingly out of nowhere, revealing itself further, in bursts of a microscopically miniscule glow that lights a part of you you've surrendered or forgotten.

At the Piazza San Marco, I inhale the damp air, before placing my Italian loafer on to a congested tiled alcove of the beloved cathedral. I feel the innovative blending of cultures; Moorish, Italian, and Mediterranean flavors romantically compressed in timeless embrace. They aromatically press into us, so that we may see how it's possible to gradually open ourselves up to more; telling us not to settle for taking in only lesser juxtapositions. They tell of a timeless imperative; that of inspiring each other.

The piazza brims with the evening energy of the timeless Italian art of *passagiata*—the culture held together by the buzzing of lives; like bees they swarm with the sound of clinking glasses, lilts of laughter, heels clicking upon pavements, the incessant chatter of the marketplace, and the theatrical telling of tall tales. For this piazza is born of the power of preposition, the with, to, from, in and of—the little connections that make life full and worthwhile.

Venice is surreal proof of how artful space brings out artful life.

Though I'm sentimentally attached to the beauty of the eastern coastline of New York, it's less compelling for me than this bastion of pelagic energy. Like all true masterpieces, Venezia is almost too magically wired both inside and out. And this is precisely why it appears too complicated to know it. Instead, it begs to be perceived. I live for this unique crossroad of artistic juxtaposition; alive and ever present, in an exact longitude of great conjuring. Venice sits inside that cradle where one's awareness protrudes against the discovery of unknown forces.

Ritualistically, I remain spoiled by the comforting ambience of the Belmont Ciprianni, where I've stayed since my first visit with my parents, a many moons ago gift for high school graduation. It's not a place conducive to the groove of solitaire. Every crevice of each narrow alley with its cobbling and ancient facades, its shops and shrines, repeatedly shares the same special secret, it faithfully tells me that the true magic of this life is simply and only love. I'm a devotee of the ideal.

"*Buonasera,* Michello," greeted Guiseppe Franco, the famed proprietor of the La Coppia on Calle dei Fuseri. I remember when he took it over years ago from Massimo, who my father knew from summers as a boy in Tuscany. The glue of the ristorante is Carina, the *cucina* maestro solely responsible for adding inches to the waists of infamous icons and hungry, appreciative Italians like myself.

"I am here for two nights on business, hopefully my *amata* will be joining me on the third evening."

"Poor bambino, Michello. To be in Venezia, alone, for two moons is not good for a man's constitution, *capisce*? You must let Carina conjure something masterful to properly console you. Maybe a delectable bronzino tonight?"

"Say no more, my mouth is watering. *Dille di sorprendermi.*"

"For now, an *aperitivo,* Michello. You must dine tonight as my guest, yes?"

A young German gentleman seated alone at a nearby table who overheard our banter seemed to intuit that I hadn't heard back yet from Chloe said, "If you've never eaten while crying, you don't know what life tastes like."

"Goethe, I believe."

Guiseppe invited Ludvig to join us with a hand gesture. "I see exactly where we three stand. Weary boys, perhaps awaiting our next divine prompting. You know this Michello, and Ludvig, obviously you are also a very wise fellow. We are precisely all here for a reason. And in Venice. How extraordinary is our fate? You know how certain places are legendarily known for magical energy?"

"Venice is an energy vortex of a sensual kind," said Ludvig.

"A Dolmen Arch of appetite," I said.

"The Pyramids."

"Bali."

"Ayers Rock."

"Machu Picchu."

"Here in Venice, there is a subtle layer of difference from them all," Giuseppe interrupted. "Here, unlike anywhere else, we do not have to make the first move to find our magic. In Venice, the magic does not wait patiently for anyone. It whispers as you pass by; and when it calls, it comes only for you and you alone; and before you know it, you are magically, literally, drawn into it. You see, there is something lingering here that knows us. I believe personally, it is an ancient knowing that resides in the mix of the air and the water here. It is as if we are drenched in a spiritual microclimate and its influence is around us in ways that we cannot see. We breathe it in unknowingly while it alters our perception and understanding."

Ludvig and I listened in silent appreciation.

"You may think that I make this up to romantically entertain my guests, no? But trust me, the truth of this is far greater than my words. You see, once you are here, even if one time only, the elixir of which I speak is infused inside your bones. No one can escape it, especially in the Italian night, a drowning drop of ardent possibility upon this broken planet. Venezia, she alone is the trusted land where the Sacred Feminine meets her King."

"*Perfettamente messo*, Giuseppe. You are an inspiration, my friend," I said, recalling the sacred treasure of Chintamani. "What a concept! I love the heart of this magnificent idea."

"I pity those who have not yet come to Venice to meet this mysterious invisible force. Plainly my guests, there is absolutely no room for anything that does not uphold the magic of life and art. Here, it is all about the life that is art and the art that is life. But they are one and the same and separating them brings nothing but despair. Venice will never be too old to matter because art is the only means by which we are to avoid obsolescence. You see my point, no?"

"Art and appreciating its essence is everything and holds the ancient secret of immortality. And I also know that physics is the easiest part," I said to our German brother.

"I won't argue your point," Ludvig answered.

"Try the incredible Mediterranean oysters," Giuseppe said, gesturing to the *cameriere* to bring more. "They are smaller than their Atlantic cousins, but far more tasty. And do you know why? In the Atlantic the little fellows spend hours each day out of the water when the Atlantic tides pull back for the shore beds where they nest. Your *ostriche* must work much harder than ours to survive and as a result they become heftier."

"I think working harder makes you better. I think it might be the same for oysters as for people." Ludvig said.

"Ah no no no." Giuseppe insisted. "Strife is never what makes us greater. *Mangiare. Gettarsi.* See, gastronomy is also art, my friends. All art is made of the same divine threads. We are lucky to be beneficiaries of such a talented weaver as Carmina, *sì?*"

"Speaking of art. Do you know why I'm here on such a moon-drenched night as this?"

"Ah, I surmise perhaps for a few coveted artistic appointments? Through the grapevine I hear there are a few very rare pieces circulating, and I hear there are others here on the same mission."

"Yes, of course there are. Tomorrow morning I'm viewing an 18th century canvas by none other than Tiepolo."

Just then, an awe inspiriting antipasto was ceremoniously served. "Food may not be as eternal as Tiepolo, but try making great art without feeding the artist," said Ludvig. "I hereby second the need for robust aperitif, for skillful accompaniment is an art form in and of itself, however underrated as it may seem to those in other lands."

"So then tonight you eat and tomorrow you nibble. Our grandmothers say it is the old and best way. I believe, it still works very well, no? The new generation is obsessed with dieting because they will not love themselves enough from the inside out. Such depravity, it saddens me. It isn't God's way. People who love to eat are always the best people.[iv] Oh, but back to the prized secret showing of yours tomorrow; I toast you, Michello, and the lost work you seek, but you see, I also know that it has already been found; and you are here now only to claim it for yourself. And this young man here, Ludvig, our new comrade, I believe he too appreciates the quest. I am very sure of it."

I raised my glass. "Then let us toast to the quest and to finding our blundering way to our best future."

"Here's to the magic of that," toasted Ludvig. "And as to the magic of the quest, I will be joining you in the morning at the Tiepolo, Michello. I've heard your name spoken often in the galleries of Hamburg and Berlin. They say you are a formidable player. It's a pleasure to finally meet you."

34 Eldritch

Italy

I'm in the dark. I'm in freefall. My godfather Gio passed away Friday afternoon, and I cannot find the bottom of the hole in my heart. He wasn't sick a day, so that's good, but his heart was full so why he had to leave so suddenly will haunt me. I have the tickets I bought to the Mont tucked in my trusty portmanteau. It was never made to carry such sadness. We'll never make it to Prince's palace together to marvel at Leonardo together. We'll never stop for Stracciatella again on our way to a museum. So many things, so many things, never to be again. The not-at-homeness that Gio told me of on the phone wasn't philosophical. It was premonitory, and he half knew it though he denied it was so.

If you're lucky, there are people in your life who you don't have to see often but are somehow always there for you. It's as if you've known each other for centuries, not years, so the small passing of time seems inconsequential. But every moment you spend with them, even if in quiet company, marks your soul in ways you cannot measure. This was how it always was with the magical entity that was Gio.

As soon as I knew Gio was gone, I called Prince, knowing he would drop everything to come to bid his beloved mentor farewell. Prince consoled me that Friday is the holiest day to die in the Jewish, Catholic, and Muslim traditions. Whether it's because it's the eve of Shabbat or because Christ died on Good Friday, these three monotheistic faiths share the idea that a believer who dies on Friday goes straight to the sacred gate without delay.

With the funeral days away and everything in my life hanging in

211

desolation by tiny threads, I am at a loss in ways that are too vast to fathom. It's as if I've fallen into a deep well and want to scream at the top of my lungs, but no sound will come out. Like Munch in "The Scream" I am beyond disconsolate and can't face my own guilt about delaying my visit with Gio, even after I had the premonition. I was but a day too late to see him, or to be with him when he died; or to have been there so that he would not have died; or just to be able to say goodbye.

The only thing I could muster was to unravel with Prince as my wingman. Chloe was immersed in a new gallery in Brussels and she had still not responded back to my calls or texts. The best-laid plans are worthless when executed too late to matter. Here I was tying up loose ends in Venice, about to see Gio and then intending to devote myself to getting Chloe's attention—and a day later, here I am, alone, without Gio, without Chloe and without my sanity or my heart intact. I must face that I've waited too long for everything I hold dear, and the aftermath of this realization is a bleak emptiness beyond even what Athena had warned.

"Prince, I'm sorry for calling so late but Gio has died. I'm annihilated. I was on my way to see him, but I was too late. P, I've been too late for everything I fear, as even Chloe has seemingly given up on me."

"Mitch, I feel partly to blame as I kept you unexpectedly away too long."

"Had I not been with you to fully experience the miracle of the vault's secrets and the Leonardo, I don't think I'd be able to admit the err of my ways. Becoming is such a gradual process Prince and I am a certifiable idiot, I'm afraid."

"Yes, my friend, we are both afraid; this I know we also have in common. The circumstances are different, but the fear is the same."

"I know I've spoken to you about mending my ways but I'm distraught that I've yet to do any of it."

"I do see however that you have been preparing yourself though."

"To no avail. While I'm getting ready for something, every opportunity to do it is gone. What good is preparation if it lasts beyond its usefulness?"

"Maybe now you will be able to get out of your own way and step-up anew, like the lich you told me about."

"There's no maybe for me anymore, P. I must become a man who is steadfast in action, or I must die trying."

"No more of dying, Mitch. We have had two deaths in the family already now. We must heal ourselves and each other."

"P, if Chloe isn't there for me, I will be the likely third, dying of a broken heart."

"What will be will be. Know that I will fly in for Gio's service. I owe that man so much love and respect. Tell me what day I need to come and know I will be there for you."

35 Overstitch

Italy

Prince arrived by Blackhawk helicopter. As I walked under its whirring blades to greet my friend, my sunglasses blew off my head; the sadness so thick around me that I secretly hoped the blades would end the pain and grant me a future peace.

After the viewing ceremony, Prince whispered me aside that I shouldn't let them close the casket yet. I was too numb to ask why and went along, informing the funeral director that only the two of us would return that evening to close the casket privately. We walked to my car. I took a bottle of spring water from the door holder and poured it on my head to startle me into demi-coherence.

"I'm running out of air to breathe. P, tell me what on earth you're thinking."

"Mitch, I've brought the magic ball with me."

"You what?"

"I don't want it in my life. I want to safeguard it from every savage outcome that might befall it. Who else could I safely trust it to but Gio? If anyone would know what to do with it, it would be him. And suppose it's true you know, what the ancients say about the crossing?"

"What do you mean?"

"You know, the toll to pay when crossing the River Styx."

"Gio, though a metaphysician is Roman Catholic, P."

"And I a Muslim, but no one I know of has ever returned to tell us what crossing over to the other side is like. The magic orb will gain Gio good voyage no matter where he arrives. The ball needs to go back to wherever it came from. It surely doesn't belong here, tormenting and tempting us weak-willed mortals. Loved ones put mementos in deceased family member's caskets all the time. The ball's just not an ordinary departing gift, that's all."

"But Mitch, you also have a ball that you've told me about."

"I suppose. But mine isn't a real magic ball."

"Are you sure? You foresaw Gio's death in it."

"Prince, I'm not owning-up to anything about the voodoo moment I had. I still have no clear idea what really happened."

"Oh, yes you do. That you had a ball, all the while, and that you had the premonition while you were engaged with it, is something altogether different than what you're pretending to yourself. Lying to yourself is an art I've watched you practice for years. "

"I could object but now's not the time, and I know that it's also lovingly appropriate, however bizarre your plan seems. But it doesn't matter anyway. I don't have the ball with me."

"But Mitch, I took the liberty of calling Terry right after I received your call about Gio's passing. I had him retrieve the ball from your apartment and express it to me at the palace. Mitch, I have your ball with me, here. That is, I have both our balls with me."

"Prince, this is beyond sensical. I can't believe you took it upon yourself to do this and actually arrange it."

"You would be quite surprised at how independent this king has become lately, since I must take care of all my secret things, all in secret."

"Let me get this straight. You have both balls with you, and you want us to gift them both to Gio, tonight before we close his casket?"

"Yes, exactly. That is if you do."

I didn't answer trying to wrestle through it without verbal success.

"I know you can't process this all right now, but you do trust me?"

"Yes, of course, I trust you with my life. We are bonded in ways I cannot comprehend. Your being here with me and being here for Gio, means the world to me."

After a brief rehearsal to assist me in collecting my thoughts, I'd become remarkably comfortable with the idea. Prince and I made our way back to the funeral home before sunset. The director led us into Gio's viewing parlor. Once the director closed the doors, we privately knelt before the open casket, expressing our thoughts silently. I began to cry. Prince put his hand on my shoulder. "Here, Mitch, it's time" he said handing me his father's crystal ball, wrapped in a black velvet sack with a silk tie that made my mind jump to an image of Gio once handing a bottle of grappa wrapped in velvet to my mother. Psyche is an incessant gamer who pricks us awake.

"You first, P. After all, yours is the real magic ball."

Prince unwrapped the ball from the sac and carefully placed it to the left of Gio's head. Prince bowed to his mentor. "Here you go my dearest Merlin. Thank you for taking these from us. You are the entrusted one."

Then Prince handed me the second sac which contained my innocuous orb. I dutifully unwrapped it and nestled it at the right of Gio's head. "Here you go my enlightened Padrino. We are not equipped to handle such power here. Know that I will love and miss you forevermore." Tears were streaming down both our faces now; though our eyes indicated that inside we were smiling at the possibility of Gio somehow knowing of our gesture, and the pure release we felt from letting go of all control and trusting in the unknown.

But as soon as I placed the second ball, both orbs began to illuminate. As we moved our hands closer to the casket again, we marveled at what was happening right before our eyes. We stared in disbelief without blinking for fear of missing something. The sense of joy we felt was incomprehensible. But neither the new king nor I had ever witnessed anything like this with either ball.

However long it was that we watched and waited, staring at the aglow orbs, neither of us dared to utter a sound. Our eyes were transfixed on the lighted spheres, the white glow emanating from both orbs simultaneously. When I put my hand on the lid to begin to close the casket, the luminescence of the balls softened to a tender glow and three starry pinpoints of light appeared in their middle. Suspended in the magical moment, I'd lost all sense of time until I heard the funeral director re-enter the parlor. I quickly pulled the heavy casket lid closed. I asked the director to lock it and give me the key. Prince and I exited the parlor's double doors, like startled altar boys, nervously crossing the parking lot to seek refuge inside my car. Once inside, we simultaneously exhaled and turned to each other in exasperated amazement.

"Well that certainly debunks the cauldron of deniability," Prince said.

I attested, "And that deflates the claims of the atheists I know. P, the three specks of light again?"

"Yes, the Chintamani lives on for us, Mitch."

"Orion's belt, perhaps that is where our dear uncle is headed."

"Clearly, he is well equipped for any journey," Prince said assuredly.

I could only sigh. "Pure magic, purest magic, beautiful magic." Everything had become crystal clear from the clarity that only springs from deep knowing. I knew an unmistakable part of me, one that's lived through many lifetimes, comprehended exactly what was happening and that Gio graced us to receive his gift. As grateful watchers, Prince and I once again witnessed the power of two. At this celestial moment our souls could not deny the abiding sacred truth. We are magic. *'God's in his heaven, all's right with the world'.*'"

36 Ostrich

New York

Like the ostrich who buries its head in the sand, we look away from whatever we fear facing. As it turns out, this impressively strong bird is a warrior unlikely to flinch from confronting anything. Instead, the head burying is how the ostrich prepares its nest, digging a deep hole to safely bury its eggs. Unlike this creature, I have no such excuse for my head-burying.

Mine went on for years without my admitting, and when I received hints about it, I chose to make sure nothing diverted my attention from commerce and the so-called successful life which I'd built, and most of all, from my monogamous devotion to art. Had I pursued more of the ancient ideal of balance, which was innate in the art I chased, I wouldn't have been left with all of only one and not the other.

A triptych of tsunamic personal events has conspired to make it mandatory that I take my head out of the sand. Leonardo's *Salvatore Mundi* was the first. I was dazed, inebriated, and humbled to be in its presence. I felt it in parts of my being I'd only speculated existed. Gio's death was the second, decapitating my heart. And third, the glowing orbs at the casket, a life-altering moment.

And now—steady boy, steady—the critical crossroad as foretold is before me. This morning, I awakened sweat soaked from a dream. Scrawled on a wall in the dream was a sign: WARNING. THE UMBILICAL CORD IS A NOOSE. The dream was a still shot photo montage of me, age 12 to current. The dream's nemesis shocked me. It was my godfather, Gio, my mother, father, and uncles were at the head of a line of walk-ons.

I've been back in New York for weeks, and throughout I've remembered each night's dream in detail. I've tried to defuse the dreaming's pattern: attending a Jeff Weiss play at The Kitchen; puzzling over Brice Marden's calligraphy at the Modern; rereading Kipling's unwoke masterpiece, *Kim*; trying to slip alternative material over the transom to my psyche. But when sleep finally must be served, despite kneading my subconscious with VOGA, the same dreaming occurs.

I'm aware that the dream warning on the wall—it also appears on given nights on the sides of buses and Amazon delivery vans, as subway graffiti, on Times Square billboards, on bikers' tattooed forearms—I'm aware that it isn't about the childbirth lifeline. It's about my co-dependent relationship to the underwriter of who I am, and I'm shaken at the sense of release this warning calls on me to accept. I would never have dreamed such dreams, if I wasn't already so topsy-turvy that the pleadings of my analytic brain against them were drowned out.

"Is there anything that you would not want to know?" Athena had asked me, "because we cannot un-know anything once we know it." What shocks me is that the part of me that's always itched at my unfulfillment feels thankful that it's all happened.

And as if this heretical challenge to my lifelong assumptions wasn't sufficiently unsettling, the unresolved matter of my thin ice relationship with my would-be soul mate, Chloe Joubert, is heavily upon me.

Since Venice, I've deluged her with unanswered voice mails, texts, and emails. I've interrogated our mutual friend Genevieve who introduced us. "I warned you that my French sister brooks no BS before I gave you her cell," she said. "I know exactly why she's giving you the cold shoulder, but so do you." She chucked me under the chin, pointed a gun finger at me, mockingly called me Mitchy-poo, and ushered me out of her workshop.

And so, having showered, shaved, and completed my toiletries, I sat down at my desk, turned on my MacBook, scrolled through an online art catalogue Terry sent me, and purchased a mandala painting in his name by the American artist, Clarence H. Carter.

It's not lost on me that mandala is Sanskrit for circle, and as of late my life has been overrun with orbs. But Carter's paintings have never been on my treasure hunting menu.

Irony of ironies, the fleeting French phantom of late, has apparently made a read on this underserved clientele and opened a pop-up showroom on west Broadway, six blocks from my atelier, to exhibit what her catalogue calls Underappreciated American Artists.

I'll let the part of her catalog that applies to my purchase speak for itself.

"In the field of abstract surrealism, I believe that Clarence H. Carter will soon be considered at the head of the class. His vision is exceptionally pure and his technique is unsurpassed, producing a union of great visual impact and tactile delight. Carter's mandalas consist of a series of superimposed translucent egg-shapes floating in space. They are beautifully intricate and each comes to focus in a series of increasingly smaller shapes which end in a minute brilliantly colored central image, out of which all the other forms seem to expand. Color is sovereign. The result is a marvelous blend of harmonious movement."

This Carter purchase is my final play to break through the wall of silence to my would-be lover. Two weeks ago, I expressed what could be taken for a proposal of marriage to Chloe's gallery. Rule of thumb: you can ignore texts, emails, voice mails; you can throw a letter in the trash; but I know you will open a Fedex. Being honest with myself though I'm quitting my unwillingness to love a mortal as much as I love art, cold turkey doesn't cleanse the soul of an entrenched way of life all at once. How Chloe takes my message will be the determinant. Here's what I said:

Dear Chloe,

> *You stood me up in Venice; you stood me up at my Padrino's services; and for weeks I've been home and trying to reach you by email, text, and voice message, niente, silencio, no avail. I've seized on fedex as a last resort.*
>
> *Before giving me your cell, Genevieve told me that you don't suffer fools. I've been a fool, married to art to protect my heart. I'm suing Titian, Rafael and the cast of characters for divorce. I'm in love with you. You're the accomplice I need to be fully me. I hope you still feel as I do. Voici a la magie d'une vie pleine.*

Michello

A week has gone by, sans reply.

I regretfully recall telling Prince when he was immersed in self-doubt to not focus on how it ends. I encouraged him to take action to get past dwelling on the end game. Though I thought it to be good advice at the time, ever since having the magical revelation at Gio's casket, I know that it isn't true.

Despite however it appears, nothing really ends. We may call it an ending when we can't see past where we are to the next; but the truth is, there is no end to anything. The journey is never linear; far more beguiling, it is perfectly round. Like the glorious orbs and the mandala, the circle tells us that everything goes on, with or without our knowing—and thankfully, I can heartfully now see, come what may—the magic goes on.

The Art of Possibility

Everywhere

The conjuring is readily at hand by all who know.
      Nostradamus

no matter what the art, all creation is born of conjuring.
all creativity, literally each tiny ounce
of every idea, every challenging speck
or smitch of possibility, every embryo of imagination
that's ever been conceived by anyone, anywhere,
since the first of time, begins with an incandescent disturbance,
a primordial itch which stirs despite our apprehension.

we live day to day pretending to know
more about it than we do;
but no one knows exactly why things unfold as they must.
the perplexing itch, from where does it stir?
traveling from invisible recesses
to surface in this fleeting space called real time,
it boroughs and beguiles.

it calls us in like an ancient Greek siren
mysteriously urging us by way of unmet sensation,
relentlessly luring us to tango.
peering out from its bunker it beckons
drawing us in to tandem bardo,
suggesting a hint of relief might await in the wings.
still unhinged, we comply in a choreographed flow
of cosmic reciprocity.

despite the sensational melee, the itch asserts,
urging us to make room for something yet to come.
whether physical or metaphoric,
the itch demands our unfettered attention,
usurping our ability to focus on anything
but quelling its urge.
thwarting every inclination it insists
we acknowledge, no matter when it comes,
in day or night, dark or light, sleep or waking.

only upon surrendering to its prodding
can we begin to persuade its retirement.
and so, in retrospect, the simple itch
like all self-directed awareness,
is at best, a cosmic hint.
born from out of impenetrable fog,
the itch is in itself, an irresistible force.

though we yearn for the possibility
of fusion in its summons,
inside the dynamic beguiling,
we are fated to hold both spaces,
the itched and the scratched.

…And with the two-step design
a universal rhythm is honored.
like the revelatory exchange between life and art,
love and longing, actor and audience,
performer and watcher,
it is only by answering both calls
that we can see that both
the itching and the scratching are good.

ABOUT THE AUTHOR

Harper St. Clair writes spiritual mysteries under the desert moon of Arizona and believes in the magic that comes from sharing our spheres of influence with each other.

The author believes that fiction is a critical part of our reality; as our imaginations are woven into our fiber, as much as the logics. The world in which we dwell, that is, the one inside our heads, lives side by side; amidst alternative realities set upon blurry lines and squiggles. The parallels between reality and fiction are readily called upon by the story's characters in order to advance self-discovery. Mixing truths with rumor, hearsay, and creative or imaginary connections is after all, how literary batter is baked. Like Truman Capote said, all literature is gossip.

…May we as readers (and writers) become believers in more…not less…and inspire each other to refine our truth, no matter where it dwells; here, there or in that certain somewhere…between the worlds.

www.harperstclair.com

END NOTES

---

[i] David Wang, Environmental and Architectural Phenomenology, 2007
[ii] Nicholas Roerich
[iii] Credit: TS Eliot/J Alfred Prufrock
[iv] Julia Child
[v] R. Browning